I0523906

Shadows

When the shadows of the past gather,
trouble isn't far behind ...

Wongan Creek Series
Book 3

Juanita Kees

WONGAN CREEK SERIES

JUANITA KEES

Published by Juanita Kees (Kees2Create)

eBook ISBN: 9780645631975

Paperback ISBN: 9780645631982

Cover Design Copyright © by Paradox Book Cover Designs & formatting.

Shadows

Juanita Kees

When the shadows of the past gather, trouble isn't far behind ...

Fenella Rose-Waterman is happy running The Cranky Lizard winery until a broken relationship lifts the lid on the Pandora's Box of her past. After years of repressed memories haunting her dreams, she is forced to face the truth to find justice. But with truth comes a danger that puts everyone she loves at risk.

Kieran Murphy left Wongan Creek a newlywed and returned a widower. He believes he and his young son will find healing in the town that healed him once before. Instead, he finds the woman he once loved running scared, her life in turmoil and her business under threat.

As the shadows of the past gather on the horizon, will they lose their chance of happiness, or will they find healing together?

About the Author

Finding hope in country towns with dark secrets ...

Juanita escapes the real world to create emotionally engaging stories steeped in crime, suspense, mystery and intrigue. Her books are set in dusty, rural outback Australia and on the NASCAR racetracks of America. Her small-town USA and Australian rural stories have made the Amazon bestseller and top 100 lists. Juanita also likes to dabble in the ponds of fantasy and paranormal with Greek gods brought to life in the 21st century.

Juanita graduated college with distinctions and a diploma in Proofreading, Editing and Publishing in 2011 and started her freelance writing business, Kees2Create Words. As a developmental and structural editor, she assists writers to polish their manuscripts for submission. In 2012, she achieved her dream of becoming a published author and now has multiple novels on the market.

When she's not working, writing, editing or proofreading, Juanita enjoys travelling to discover new worlds for inspiration. Mother to two handsome heroes and partner to a car enthusiast, Juanita also has a passion for fast cars and country living.

Juanita loves to talk books with readers and would love to connect. Contact her via:

Website:
https://juanitakees.com/contact/
Kees2Create Words Editing:
https://kees2createwords.com/
Bookbub:
https://www.bookbub.com/authors/juanita-kees
Newsletter:
https://kees2createwords.substack.com/embed
Goodreads:
https://www.goodreads.com/author/show/6454477.
Juanita_Kees
Book Love Book Club:
https://www.facebook.com/groups/607880523038543

Chapter One

Fen drew in a deep breath and let it out on a sigh as she lined up shot glasses on the scarred wooden bar at The Cranky Lizard winery. 'How could I have been so stupid, Sarge?'

'There's nothing stupid about you, Fenella. You were simply an easy mark.' Sergeant Riggs closed his notepad and tucked it into his uniform pocket. 'It's not a reflection on your intelligence. It's more a sign of how smart organised crime is becoming and how easy it is for these guys to target people like you and Liv.'

'You'd think I'd have recognised the tactics though.' Luke Sampson had charmed his way into her heart and home, then he'd wormed his way into the winery accounts and stolen Murray and Liv's lifetime of hard work. All because she'd believed the lies of a thief.

'Men like Sampson see the scars, the wristbands, the

1

piercings and the dark clothing, and they see a rebel, someone who has a score to settle with the world. They don't see where you've come from or where you've been. They don't know who you've grown into or what you've become. They only see the wounds from a past that can be reopened and made to fester.'

And no matter how hard she tried to ignore her past, it kept coming back to slap her on the arse. The rebellious child nobody had wanted because she self-harmed. The inexplicable, deep-seated fear that haunted the shadows at night, the ingrained terror of a memory that refused to surface. And the confusion of being shunted from one foster family to another, not knowing how long she'd be there before her actions would have her carers rethinking their decision.

No-one had understood the devil that drove her until the Watermans had taken her in and helped her turn her life around. Liv had been more of a mum to her than Antoinette had ever been.

Fen shook off the thought of Antoinette the way she always did, the same way she pushed aside the nightmares that caught her unaware in the middle of the night. 'So, what happens now?'

'There'll be an investigation. Fraud squad will take over and turn your life upside down. They'll go through the winery's books with a fine-tooth comb. Every transaction, every movement will be scrutinised. You'll be questioned and cross-questioned until they can eliminate you as an accomplice, given your intimate relationship with Sampson.'

She pulled a face. 'If only I hadn't given in to his nagging for a date. But he wouldn't give up until I said yes.' It had seemed like the perfect way to take a step forward, out of her comfort zone, away from the hope that, one day, Kieran Murphy might come home. 'Showing up here every day in his lunch break, on weekends. Making me believe how much he hated his job at the mine.'

Riggs chuckled. 'Unfortunately, there are good people and bad people in this world, young lady, and sometimes it's hard to tell them apart. Sometimes they pretend to care, yet all the time they're carrying a knife in their lunchbox, waiting for the opportunity to stab you in the back with it. You were unlucky to get one of those. Not that I'm surprised he picked you. You've grown into a fine young lass. A man would have to have rocks in his head not to notice that. If you were my daughter, I'd have the shotgun loaded twenty-four-seven.'

Fen leaned across the bar and patted his arms. 'Cheers for that.'

Riggs' smile faded back into his usual mask of seriousness. 'Be careful, Fen. The men Sampson answers to don't play games. There's a reason they infiltrate small towns. It's much easier to hide things out here.'

Fen shivered. 'I found that out the hard way, Sarge.'

Her jaw still ached where Luke's knuckles had made contact the day she'd found his cuts hidden in a box under their bed and dared to ask about them. That had been her final clue that Luke Sampson wasn't the guy who liked red wine and sunsets and walks on the beach or hitting the surf with his board on a Sunday morning. And his Harley wasn't for recreation only.

All the other clues had been there in plain sight, except she'd been too blind to see them. And by the time she'd had the blinkers ripped off, it was too late. He'd taken off with a million dollars of their bank balance and left her with a hectare of growth down the back paddock — that *wasn't* grapevines — to explain to police.

'He'll pay for that too, Fen. I promise you that.' Riggs straightened and slapped a hand on the bar. 'I've got to get back into town. Say hi to Liv for me, okay?'

A rowdy group entered the cellar, led by their tour group operator. Her travelling bachelor party had arrived. 'Will do, Sarge.'

He paused and looked across to where Liv stood in deep conversation with a man Fen had been trying not to look at since he'd stepped through the door. 'You'd be happy Murphy's back in town?'

Her heart did that little skip-dance it always did whenever she thought of Kieran. 'I'm happy he answered the ad for a new manager. He has the skills and experience. Turning the winery around and fixing the mess I've made is all that matters now.' There, she'd put him in the safety zone where he couldn't rock her world again. Not when it had already been rocked because she'd taken a wrong turn trying to get over him.

Riggs studied her intently for a minute before making way for the tour group. 'Don't keep your blinkers on forever, okay? Wounds heal, and we forget our mistakes. Eventually. Take care, Fen. I'll be in touch.' He turned to the group. 'You boys stay out of trouble now. I don't want to have to come back here today.'

As she poured the first round for the group, Fen realised Liv was right about one thing — getting back to business was a whole lot better for her than crying into a coffee mug over a no-good, lying thief who didn't deserve her tears. Her relationship with Luke Sampson had only proved what she'd already suspected. Men were trouble.

Not all men are bastards, Fen love. You need to believe that, or you'll never find happiness.

Liv's words echoed through her thoughts. Confident words from a woman who'd been married to her soulmate, a gentle giant and true hero, whose sudden passing from a heart attack had left a huge gap in their lives. He'd gone into town for supplies and he hadn't come back. There one day, gone the next.

She let her gaze stray towards Liv, deep in

conversation with the man who had once been her rock and confidante. Kieran Murphy. Her heart hovered between stop and go. She'd loved him with every essence of her being. Until he'd tilted her world on an axis that had only just found balance and married Diane.

She steadied her hand as she poured a liqueur and concentrated on not spilling any. She shouldn't be this happy to see him when she'd lost him all those years ago, and the bond between them had been broken by distance and jealousy.

From across the room, those see-all eyes met hers with a flash of pleasure that took her breath away. Kieran had always had that power. A wave of memories played through her mind. There'd been a time when he'd brought happiness and light to her world of darkness. Until distance had silenced it all. The smile. The love. The friendship. Everything.

Strong fingers clamped around her leather wristband, the rough edges of the rawhide scraping against her scars, startling her out of her musings.

'I *said*, could I have a tasting round, please.'

Something in the man's tone — an inflection, a bite — had her stiffening as his hold tightened. Her gaze shot to his, caught sight of the tattoo under his left eye. The same teardrop design Luke wore on his left bicep, the only difference being this man's one had been coloured in whereas Luke's had been clear.

She shivered against the unease that knotted her belly and tried to keep her voice steady. 'If you let go of my hand, I'll pour you a drink. The prices are on the wine list.'

'A nice girl like you should pay more attention to her surroundings. Someone could get hurt while you're not looking.' He delivered the words through lips pulled tight over yellowed teeth, his soulless grey eyes set in a round face, tanned by the sun and weathered by the wind.

Memories swirled through her mind. A past that should stay forgotten in a place with dark hallways and shadowy corners. Men with secrets to keep, and Antoinette, the woman who serviced them. Men just like this one from a dark and dirty underworld where crime paid for sex and drugs. A life no child should be exposed to. Nausea burned in her throat, perspiration dampened the collar of her shirt and terror crept in from the shadows of her mind as the scars under her wristbands itched.

Kieran's warmth and solid strength filled the space behind her. 'Do we have a problem here?'

The man removed his fingers from her wrist. 'Your bartender here is a little slow. I was just trying to catch her attention.' He straightened, the faded patches on his worn leather vest coming into view. 'But it's okay. I'm not thirsty anymore.' He slapped ten dollars onto the bar, the rings on his tattooed knuckles catching the sunlight. 'That should cover it.' His eyes found Fen's. 'Take care now.'

Kieran crossed his arms and watched as the man made his way out the door. 'Want to tell me what that was all about?'

Fen waited until the flyscreen door closed before she turned to face him, praying he wouldn't see the terror she could almost taste. 'Unhappy customer. I had it under control.' She took slow breaths to control the hammering of her heart against her ribs and the fear that twisted her belly into knots. She was being watched by Luke's club members. The reality of that sank into her mind like a stone thrown into the koi pond out the front.

'Don't lie to me, Fen. I may have been away a while, but I still recognise trouble when I see it.'

Her heart did a backward somersault as he bent to kiss her cheek, greeting her the way he always had. Before he went away. She ignored the impulse to kiss him back, the way she would have done years ago. His long silence had hurt, their friendship the sacrifice he'd made in the name of commitment. Still, she couldn't deny the flicker of happiness that chased some of the fear from her mind. Kieran Murphy had come home, and she'd always felt safe when he was near.

'Welcome back.'

'Thank you.' The smile he offered her no longer reached his eyes or lit up his face the way it used to.

Dark shadows and a drawn look hinted at stress and sleepless nights.

Liv stepped up to the bar and sent her a look that told Fen she'd recognised the patches and the threat. 'Are you okay, love?'

'I'm okay, Mum. He's gone now.' She squeezed her mum's hand reassuringly.

Liv had enough to worry about, but it would be hard to ignore the warning in the man's presence so soon after they'd filed charges on Luke. Fen closed her thoughts to the fear that tried to sneak in again. She had to trust that Riggs would keep them safe. She wouldn't let herself be controlled by fear again. Fen turned to Kieran.

'How long do you need to think about taking the job?' One thing she could be certain of was that Kieran would know how to fix what Luke had broken. Everything except her heart.

'I can't make snap decisions here, Fen. It's not just me I have to think about.' A hint of sadness flickered in his expression and that trademark smile tugged down at the corners.

Of course, he'd have a family to consider. The tiny two-bedroomed cottage at the end of Blue Lizard Lane might not be big enough if he had children.

A lick of pain tightened her chest. Children. She rubbed at her wrists. There'd been a time once when she'd wanted to have kids, but every time she felt the itch of the scars, she was reminded of the past and all the reasons she shouldn't. A past haunted by memories that flickered out of reach on the peripheral of her mind. Monsters that lay buried until something triggered them and they rose to taunt her. Like the man at the bar.

'Fen, I'm going to take Kieran out to the cottage for a look. Would you mind keeping an eye on young Liam for us?'

'Liam?'

Kieran smiled. 'My son. He's four.' He looked at her through eyes that shone with pride and a warmth that, until now, had been missing.

A weight of regret settled in her stomach. Kieran would be a great dad. He'd overcome the monsters of his past, reached beyond the same barriers that kept her locked into their grip. The tour group leader signalled her for their bill. 'Give me a moment to take care of this, then I'm free for a while.' A distraction was exactly what she needed, and kids weren't nearly as complicated as adults or as threatening as cuts on a leather vest. 'Where is he?'

Liv waved a hand over to the play area. 'He's out there exploring. Take a bottle of apple juice out to him, would you, love?'

'Does he have a favourite topic he likes to talk about? To break the ice?'

A sad look crossed Kieran's features. 'He doesn't talk much these days.'

10

She wanted to ask why, but the grim pull to Kieran's lips had her swallowing on the question. There'd be time later for explanations. 'Okay, I'll see what I can find for him to do.'

Fen settled the tour group's bill, thanking them before she walked over to the fridge and pulled out a bottle of apple juice. If Kieran accepted the job, could she cope with watching them together every day? Her best friend, his wife and their perfect, happy family?

'Thanks.' Kieran squeezed her shoulder as he passed her to follow Liv out the door.

She watched him walk away, different yet the same, a set to his shoulders she hadn't seen since they were troubled teens arriving in Wongan Creek. With a sigh, she headed for the playground to find Liam. It stood eerily quiet and empty. Where were the sounds of a child playing? The tinkle of bells and spin of plastic blocks on metal poles, the delighted giggles of a ride down the slide.

Her breath caught in her throat as her thoughts slipped back to the man in the leather vest and the warning in his parting words. She shook them off. No, men like him didn't act on their threats immediately. And strangers wouldn't be their target. Men like him would strike at something much closer to home. Had Luke sent him to warn her to back off? As soon as things settled, she'd call Riggs with an update on the stranger's visit.

Fen pulled off the plastic seal around the top of the juice bottle and called out, 'Hey, Liam. My name is Fen. Your dad asked me to bring you an apple juice.'

Silence met her call and her heart took a little dip. Another quick look around showed all the gates surrounding the play area were closed.

'Liam?' She edged closer to the play equipment, searching the windows of a yellow cubby, the clear panel on the red tunnel that housed the interactive play boards, and the green platform with the periscope and pirate flag.

A little sniffle reached her ears from the tunnel that covered the slide. She leaned over to look inside. At the top of the slide, a little boy sat crouched over with his knees hugged to his chest and his head resting on a grubby-looking stuffed toy.

'Are you okay up there, mate?'

A mop of brown curls shivered as the little boy shook his head. A soft sob escaped his chest and he buried his face deeper into the stuffed toy.

'Okay, so your dad asked me to bring you a drink while he and my mum go and look at the cottage where you'll be staying.' Where was Diane? Why wasn't she here to take care of her son? 'Do you think you'd like to live here?'

Breath-stealing sobs echoed down the tunnel. Fen sat down on the edge of the slide. 'Why don't you come down and tell me what's making you sad? Maybe I can help.' The boy's heart-breaking sobs made her eyes sting with tears and her throat clog up. Fen patted the space next to her. 'If you come down, I'll make you a special drink. It's one of my favourites. Do you like lizards?'

At the top of the slide, Liam sucked in a breath and let it out on a word. 'Dunno.'

She'd kill for curls like his. Rich brown hair touched with caramel, just like his dad's. Did he have Diane's eyes?

'I like lizards. A lot. How about I make you a special drink called the Grumpy Lizard and you tell me if you like it or not? It comes with a lizard straw. The lizard's feet hook over the side of the cup. I'll let you keep it when you're done. Would you like that?'

Liam stretched out his legs, a teary look in his eyes the exact same shade as Kieran's. He eased forward on the slide and moved down it inch by slow inch, using his boots as a brake. Fen waited until he reached her side and his feet reached the soft-fall next to hers. She held out the apple juice, but he didn't take it.

'Want to tell me what those tears are for?'

Liam twisted the ear of a worn stuffed sheep and his mouth formed a pout. 'I don't want to live here.'

'Why not? We have lambs like the one you're holding. Real live ones. Down in the paddock near the river.'

'But I want to live where my mummy is.'

Fenella's heart skipped a beat. Had Kieran and Diane separated? 'Okay. And where is that, mate?'

Tears slid down his cheeks. 'She's an angel.'

～

Up at the cottage, Liv held out her hand and Kieran shook it. 'We have a deal.' He and Liam needed this. A clean break, a new start.

'It's going to be a challenge, Kieran. I can't promise you any different. Luke Sampson left this place in a mess and it's going to take some time to recover from it.' Her smile faded. 'Muzz will be turning in his grave knowing what that man did to us.'

Kieran shifted on his feet. He still couldn't believe Muzz was gone. A man larger than life with the patience of a saint and an infectious belly laugh. A man who could fix anything from heavy machinery to electronics, even teenage kids with attitude. 'I'm sorry, Liv. I'll do my best to turn it around for you.'

'I have complete faith in you. Fen blames herself for what happened. I've tried so hard to help her understand that it wasn't anyone's fault except that scoundrel Luke's.' Liv put her arm through his and they strolled back through the vines to the cellar door. 'Will Diane come over once you've settled in?'

And there it was, the question he'd known he wouldn't be able to avoid. The failure he preferred not to think about without a glass of something in his hand to make him forget. Kieran pushed open the gate leading into the gardens outside the cellar building. 'It's just Liam and I now. Diane passed away twelve months ago.'

'Oh, Kieran, I'm so sorry to hear that.' She squeezed his arm.

He let out a breath against the tightness in his chest. He'd never get over hearing those awful words that had echoed through the hospital corridors that day. *She's gone, mate, sorry. We did what we could to save her.*

'Thanks, Liv.'

The sound of crying reached his ears as they made their way into the play area. Kieran's heart tripped. He knew that cry well. He'd heard it so many times over the last twelve months. Had spent many a night holding back his own fears and doubts while he tried to still it. If only Liam hadn't been in the car with Diane that day then the nightmares that haunted his dreams, and sometimes his waking hours, wouldn't keep resurfacing. If only Kieran had paid closer attention to his wife.

'Oh dear,' Liv whispered. 'He sounds heartbroken.'

'Excuse me for a moment, Liv?'

'Of course, go to him.'

He hurried into the play area, fighting the ache in his chest that tried to slow his steps. Fen sat on the edge of the slide with Liam gathered in her lap, her arms around him, a glimmer of tears on her cheeks. He understood

15

how she felt hearing those cries. Helpless, useless, powerless. Because he could never give Liam what his son needed most. His mother.

He knelt next to them and brushed a hand over his son's hair. 'Hey, mate. What's up?'

Liam stuck his thumb in his mouth and reached for Kieran with his other hand. As Fen's arms dropped away, he gathered his son to his chest and stood. Liam cuddled into him, his damp face buried against Kieran's neck.

'I'm so sorry. I had no idea,' Fen whispered.

He heard the regret in her voice and tried to keep the pain from his own. 'It's okay.' Except it wasn't. It might never be okay again. Not for Liam. 'It's been a long day for you, hasn't it, mate?' Kieran turned to Liv. 'Will it be alright if I swing by and sign the contract tomorrow?'

'Of course, love.'

'Thank you.' He turned back to Fen. 'Thank you for taking care of him. I appreciate it.'

'No problem.' She hugged her arms under her breasts, her eyes full of conflict and sadness.

He knew the thoughts that would be churning through her mind. He'd once been close enough to her to know her deepest, darkest secrets. Fen would be remembering what it was like to be abandoned, unwanted, unloved. To lose a mother the way he'd lost a father. To be adrift in a cold, hard world until they'd found peace and a home in the hearts of Wongan Creek.

Here, Liam could be with him out amongst the vineyards, away from the sad memories, and he'd have new people around him. As much as he owed the Vincents for giving him a chance in life, their grief at losing their daughter consumed them to the point where they no longer had a place in their hearts for Liam. Or him.

'Why don't you stay here tonight, Kieran?' Liv's suggestion fell into the silence that had settled awkwardly between them. 'Go into town and collect your things. Liam might feel better if he's settled sooner rather than later.'

No point delaying things further. It wasn't as if they had anything to keep them in town. All they'd brought with them from Sydney were clothes and toys. Everything else had been put into storage until he or the Vincents could deal with the sad memories and pain of parting with Diane's possessions.

'Are you sure?'

'Of course.' Liv patted his arm. 'We'll be ready for you when you come back. Take a couple of days to settle in. We have a wedding to cater for on Saturday, so we'll be busy all day. On Sunday we have breakfasts, lunches and tasting tours all booked. You can sit back and see what we do to get through the winter season before we put you to work on the clean-up in the vineyard.'

Fen stood and dusted off the seat of her denims. 'Will Liam be okay?'

The concern in her voice touched his heart. It had been a long time since Fen was a foster kid, but she'd understand the fears that went with strange places and people. 'He has a few favourite things he's brought over with him. I'll bring them over.'

'We'll make the transition as easy as possible for him.' She glanced at her watch. 'Okay, I'd better go and clean up. Those glasses won't wash themselves.' Fen brushed against him as she leaned over to pat Liam's back. 'See you later, mate. I'll save that Grumpy Lizard for when you come back.'

Liam's head moved under Kieran's chin as he looked at Fen and nodded. 'K.'

The single sound drifted out quietly from his son's lips and warmed some of the ice that gripped Kieran's soul. Liam was at least responding. It was more than he could ever have hoped for so soon. Perhaps in Fen his son had found a kindred spirit, a loner just like him.

Kieran tried to inject a lighter note into his voice he didn't feel and let a glimmer of hope warm him. Maybe coming home to Wongan Creek was a good idea after all. 'Right, we'll see you later then.'

Liv walked him out to the car and waited as he strapped Liam into his booster seat. Stepping back, he closed the door and looked out across the valley where rows and rows of vine leaves had turned brilliant shades of autumn colours. The quiet, peaceful view eased some of the tension from his shoulders. Across the creek, the Whispering Hills rose to meet the sky, as beautiful as he remembered them. He hadn't realised how much he'd missed them. So different from Sydney and the Blue Mountains, yet no less beautiful. If only Diane had loved Wongan Creek the way he did.

'It takes a while, love.' Liv's touch was soft on his sleeve. 'But time will heal the hurt and ease the loss.'

He shook his head slowly, hands on his hips as he watched an eagle soar over the ridge. If Liv only knew the full story … It would take more than time to heal, especially for Liam. But the less people knew about the way Diane died, the better. No matter what she'd done, he had to look after his son's interests first. Liam was his focus now.

'I hope so, Liv.' Because second chances and forgiveness were damn hard to earn.

Chapter Two

Fen retrieved a Cranky Lizard plastic drinking cup and set it aside for Liam, along with a lizard straw for him to use. His tears had shaken her, but his words had broken her heart.

The screen door opened, and a crowd of guests filled the space around the bar as the rear lights of Kieran's rental car disappeared up the drive. He'd be back, and her heart shouldn't be bunny-hopping the way it was. They weren't friends anymore, they were strangers. Gone were the two street kids who'd found friendship and trust in each other, cast into the unknown in a strange town. They'd lived, loved and lost, and now there was a desert and a decade between them. Yet somehow knowing Kieran was home again took the edge off the mess with Luke.

'Turn up the wattage on that smile, sweetheart.

You're scaring the customers with the frown.' Liv gave her a little nudge. 'You take the shots, I'll take the wine-tasting.'

Fen grinned and assessed the audience as she twirled a bottle of butterscotch-flavoured liqueur before putting it down on the bar. 'G'day, folks, and welcome to The Cranky Lizard. Ten bucks gives you five shots and another ten gives you a sneak peek at some mixes to play with when you take home a few Lizards today. Who's first?'

The hour-long session flew by with a responsive audience. This was what she loved best — the interaction, the appreciation on the faces and lips of the tasters and knowing that what they produced was high quality they could be proud of. Luke might have stolen money from them, but that's all she'd let him take. The group walked out the door loaded up with cases of wine and spirits, and Liv's smile grew with every sale. Liv's happiness was all that counted.

As the bus pulled out, Fen delivered a double-handed high five against her mum's. 'Go you!'

'Team effort.' Liv hugged her tightly. 'We'll fix this, darling. You know we will.'

'I know, Mum. I only wish I'd been paying closer attention to what Luke was up to.' She ran a hand across the wood of the bar counter in a place that held her happiest memories. 'I almost lost you everything.'

'Stop that now. You had your hands full with the

renovations. Painters, builders, decorators. You couldn't be everywhere. And Luke had me fooled too. I trusted him as much as you did. He seemed like such a *nice* guy.' Liv cleared the glasses and began washing them out. 'How do you feel about Kieran taking the job?'

'I have faith he'll get us back to where we need to be.'

'And maybe rekindle that friendship again?'

'Don't you go getting any ideas.' Fen shook her finger at Liv. 'I'm not in the market for romance after what Luke did, and Kieran —'

Kieran had to be heartbroken over Diane. He'd loved her so much. Fen pushed away the stab of pain. He'd never love her the same way. She'd always be the girl he'd shared a ride with in the back of Martha Wallace's car, the mate who'd had his back through the adjustment period in their new foster homes. It had to be enough. They could only ever be friends. Anything else would change that bond between them in a way they could never mend again if things didn't work out.

'Little Liam is cute.'

'So are kittens.' Fen tossed a damp tea towel into the laundry basket under the bar counter. 'You want romance, I could always organise you a date with Harry Murchison.'

Liv laughed. 'Harry wouldn't remember we had a date. I'd be lucky if he remembered who I was. Poor soul, his Alzheimer's is getting worse. Still, he's such a character. Heather and Travis have their hands full taking care of him, but they love it. I think little Casey will be good for Liam.'

'You're packaging again, Liv. Heather and Travis. Casey and Liam. Kieran and I can't be a package.'

'Can't you, love? You and Kieran were close once.'

Until Diane. 'We were lost kids with dubious pasts and doubtful futures, but all that changed thanks to you.' She kissed her mum's cheek.

'All I did was love you. You were easy to love, even when you were fighting it. So sad about Diane.' Liv shook her head. 'So young. She had so much talent too. Such a good artist.'

'I remember seeing her art on the walls at the library. I hope they were happy together.'

Liv sighed. 'He broke your heart when he moved away. Have you forgiven him for that?'

'It was a long time ago, Mum.' Forgiveness hadn't been easy, acceptance even harder, but Kieran had loved Diane and Fen hadn't been able to deny him that happiness. Even when it meant giving up the boy she'd loved with all her heart. 'Can you finish up here while I go up to the cottage to make the beds?'

Liv turned to hug her. 'Of course, sweetheart, thank you. Look in the storeroom to see if you can find a few things that will make young Liam's room more welcoming.'

'Will do.' A room could feel so cold and

unwelcoming to a child. Very often that room never grew warmer or more comfortable. Fen knew that better than most. She smiled and hugged her mum back. 'Thanks.'

When she'd come to Muzz and Liv's, they'd had love in abundance to give away. Fen had tested their patience as a sullen, rebellious teenager, yet not once had they ever given up on her. Not even when screams had haunted her dreams at night and echoed off the walls of the house. Nor when the demons that haunted her memories tried to surface, but flitted out of reach again, denying her mind the healing it needed.

She'd lost count of the foster homes she'd been forced to leave, the names she'd been called — devil child, manic depressive, unstable — when all she'd wanted was someone to understand her, to silence the voices that kept her from sleep. And the doctors who'd prodded and probed her mind, only to label her behaviour a result of the circumstances that had made her an orphan. Repressed memories that remained trapped in the corridors of her mind, locked behind doors she couldn't open.

Fen made her way to the storeroom where they kept all things lost and found. She picked her way through perfumes, wine bottles and a collection of souvenirs until she struck gold with a couple of boxes of building blocks from back when wizards and magic were a thing, a puzzle with cartoon sheep on it and a bundle of books written by a local children's author for Liam's age group. She dropped her treasure into a wicker picnic basket she found on the bottom shelf next to a bedside lamp.

The lamp. A smile touched her lips. God, she'd forgotten about it. A wooden base with a hand-painted shade full of crawling lizards. Her smile grew wider even as her chest tightened with the memory.

She and Liv had painted it together a long while after Fen had destroyed the original shade. In a fit of frustration when she'd been angry at the world, she'd hurled it across the room. Liv hadn't even flinched. Instead, she'd picked up the lamp, removed the twisted metal, material-covered frame and tucked the base under her arm.

'We can fix this or we can throw it away, Fenella,' she'd said in that quiet, patient tone that reached inside Fen's heart every time whether she'd wanted it to or not.

'I hate this place. I want to go back to the city.'

'To what, love?'

To what? To an endless roll call of foster families, some of whom cared and some who didn't about a child who curled up in a corner and sliced at her wrists. To a phantom father whose name was taboo. To the place where her drug-addicted mother had died in a room off the dark and dingy corridors of a gentlemen's club, where most of the members were far from deserving of the title. Back to the streets of Perth, where she'd end up exactly like Antoinette. So, she'd stayed, and Liv had taught her all about the resilience of lizards then they'd made the new lampshade.

Be a lizard, Fen. You can grow a new tail, or you can keep searching for the old one you lost, only to find its useless to you. Your choice.

She'd chosen to grow a new tail and hadn't looked back. Fen sighed. Not the sort of story you could tell a four-year-old who'd lost his mum, but hopefully he'd like the lizards anyway. She added the lamp to the basket and reached for the linen trolley to drag it closer.

Two sets of sheets and towels. Fen dropped them into the linen bag and placed the basket and lamp on top. The cottage already had the basic cleaning products and toiletries, so she overlooked those to reach for a pile of tea towels then flicked the light switch that would coat the storeroom in darkness.

A brief smile touched her lips along with the fleeting memory of Kieran's lips on hers. A long time ago in this same storeroom. She'd lost her head around him, desperate not to say goodbye, knowing he'd be lost to her for good. Days before Diane had whipped him away across the Eyre Highway.

I'll miss you, Fen.

She'd had to let him go, cut the anchor loose, lose another tail, learn to go on without him, or revert to that inner, scared child who curled up in shadowy corners with a knife. She'd refused to become that girl again, so she'd focused on the vineyard and growing the business with the people who loved her unconditionally.

Fen pulled the door closed and pushed the trolley down the hallway, out the door and up the concrete path leading to the manager's cottage. On either side of the walkway, kangaroo paws flowered in brilliant shades of red, green, pink and yellow. Her favourite native flower with their blooms shaped like a kangaroo's paw and the long, rough stems reaching for the sky. Two blue wrens flirted with each other over a hedge of lavender. God, she loved the country. A sense of peace settled around her as she pushed her load up the gentle incline.

The cottage had a view almost as good as the one from the main house. From its vantage point on the hill, the manager had a three-sixty-degree view of the vineyard and the flow of the Whispering Hills that formed the backbone of Wongan Creek. Except for the growing scar on the landscape created by Wongan Creek Mining Company a little further south, the view flowed on unmarred.

Life was changing, like the leaves on the vines as they headed towards the end of autumn. And here she was feeling like she'd come full circle, with Kieran back in town, even more inaccessible than he'd been before.

In the car park outside the pub, Kieran sighed as Liam resisted the tug on his hand. 'Come on, mate. You'll love it, I promise. You get to play in that cool playground whenever you want to.'

'Don't wanna.' Liam's lip quivered as he tightened his grip on the woolly toy sheep under his arm.

'It's getting late. Aren't you hungry? When we get there, I can make you those noodles you like so much.'

'No!' Liam stamped a booted foot on the gravel in the pub car park and yelled, 'I hate you. I want Mummy.'

The words stung, but it hurt more that he couldn't give Liam what he wanted. 'No, you don't, mate. It's late. We're both tired. I'm hungry too. The sooner we get to our new home, the sooner we can eat.'

'Not hungry,' he wailed. Tears slipped down Liam's cheeks as he threw his toy on the ground.

Great. The last thing Kieran needed was a full-blown temper tantrum in the middle of Wongan Creek's Main Street when curious eyes were already shifting his way. He returned Virginia Turner's wave and winced as she crossed the street. Had she retired now? God, he hoped so otherwise Liam was in for a tough time. The school principal took no prisoners. She'd been a tough nut back then. Hopefully she'd mellowed with time.

He turned his attention back to his son who'd thrown himself down next to his toy. Kieran ran a hand through his hair. Jesus, he wasn't cut out to do this alone. Diane's crippling pre- and post-natal depression had left him holding the baby, literally. For almost five years he'd struggled to hold down a job, raise his child and look after Diane.

You're the only one who can manage her. The Vincents had tried and failed. Watching their daughter sink deeper into the black hole of depression had been too much for them to handle. He'd tried so hard to coax Diane back from the edge. His failure weighed heavily on his shoulders.

On the ground, Liam lay on his back, kicking against the back wheel of the car and wailing loudly. Kieran knelt beside him, his heart aching and embarrassment burning in his face. Normally he'd step away, ignore the tantrum until Liam settled and then go through the steps of dealing with it just like all the parenting books and Liam's therapist suggested. Today there was no time for that.

Ms Turner back-tracked on her way to Mama Bella's Café and came to stand beside him, one hand on her cane, the other on her hip. 'Is it really you, Kieran Murphy?'

Kieran stood to greet her. Liam's yells reduced to loud moans as he turned his head to look at the newcomer. Yes, Ms Turner still had the power.

'It is. Hello, Ms Turner.'

'Hmmm. You may call me Virginia. You're not a schoolboy anymore.'

Kieran lodged his hands on his hips and looked at Liam who'd reached for his sheep and clutched it to his chest. 'Virginia, lovely to see you.'

She snorted. 'Bollocks. You were never very good at lying, boy. Is this your son?'

He gritted his teeth and waited for the lecture he'd heard so many times before from well-meaning people who knew everything about raising kids and nothing about their circumstances. 'Yes.'

'I'd imagine he's a sweet boy when he's not throwing a tantrum.'

'He is.'

'Hmm.' She prodded the stuffed sheep lightly with her cane. 'What's the sheep's name?'

Liam's moans hitched in his throat and became whimpers. 'Go *away*.' His arms tightened around the toy.

'Liam …' Kieran began, mortified by his son's disrespect.

Virginia held up her hand and shook her head. 'I'll deal with it, young man.' She turned her attention back to his son. 'Liam is a funny name for a sheep. Does he have another one?'

'No.' Out came the lip, but Liam pushed himself up into a sitting position. 'I'm Liam.'

'So, is the sheep's name Go Away?' Virginia shook her head. 'I've never heard of a name like that before.'

'Nooo,' Liam wailed.

'So, tell me his name then.'

Liam hiccupped on a sob. 'Woolly.'

'Well, that's original. Can I see him?'

Liam hesitated a moment before holding the sheep out to her.

Virginia extended her hand. 'You'll have to get up off the road, young man. I can't reach that far.'

Liam shuffled to his feet, squashing poor Woolly's face into the ground.

Virginia ran a hand over the soft toy then tapped her cane on the gravel. 'That's a very nice friend you have there, young man. He looks tired and hungry though. Do you think he should go home for a nap?'

Liam nodded. 'He camed all the way from Sydney.'

'Came,' corrected Virginia. 'And that's a very long way for a young lamb like him to come. Why don't you go home with your dad so Woolly can rest? Friends always take good care of each other.'

'K,' agreed Liam as he tucked Woolly under his arm.

Kieran let out a quiet sigh of relief and opened the back door to let his son scramble inside and climb into his booster seat. He turned to Virginia. 'Thank you.'

A ghost of a smile tugged at the stern school principal's lips. 'You're welcome. I've had many, many years of practice.' She patted his arm gently. 'I'm really sorry to hear about Diane. Elaine told me what happened. You did the right thing coming home with the boy.'

31

He wondered how much his mother-in-law had told her, but at least he could trust Virginia Turner to keep the information to herself. No gossip ever passed those stern lips. Kieran leaned hard on the car door frame. 'I hope so, Ms Turner.'

'Virginia. Did Liv give you the job?'

How did she even know that already? She might not share gossip, but she sure had an ear on the grapevine. He hadn't told a soul he was going for that interview, not even Elaine. He'd forgotten the power of small-town gossip. 'Yes, thank you. We're on our way over there now to settle Liam into the cottage.'

'Good. No point in mucking about. So, you've seen Fenella then?'

His heart did that little thing it always did at the mention of her name. That arrhythmic stutter that made him feel guilty because Diane's name had never had the same effect, no matter how hard he'd tried to love her. 'Yes.'

Virginia tapped her cane on the gravel. 'No-one knows better than you and Fenella how hard this is for your boy, and to understand what's happening in Liam's head right now. The Cranky Lizard is the best place for you.'

Kieran nodded even though he wasn't convinced. He'd agonised over the move back to Western Australia, over taking Liam so far away from the only grandparents he had, over so many things. He'd answered Liv's ad in the paper half-heartedly, not even sure he wanted to come back to Wongan Creek, not really knowing what he wanted at all.

For God's sake, he hadn't managed a vineyard in years. Not since Diane had insisted on moving from the Blue Mountains to the city. He'd done it for her, in the vain hope that it might cure what ailed her. But he'd realised his mistake too late and it cost him his wife and almost his son too.

'Right. Well, I'll get on now. I'm on my way to a CWA meeting. We're planning the winter festival. Drive carefully. And when you have a chance to breathe, get in touch with Travis Bailey. His niece, Casey, is a couple of years older than Liam. She lost her mum in that nasty business with that Bannister boy.'

Kieran shuddered. He'd read about it in the papers online. How they'd caught Zac Bannister, found enough evidence to convict him of the murder of Travis's twin sister years after her death. 'I will, thanks.'

Virginia waved goodbye and found her way back onto the walkway that would lead her to Mama Bella's Café and the meeting with the CWA ladies. He wondered if Marge Everett was still driving the school bus. Mama Bella's still held pride of place on Main Street. He'd have to treat Liam to one of Bella's famous milkshakes once they'd settled in.

'Daddy?'

Kieran moved from his leaning position on the door

and dipped into the back of the car to secure the seat safety harness around Liam. 'Are you and Woolly ready for an adventure?'

'Woolly's hungry.'

He smiled, almost laughed for the first time in way too long. At last, a good sign after months of a waning appetite. 'Let's get you home then. Chicken noodles with a side of Vegemite toast coming right up.'

He closed the door and got into the driver's seat. Could the cottage at the vineyard be a home for them? Could it be the catalyst for happiness after years of struggle? With a sense of determination to make it so for Liam's sake, Kieran turned the key in the ignition of his rental car and directed the nose in the direction of The Cranky Lizard.

Chapter Three

Fen flicked her fringe away from her eyes, tucked the sheet under the mattress on Kieran's bed and tried hard not to think about him sleeping there. Alone.

Sometimes it felt like a lifetime since they'd first met in that cold and soulless partitioned space at the Department of Child Protection and Family Support office in Armadale. Yet there were days when it felt like yesterday that the equally soulless caseworker, Martha Wallace, had sat opposite them in her imposing chair and looked at them as if she held no hope for their futures.

'We have two families in Wongan Creek prepared to take you.'

Like two-pound dogs waiting to be rescued then rejected because they were too vicious for the family.

She'd looked at Kieran in his threadbare denim jeans and flannel shirt over a black T-shirt. He'd looked at her dressed in loose black as she'd twisted her leather cuffs against the itch on the skin under them, and an unspoken pact had passed between them. They'd stick together until the pain of their pasts subsided, and when the hope of finding a forever family faded and they were lobbed back into the system again, they'd have each other's backs.

Fen tucked the quilt into the cover and shook it out, letting it settle over the bed. She smoothed out the air pockets with the palms of her hands. Was Martha Wallace still alive? She'd been an ancient old dragon even back then. Luckily things had worked out for her and Kieran, and they'd never had to have much to do with her again, except for suffering through the occasional home visit.

The sound of a car pulling into the carport next to the cottage dragged her out of the past. Nerves jiggled in her stomach. Kieran and Liam were here. Another chapter of their lives, so intricately entwined yet worlds apart, was about to begin. Would Liam like his room? Would Kieran stay? Could they rekindle what they'd had and chase the sadness from his eyes? She hated seeing him like that again. Broken. Beaten. The way he'd been in the office that day so long ago. Except this time his bruises weren't physical. They couldn't be treated with arnica and a bandaid. With one last fluff of the pillows, Fen walked out of the room and down the hallway to open the front door.

'You made it back,' she greeted as Kieran got out the car.

'Yeah.' He ran a hand through his hair.

'Trouble?'

He looked so tired, so empty. Diane had been his life. Fen pushed down on the niggle of jealousy. She had no right to feel it. Growing apart as they grew up had always been inevitable.

Kieran helped Liam out of the car and set him on his feet on the ground. The poor kid had a rumpled look about him that paid testament to a rough day. Hopefully he'd be happy in his lizard room and not creeped out by it or it could be a long night for Kieran. One of many, she suspected.

'A little. I bumped into Virginia Turner. She dealt with it.' He ruffled Liam's curls and the action earned him a grumpy frown. 'Nothing a tummy full of food and a nice warm bed won't fix, isn't that right, mate?'

'I hope you're hungry then. Liv sent up a dish of her famous mac 'n cheese with bacon and tomato. It's warming in the oven for you.' Fen stepped off the verandah and walked towards them. 'Need a hand to get everything inside?'

'That would be great, thanks. Liv's macaroni cheese sounds better than the Vegemite sandwich and instant chicken noodles I had planned.' Some of the stress eased from Kieran's brow only to sneak back in again as Liam latched onto his leg. He leaned down to sweep the little guy into his arms. 'It's been a long day, hasn't it, mate?'

The resignation in his voice told her it would be an equally long night. How had it come to this? The bond between father and son was strong. Fen could almost feel it, touch it, and didn't doubt for a milli-second that Kieran adored Liam. How long had he been struggling alone and what had prompted him to come back?

'Hey, Liam, I've got a surprise in the kitchen for you. Why don't you come inside and see it?'

She hoped The Cranky Lizard kid's cup would impress Liam and that Kieran wouldn't object to the fairy bread snack she'd prepared. Kieran's lips curved in a smile that almost reached his eyes before he walked towards her, long denim-clad legs eating up the short distance between them. God damn him, he still had that sexy swagger. And those eyes that looked right inside her soul. Eyes that had seen through the wall she'd built all those years ago.

He planted a kiss on her cheek, his beard brushing her skin, his lips warm and affectionate. 'You're a champ, Fen. Thanks.'

'You're welcome.' She tried to cover the quiver in her voice with a cough.

Liam lifted his head from his father's shoulder, interest sparking in his tear-stained eyes. 'Grumpy Lizard?'

Fen grinned. 'Yep. And fairy bread.' She let her gaze slide to Kieran's and felt the full force of his eyes on her. 'If that's okay with you?'

'Perfect. Thanks, mate.'

The erratic beat of her heart stilled and the thrill of his gaze eased as reality sunk in once again. That's all she'd ever be for Kieran. The mate who had his back.

'Great.' Her smile felt tight on her lips as she turned away and walked back into the house. 'Come inside then. I wasn't sure Liam would like macaroni cheese, so I figured a snack wouldn't hurt.' She rubbed at the ache in her chest and swallowed against the tightness that gripped her throat. God damn it, she wouldn't cry. He was nothing to her and she was nothing to him, except a friend. That was all she wanted. All he needed.

'There are a few beers in the fridge, some milk, your choice of red or white Cranky Lizards, soft drinks and bottled water. Fresh bread will be delivered to your door around six in the morning along with half a dozen fresh eggs. If there is anything else you need, ring down to reception and I'll bring it up.'

Pull yourself together, Fenella. He'd see through her psycho-babble. He always had. And then things would get more awkward than they were already.

'Chickens?' Liam's interest sparked.

'And lambs.' Fen patted the toy sheep the boy held.

'Where?'

'Come into the kitchen and your dad can show you

the lambs from the window. They're Harry's lambs from across the creek, but he doesn't mind sharing them with us. Sometimes he forgets they're here and they stay a few days. It's good for the grass and clears the weeds. The chickens are up at the main house. I'll show you those tomorrow if you like?'

Liam nodded, his eyes still too serious for a smile. 'K.'

She led them to the kitchen and watched Kieran take Liam over to the window so he could point out the sheep.

'Have you scheduled pruning back the vines, Fen?'

'Liv has organised a team to come in from Wednesday next week. And we have a couple of grey nomads signed up too. The schedule is on the desk in your office. Induction is set for Tuesday at six am. We've got a few old vines we need to replace. The bobcat is booked for Friday.'

'Sounds good.'

Fen wanted to believe him, except the exhaustion in his voice erased any enthusiasm he might have left. 'Worry about it on Monday, Kieran. We're on track with the schedule. You have more important things to worry about tonight. I'll leave you and Liam alone to settle in. The water in the heater should be warm enough to run a bath or shower.'

He turned from the window to face her. She hated the drawn look and dark circles that bruised his eyes.

Maybe the country air would do him good. Maybe the awkwardness between them would fade.

'Right, well, I'll leave you to settle in. I'll be back with your breakfast basket in the morning.'

'Thanks, Fen. It's good to be home.' His eyes searched hers, filled with something she couldn't identify. Not with the link between them broken, the distance between them more than just miles across the desert and Diane's ghost present in the room.

Early morning sunlight teased the sky over the vines as dawn broke through the clouds. Kieran watched his son sleep. As comfortable and welcoming as Fen had made Liam's bedroom, he hadn't been ready to sleep there alone. So, he'd spent another long, almost sleepless night with Liam clinging to his side, whimpering in his sleep as Kieran brushed a soothing hand over the dark brown curls.

God, he loved his son with all his heart, but he really needed a good night's sleep. Perhaps the fresh air and exercise out here in the country would eventually tire Liam out enough to sleep peacefully. With a bit of luck his son would make friends in the community and gain some confidence too, begin to forget the horror of the last twelve months.

Clean up and pruning would be exhausting over the

next few weeks. He hoped he could cope with the long, back-breaking hours on minimal sleep and that he wouldn't let Liv and Fen down. Fen with her dark pixie-cut, black clothes and the wristbands that hid a world of hurt.

Diane's insane jealousy meant he'd cut all ties with Fen and focused on keeping his wife happy, protecting his in-laws from the highs and lower-than-lows of her moods. Moods they'd had no idea how to deal with. He'd tried so damn hard not to crumble under the pressure as his marriage had descended into a hell neither of them could escape from.

Liam stirred and stretched. Another day, a new start. Kieran prayed that he'd made the right choice coming back to the place where he'd been given a second chance, where he hoped the people had it in their hearts to give him another.

'I'm hungry, Daddy.' Liam looked at him with eyes still heavy from sleep and tears.

Kieran smiled. He'd never imagined that those two words could come to mean so much. 'Are you, mate? What would you like for breakfast?'

'Chocolate.'

He chuckled. 'Maybe later, okay? First, I think Fen said there'd be nice fresh bread. Should we go look outside?'

Liam pushed himself up on the mattress to sit on his knees. 'Can we see the chooks?'

'I'm sure we can, mate. First things first, okay? Breakfast, brush teeth and get dressed.' He tickled the ribs that poked out from his son's too skinny side.

Liam giggled and pushed his hand away. 'Need to pee, Daddy.'

Kieran pulled a face. 'Off you go then. Don't forget to lift the seat. I'll go see if we have bread.'

'And peanut butter.'

'Yep, that too.'

'And Vegemite.' Liam called out as he made his way to the bathroom.

'Righto.'

Kieran threw back the covers and eased his legs over the edge of the bed. He found his track pants on the floor where he'd left them and tugged them on before walking down the short hallway to the front door. Pulling it open, he let his gaze travel the early morning vista. A smoky haze fell across the Whispering Hills, a remnant from the wood-burning fireplaces warming the homes of the town's residents. With winter only days away, the mornings had become cooler. Soon the dew would turn to frost. The once lush vines would lose their green and gold, leaving them naked to the harshness of winter. Already some of the leaves had turned brown and shrivelled, ready to fall to the ground with the breeze.

Across the creek in the distance, sheep grazed the last remaining summer weeds from Travis Bailey's canola fields. Kieran made a mental note to call him, touch base, see how things were going. So much had changed in Wongan Creek since gold fever had struck the region, even the landscape and the dynamics of the town. Still, it was far away from the Castle Cove house he'd shared with Diane and the endless, peaceful view across the water.

He'd hoped the bright and cheerful two-storey home with its picture-perfect, sunny windows and airy feel would lift Diane's spirits. It hadn't. Nothing had given her peace. She'd no longer wanted to paint and release her dark thoughts on canvas. The home had become a trap for the unseen demons she'd no longer wished to battle.

With a sigh, Kieran reached for the covered picnic basket on the table near the door. He lifted the cloth and inhaled the mouth-watering aroma of freshly baked bread. Still warm. It couldn't have been too long ago that Fen would have placed the basket on the table.

His gut pulled tight with affection he couldn't afford to explore. Fen was off limits. All women were off limits until he could erase the sadness from his son's eyes and the guilt from his own mind. Right now, he couldn't see past Diane's ghost even though their marriage had failed long before Liam was born.

He looked up and spotted Fen on the wooden bridge that spanned the koi pond outside the cellar door. Short black jacket and black jeans that hugged her curves as she leaned over to toss fish food into the pond.

'Morning, Fen. Thanks for the bread,' he called out, his voice carrying easily through the quiet morning.

She turned and waved, her fringe flopping across her face, too far away for him to read her expression. She turned and walked away towards the cellar. Disappointment flooded him, a part of him hoping she'd come over for a chat, but it seemed Fen was as keen to distance herself from him as he should be to keep the barrier between them.

Liam tugged on the leg of his track pants. 'Did we get bread, Daddy?'

He looked down at the still tousled head. 'Yes, we did.' He held the basket at Liam's level. 'Can you smell that? Does it smell good?'

Liam sniffed at the basket. 'Yum.'

'Fen put some jam in there too. Strawberry. Do you think it's homemade?'

Liam shrugged. 'Can I see the fish?' He pointed to the pond.

Kieran ruffled Liam's hair and laughed, the sound unfamiliarly uplifting. 'Let's get breakfast out of the way and then we can explore. Deal?' He held out his fist for a bump.

'K.' Liam's knuckles met his.

Liam didn't need a lot of persuasion to eat his breakfast, devouring a good chunk of the fluffy bread and making an impressive dip into the jam. Kieran let a glimmer of hope grow in his heart that maybe he could make his son happy and healthy again.

Kitchen cleaned, Liam dressed, and the remnants of breakfast scrubbed from his cheeks, Kieran held out a pair of bright blue wellies patterned with dinosaurs.

'Put these on and we'll go have a look at the chooks.'

'And the fish?'

'Yep.'

'And the lambs too?' Liam sat down on the floor and tugged on his boots.

'Sure.' Kieran held out a jacket. 'Put this on too, mate. It's a little cool outside still.'

'K, Daddy.' Liam obeyed then he picked up his ever-present toy sheep and cuddled it.

Kieran shrugged into his own jacket and pulled on leather steel-capped boots. 'Fish or chooks first?'

'Fish!'

'Come on then.'

He opened the door and let his son clamber out into the weak, early morning sun. Later it would warm up to a nice comfortable temperature and they could enjoy the last of autumn's warmth. Liam stopped under the white street sign sporting a picture of a blue-tongue lizard and bolted on top of a blue lamp post. Kieran snapped a photo with his phone of Liam pointing up at it, his smile wide. Perhaps it would help the Vincents overcome their grief if they could see their only grandchild on the road to recovery too. He tapped the share button and hit send to their email address.

Liam tensed as they approached the pond, his enthusiasm waning fast, descending quickly into reluctance as the body of water loomed. To him it would seem more like a lake than a pond, its depths and watery secrets unknown, raising memories of another place, another time when water had held a fear larger than life. He slipped his hand into Kieran's and lost the spring to his step.

Kieran let his hand tighten around his son's, his grip reassuring. 'It's okay, mate. Hold on tight. Did you want to go and see the chooks instead?'

'Dunno, Daddy.'

'Let's go a bit closer then, okay? You tell me when you want to stop.' Maybe today they'd have a breakthrough. Maybe this time Liam would take a step closer to forgetting.

Muzz had outdone himself on the pond. About three metres wide and seven metres long with water cascading from a rocky waterfall, the sound of splashing filled the air. Amongst the rockery edging the pond, tufts of Mondo grass added green to the brown. Brightly coloured pink, red and white waterlilies floated across the surface of the water giving shelter to the koi. He calculated the depth as he looked past the waterlilies to the bottom of the pond. Less than a metre. Not too deep.

Shallow enough to stand in. Or for a little kid like Liam to keep his head above water if he accidentally fell in.

Liam's footsteps faltered as they went to step onto the wooden bridge that crossed the pond. 'Don't wanna see the fish anymore.'

Kieran's heart contracted. The therapist had promised Liam would get over his fear, that his memories would fade as he grew, that he'd forget the trauma of being trapped underwater. It had been twelve months already, for God's sake. How much longer would his son have to bear the nightmares that had resulted from immersion in a watery grave?

'It's okay if you don't want to, mate. We can come back later if you like.'

'No, Daddy.'

His booted foot kicked at the step onto the bridge and in that instant, Kieran's beautiful, even-tempered son became the child from hell. Haunted by memories, traumatised by the actions of an unstable mother, terrified by a mass body of water that probably wasn't even deep enough cover him up to his shoulders, he screamed and cried and tugged hard on Kieran's hand.

Liv and Fen came running as the screams reached fever pitch, tearing at his eardrums, making his head pound and the familiar ache of helplessness spread through him. He swept Liam up into his arms, stroked his back and held him close even as the little boy strained against his hold and pounded at him.

'It's okay. Daddy's here. I won't let anything hurt you.'

He whispered the words over and over into his son's curls, each syllable tearing from his throat, each one as ineffective as the little fists that connected with his face and shoulder. Each 'I hate you' an echo of Diane's words that ripped his heart to shreds. Stepping away from the bridge, he walked around the pond onto the path to the main house.

Fen reached him first, her eyes full of questions he didn't want to have to answer but knew he couldn't avoid if they were going to stay in Wongan Creek.

'Is he okay? Is he hurt?' Breathless, Fen stopped in front of him.

Kieran shook his head, unable to speak past the pain in his throat.

Liv caught up. 'Can I help?'

Kieran shook his head again. No-one could do anything that months of therapy hadn't been able to fix. All he could do was hold his son until the storm passed and keep praying for a miracle.

Breaking point. He'd reached it, denied it the right to cripple him and fought back the burn that stung his eyes. He was a survivor, for God's sake. He'd survived living on the streets until he was thrown into the system. He'd lived through the beatings and neglect that preceded his life as a runaway. He could get through this. Had to because he didn't want to fail his son the way he had his wife.

Fen picked up the toy sheep Liam had thrown to the ground. The bribe Diane had given Liam that fateful day to make him get into the car with her. She dusted it off and pressed it against his chest next to where Liam's face was pressed against his shirt.

Liam crushed it to him, his screams morphing into body-wracking sobs. Liv stroked his back, a movement that took the stiffness from his spine and had his little body relaxing against Kieran's chest as the minutes ticked by in silence and the humiliation grew.

When the fight left his son's body, Liv asked, 'Would you like to feed the chooks with me, Liam? I've been waiting for you to come.'

Seconds passed in which Kieran thought his son might start another spectacular tantrum, but instead he turned his face to Liv. She held out her arms. He hesitated only a moment longer before pushing away from Kieran and leaning over to Liv. She took his weight, adjusted him on her hip, smoothed his damp fringe from his eyes and talked as she walked away.

Arms empty and shirt damp, Kieran watched them. When would this nightmare end?

Chapter Four

Fen let her gaze travel his face, take in the lines of exhaustion drawn on his cheeks, the dullness in his eyes that spoke volumes of a hurt far deeper than he'd ever let on.

No, Mr Kieran Hard-Arse Murphy would hide behind his tough street-born exterior and continue to bottle up whatever had caused his son's meltdown. So, she'd drip-feed him coffee, be the mate she'd always been, and have his back.

'Come over to the café. I've put the coffee machine on.'

He rubbed a hand over his face, ran it across the back of his neck and stared at the ground. 'I'll be down in a minute.'

'I'll be there, waiting for you.' The way she'd been through the toughest times. The way she would have been if she'd known about his loss. Fen wished they weren't the strangers the missing years had made them.

She waited a moment longer, watched him retrace his steps and walk to the middle of the bridge. He leaned over the railing, elbows resting on the wood, hands clasped together, head bowed, and her heart ached for whatever turmoil he was fighting inside him.

She turned away and headed for the cellar wishing it was a little later in the day to warrant a dash of something stronger in the coffee. They sure as hell both needed it.

Pushing open the door, she walked across to the coffee machine set up in the small café area to the left of the bar. She loved how Muzz and Liv had sectioned off areas of The Cranky Lizard, making it totally family-friendly.

Securing a deal with a major coffee house meant they could run a supplier-sponsored café to cater to a generic lunch crowd as well as those visitors seeking out the taste of boutique wines and liqueurs.

Luke had almost ruined it all. A shiver ran through her, the unease returning. Last night, she'd called Riggs to tell him about the man in the bar, the veiled threat, and the tattoo and cuts that identified him as part of Luke's club.

A threat that had her tossing all night from an intangible fear that threaded through her dreams and phantom memories stealing around in shadowy corners she couldn't quite reach into.

Nightmares that had her curled in a ball in the corner of her room, eyes squeezed shut against the darkness, her mind clamping down on the screams that echoed in her head, the thumps and shouts receding into strangled silence, the smell of sweat and blood and anger still ripe in the air.

Years of therapy had yet to release the cause and trigger of those nightmares, what they meant. Why they wouldn't stop. Why sometimes the simplest things stopped her in her tracks, filled her with fear while a memory flitted out of reach, begging to be remembered, failing to surface. Secrets refusing to reveal themselves, that made her want to stamp her feet and scream against the frustration of being unable to force them from her mind. Just like Liam.

So many things could have triggered the little boy's tantrum. She couldn't begin to imagine what Kieran had been through with Diane dying. She had so many questions she didn't feel she could ask yet. Frustration ate at her stomach. How could she help him if she didn't know what was going on in that complicated mind of his?

With a sigh, she set about making the coffee, pleased to be distracted by the steam rising from the spouts and the gurgling noise that barely disguised Kieran's footsteps on the wooden floorboards. She looked up briefly and watched him ease into a chair at one of the round white café tables. Elbows on it, he ran his fingers through his hair before sitting back and letting his hands clench in his lap. Broken.

Hands a little unsteady, she put the large cappuccino cup onto a saucer and added a bite-sized shortbread biscuit on the side from the jar. Then she put on her Fen-face with its careless smile that hid everything she wanted it to and placed the coffee in front of him on the table.

'So … does he do that often?' She pulled out the chair opposite Kieran and sat.

He shook his head. 'Not as often as he used to.'

'Do you want to talk about it?'

Kieran sighed and toyed with the spoon in the saucer in front of him. 'It's an ugly story, Fen.'

'Uglier than ours before we arrived in Wongan Creek?'

He raised his head and hit her with the full impact of cold green eyes, empty now of the emotions that had swamped them earlier. 'Way uglier.'

Fen reached across the table and covered his hand with hers. His fist was tight under her touch, as unyielding as the wall that had sprung up between them. 'I'm here for you, Kieran. I always have been.' She swallowed against the knot in her throat. Seeing him like this — emotionally drained, empty, hopeless — was far worse than the welts and bruises she'd seen on him in that dreary office in Armadale so many years ago.

He loosened his fist and weaved his fingers through hers, making a steeple on the table where their palms met. Fen stifled the shiver that ran through her. She'd missed those fleeting touches, his smile, his lousy jokes.

'Thank you.' He turned his head to stare out the window at the vines in the distance, his fingers tightening around hers. 'I guess there's no reason to put it off any longer. It will come out sooner or later, and I'd rather you hear it from me.' He took a deep breath and let it out on a deep, shuddering sigh. 'Diane wasn't well. She suffered from depression. It wasn't until after Liam was born that one of the doctors diagnosed her as bi-polar. She refused treatment from a psychiatrist but took the medication her doctor prescribed.'

Fen offered nothing to that. Diane had always come across as unstable, but back then they'd been teenagers going through the hell puberty created. No-one had blinked an eye at her temper tantrums and constant mood swings.

'Diane never wanted children. About eight years ago, that changed. She became obsessed with having a baby. We talked it over with her doctor, thinking it might help her. We tried everything, but she couldn't fall pregnant. Eventually, after three rounds of IVF, we had Liam.'

He paused to sip his coffee, not releasing her hand. Despite the pins and needles from the tight grip, Fen couldn't bring herself to break the contact. 'He's an adorable kid.'

Kieran smiled, a small movement that tugged at his lips before his mouth pulled tight again. 'Yes, he is. Diane didn't cope well with the pregnancy or the birth. She sunk further into the black hole, ignoring Liam when he cried, refusing to feed him. She became completely unreachable. Even gave up the painting she loved so much.' He released her hand and wrapped his around the cup. 'I had to take over to keep my child alive.'

'Oh, Kieran.' It would have been so much easier to simply think of Diane as selfish, but to know that it went far deeper and more serious than that made her heart ache for all of them. It hurt more that she understood how Liam might feel abandoned by his mum because damn it, her real mother had abandoned her just like Diane had abandoned her son. If it wasn't for people like Liv, she might not be alive to share his pain. 'I'm so sorry.'

Restless, he put down the cup and stood, pacing the floor until he came to stand at the window that overlooked the vines and the hills beyond. He flattened his palms against the painted sill. 'Twelve months ago, I made the call. I couldn't deal with it anymore. I'd done everything I could to help her. She was on a downhill slide, becoming increasingly abusive and uncontrollable, and I had to think of Liam's future.'

The pain and regret in his voice, the way his shoulders dragged and that haunted look she'd seen in his eyes hurt her as much as it did him. Even after all their time apart, Fen could still tune in to Kieran's emotions, forever bound by the bond they'd formed so long ago when all they'd had was each other.

All she wanted to do was go to him and hold him until the tension eased from his spine and the ache that consumed him disappeared. Instead, she sat and listened, frozen in her seat, taking the brunt of his pain.

'I applied for intervention from the Mental Health Review Tribunal to have her involuntarily committed for treatment. They took her in for assessment. Somehow, despite having her records to refer to, they let her go. She convinced them she was fine. That it was all some ridiculous plot to create grounds for a divorce. That I was having an affair and wanted to get rid of her.' He turned away from the window to face her. 'Jesus, Fen, even if I wanted to, I didn't have time for an affair. I never cheated on Diane. No matter how bad things were between us, I stuck by her side.'

Fen shifted in her seat, dread settling in the pit of her stomach. 'Kieran, you don't have to do this right now.' She hated the pain etched into his face, the way his thoughts had his knuckles white as he gripped the windowsill behind him.

'I need you to know, Fen.' He ran a hand through his hair, hooked his fingers through the belt loops on his jeans and leaned back against the window sill. 'She left the hospital in a taxi, went around to her mum's while I was at work. She took Liam and their car. They tried to stop her, but she was running on adrenaline and crazy. She drove to the Davidson Park boat ramp, sped off it and crashed the car into Middle Harbour Creek.'

'Jesus, Kieran. With Liam in the car?' Fen pushed up out of her chair, shock making her legs unsteady.

He nodded, crossing his arms over his chest. 'Yep. Luckily there were witnesses. Two men jumped in to save them. Diane was killed on impact. No seatbelt. They managed to free Liam in time.'

Cold crept into Fen's bones as she moved to where Kieran stood. 'It's not your fault. You didn't make her do it.' She placed her hand on his crossed arms and squeezed.

'It is my fault, Fen. I gave up on her.'

'She was sick.'

'And I took that marriage vow and broke it. My son has been terrified of water ever since. I can get him to take a shower, but I can't put him anywhere near a bath let alone a pool. I was hoping we'd made progress when he asked to see the fish.'

He dropped his arms to his sides and Fen sneaked

past the barrier to wrap her arms around him and lean her head against his chest like she had many times when they'd first arrived in town, strangers in a strange new world, finding comfort in each other.

'You couldn't have guessed what she'd do.'

He remained stiff in her hold. 'I should have stayed at the hospital for the assessment instead of going home and leaving her there.'

'You did what you had to do. You had a child to take care of.'

'I failed to do that too.'

Fen pulled back and shoved at his chest. 'Stop it. It's not necessary to blame yourself. I believe you did everything you could to stop her. It's not in you to be any other way. Diane made the choice to take her life, and in doing so put her son, *your* son, in danger. Liam is alive, and he needs you. That's where you need your focus.'

She turned away from him, anger building inside her. How had Kieran ended up so responsible and broken by Diane's actions? How had Diane not recognised her own need for help, especially with the support of a man like him by her side, fighting her battles? She tried hard not to resent the woman who'd taken him from her, tried to feel sorry for Diane. But empathy was buried too far beneath the horror of what Kieran and Liam's lives had become.

'Drink your coffee. It's getting cold.'

'You're angry.' The resignation in his tone suggested it was an emotion he was used to, a position he was familiar with.

'Yes, but not with you.' Damn it, yes. She was angry, for him, and especially angry for Liam, an innocent in the game Diane had played. 'Where were her parents in all this?' Until she understood everything, she couldn't forgive Diane for using Kieran the way she had.

'They had no idea how to deal with it. The only person she wanted was me. She was my wife and my responsibility.'

'She was their child. They had an equal obligation.' She couldn't forgive the Vincents for their role in leaving the sole care of their mentally unstable daughter to him. Would have trouble with forgiving them for breaking the man she'd worked so hard to fix when he'd been broken before.

'Ha!' The sound emerged hard and rough from Kieran's throat. 'They had no control over her. Do you want to know the harsh reality, Fen?'

When he said it in a tone laced with bitterness … no. She knew she'd hate what she'd hear. He stepped forward, toe to toe, and placed his hands on her shoulders as if he needed to anchor himself against the truth.

'They knew my real mother was prone to psychotic episodes. They'd studied my case file before agreeing to foster me. They thought I'd be the perfect sibling, that

I'd understand her behaviour, be able to deal with it better than a child who hadn't been exposed to mental illness.' He rubbed a hand across the back of his neck. 'Apparently I did that too well. They came to lean on me more with every episode, every tantrum, because I was the only one who could talk her around. Diane became more reliant on me. Later, when we fell into a relationship, she continued to spiral out of control and I knew I'd never be able to leave her like that. Her parents relied on me even more. I coped better with it than they did, and they were content to leave her in my care.'

'That sounds so selfish of them.'

He shrugged. 'They were helpless. They'd tried everything else. Robert was busy with his job, involved in cases that required travel across the country. Elaine tried, but she couldn't cope alone.'

All those years he'd struggled alone and never said a word. 'Did you talk to someone about it?'

'Diane had alienated all her friends. I was trying to hold onto my job and manage her care. She didn't want counselling and I didn't think anyone would understand what we were going through.'

'You could have come to me. Trusted me.' She gripped the front of his shirt in her fists. 'Kieran, I was your friend.'

'And what could you have done? What difference could you have made? I had a roof over my head, food on the table and a bed to sleep in. A lot more than I had when I arrived in this town. I owed it to them to help with their daughter because they'd given me a home and stability. She wasn't the only challenge they had going on in their lives at the time. There were rumours at the time that Robert was having an affair. That he'd had several over the years. It's one of the reasons he accepted the job over east. To get Elaine away from here and save their marriage.'

Fen let go of his shirt. She turned away and set about clearing the table, the coffee too cold to be palatable. Words failed her as her mind churned over what he'd been through. How desperate had the Vincents been that they'd needed to resort to such extreme measures? 'So, they left Diane's care solely to you?'

'I guess it's understandable that people would see that as selfish.'

'They used you, Kieran.' Disbelief tasted bitter on her tongue.

'I loved her.'

His quietly spoken words might as well have been a shout. Pain twisted the knife in her stomach. Of course, he had. He'd been devoted to her. Kieran never did things by halves.

'It wasn't all bad, Fen. There were good times. Times when I thought we could really make it work. Days when she seemed better, happier, content. Then we'd hit a downward spiral again, fuelled by God knows what. It could be anything from a bad hair day to not having the right oils to finish a painting.'

Fen's heart ached for him. He'd lost so much he could never get back. His wife. His life.

Kieran fought hard against the urge to pull Fen into his arms and anchor her against him. He wanted to let go of the anger and hurt, cry for the woman he'd buried, the wife who'd given him a son. Accept the comfort Fen offered and take the friendship she'd always been ready to give.

No matter how strong Fen had become or how willing she was to help, he wouldn't add to her load with his baggage too. He couldn't saddle her with a broken man and a traumatised child, and the ghost of a wife he couldn't lay to rest. Not until his son had completely recovered from the trauma of her death. No matter how much he wanted to let the guilt slide from his shoulders, pack away the past and move into a future.

'Now you know.' Not everything. Not yet. He didn't want her to hate him the way Diane had in the end.

She turned to face him, smoothing the flop of her fringe from her eyes. Dark, stormy grey eyes that glittered with unshed tears. For him. For Liam. And maybe for Diane too. 'I'm sorry.'

'It is what it is.' Kieran crossed is arms over his chest to stop his hands from reaching out. 'I have to get Liam over this hurdle.'

'I'll do what I can to help.'

Losing the battle not to touch her, he cupped her cheek in his palm, her skin smooth and soft against his. 'Thank you.' He gave in to the temptation to stroke her cheek with his thumb. 'I've missed you, Fen.'

Before he could stop himself, she was there, her body snuggled against him and his arms wrapped tightly around her. His lips touched the smooth, silkiness of her apple-scented hair below his chin as she pressed her face into his shirt, her hands clutching at the material at his back. And he held her. Just held her. Absorbing the warmth she generated, sinking into the comfort of having her in his arms and the familiarity of her friendship.

The sound of Liam's laugh filtered through the doors of the cellar followed by Liv's, 'Yoo-hoo! Hope that coffee machine's on.'

At the sound of little boots hammering the floor, Fen pulled out of his arms and dashed her fingers across her cheeks. She moved away from him, leaving a cold space between his arms.

He sat down at the table and watched her go through the motions of making fresh coffee as he held open those arms for his son. Pretending that moment hadn't happened and ignoring the rightness of it would be the hardest thing to do. One touch, one hug and it felt like a homecoming. So right, yet so incredibly wrong. He lifted Liam up onto his knee and reminded himself that his son's happiness and healing was all that counted.

'Hey, mate. Did you have fun feeding the chooks?'

Liam nodded, a grin on his face that warmed Kieran's heart and lessened the ache. 'Yeah, Daddy. And I got five … no … six … no four eggs. Didn't I, Liv?'

Liv ruffled his curls and sat on the seat next to Kieran. 'You sure did, clever boy. We're going to put them in a cake later, aren't we?'

'Yep. A chocolate one. With peanut butter icing.'

Kieran grimaced. 'Not sure about peanut butter icing.'

Liv laughed. 'Butter icing.'

'Ah, much better.'

Liam chattered away about the chickens and how they were going to see the sheep next.

'Harry Murchison's sheep,' Liv clarified. 'Occasionally they wander into the bottom paddock when he forgets to close the gates. Keeps the weeds down, so we don't mind.'

'And when he forgets where they are, we can let Travis know they're here or he spends ages looking for them.' Fen placed a babycino with blue lizard-shaped marshmallows on the side in front of Liam and placed a reassuring hand on Kieran's shoulder.

He let himself enjoy the comfort of her touch until

she moved away, pleased they'd slipped into a more comfortable, less confronting discussion. Harry Murchison was a much safer subject and seeing his son's bright, happy smile again warmed his heart. 'Poor Harry. Being reliant on someone else must be hard for him to accept after being independent all these years. I can't believe Alzheimer's claimed a man with a clever mind like his.' Kieran held out a protective hand as the sip-size cup trembled in Liam's hand and the tower of milk foam wobbled, threatening to spill over the edge.

Liv smiled. 'He's a tough old bugger. A fading memory won't stop him from doing what he loves most.'

Fen carried two more coffees to the table. 'I'm sure Travis would like to see you again. He's got his hands full with overseeing the building on Murchison's Run and looking after Harry, but he still finds time to help us out when he can since Luke —'

He caught the pain and guilt in her look, remembered the little Liv had told him about what Fen's ex had done and wished he could find the man and teach him a lesson. But not until he'd learned more about the damage Luke Sampson had caused and why the mention of his name had a variety of emotions, ranging from fear to sadness, flitting through Fen's eyes. 'I'll catch up with Travis. Maybe make a turn there this afternoon.'

'I think he'd like that,' Liv murmured. 'Did Fen

mention he'll be here for Harley and Tameka's wedding tomorrow? Pretty much the whole town is invited.'

'Not yet, Liv. I didn't want to scare him away.' Fen grinned. 'He's already had a run in with Virginia. I'm not sure he's ready for a community wedding.'

Liv laughed. 'Oh, come on, Fen. The old dear has mellowed some.'

'Depends on who you speak to.' She sat in the chair next to Kieran, her knee touching his as she drew her legs under the small round table.

He shifted back in the seat, the fleeting, accidental contact too personal, too tempting. He could so easily capture her hand, thread his fingers through hers and find strength in the bond they'd shared all those years ago. An unfair expectation when he'd chosen to ignore that bond for too long and the friendship they'd shared had been delegated to memories he'd used as comfort on those dark, endless nights in hell.

Liam wriggled off his knee. 'Can I go play, Daddy?'

Kieran looked around. From the table, he had a clear view of the play area. He could keep an eye on Liam through the door. 'Off you go, but be careful, okay?'

'Course, Daddy. I'm a big boy now, aren't I, Liv?'

Liv smiled and ruffled his curls. 'You sure are. But even big boys get hurt sometimes, so listen to your dad.'

Kieran ignored the message her eyes sent as their gazes met and he realised she'd been watching him watch Fen. He'd have to be careful around Liv. Fen's foster mum had an eagle eye for trouble and a reputation for matchmaking. He couldn't afford to have her getting her hopes up. Liam scampered off and Kieran picked up his coffee.

'So, tell me more about the wedding. What can I do to help?'

Liv patted his arm. 'I'm sure we can find something for you to do. There'll be a bit of organising needed in the bar to chill the whites and champagne.' She checked her watch. 'Oh dear, we'd better get a move on, Fen love. Our first group through today is a group of retirees. No alcohol allowed. They're here for a late breakfast and the grape juice we bottled last week. A bottle of red and white on each table, I think.'

Fen looked up from her coffee cup. 'Red-and-white gingham or floral for the tablecloths?' She drew the empty cups towards her and stacked them before standing up.

'Mm, the gingham, I think. And make sure we have plenty of extra napkins on the table. You know Mavis likes to wrap up the leftovers to take home with her.'

Kieran frowned. 'Wouldn't it be healthier to give her a takeaway container?'

Fen looked at him, a smile in her eyes that flipped his heart. 'Not the same. We've tried. She wraps the cookies and shortbread with a precision that would make your eyes water.'

Liv smiled. 'An excellent achievement considering her fingers are crippled with arthritis.'

From his vantage point near the door, Kieran watched Liam scamper up the ladder to the slide. He'd forgotten the eccentricities of the people of this town, the community spirit of Wongan Creek unlike anything he'd come across since. The whole reason he'd come back, hoping to find the same level of acceptance again. To build a better life for his son who shouldn't have to live with the nightmares that haunted his sleep.

He couldn't let anything interfere with his son's happiness. He couldn't let Fen's smile make his heart trip and his pulse race. Not when his focus needed to be on fixing what was broken inside him.

Fen's phone rang. She reached into the front pocket of her apron to pull it out. Her mouth drew tight. 'Excuse me while I take this.' She turned away to answer the call. 'What do you want?'

Unease curdled the coffee warming his gut. Whoever it was on the other end of the line, there was no mistaking the anger in Fen's tone. Or the dash of fear. While his fingers itched to access the winery's accounts to assess the financial damage done and turn the business around, his mind dwelled on the emotional fallout for Fen. How much hurt had Sampson caused the girl haunted by the missing patches of her past and the unsolved mystery of her life before foster care?

Kieran watched Fen move through the French doors

out onto the verandah that ran the length of the cellar building. She stood with her spine ramrod straight and stiff, the phone to her ear as she looked out across the valley towards the creek. Black jeans hugged her curves and shaped her legs as she tapped her boot against the wooden deck.

His heart hitched. She'd always done that when she was annoyed or impatient. Or afraid. The tapping would grow faster until she'd resolved the issue she confronted. He hated that she'd been placed in a difficult situation, but when she let her head drop against the palm of her hand and her shoulders hunched over, he realised Fen wasn't just battling her unseen demon, she was cornered by it.

Beside him, Liv stood, the chair scraping against the wooden floor, masking whatever Fen said next.

'What's going on, Liv?' he asked, pushing back his own chair. 'This isn't as simple as your manager dipping his fingers in the cash register, is it?'

'Unfortunately not, but I'm not sure how much I can tell you with the level of investigation going on.'

'Then tell me what you've reported to the police.'

Liv chewed on her lip before answering. 'Luke was involved with an outlaw motorcycle club. We didn't suspect a thing. He was clean-cut, a little on the nerdy side. Until he let his true colours show.'

He hated the sadness in Liv's eyes and the questions her words raised in his mind. The possible answers scared him even more. 'The guy who showed up here yesterday, was he from the same club as Luke?'

'Yes.' Liv's eyes flickered with the same fear he'd seen in Fen's.

'Beyond Hell's Reach. Damn it, Liv, those guys are notorious for making trouble.'

Framed by the opened doors, Fen gripped the phone hard enough for Kieran to see her knuckles whiten. Then she turned to Liv, her face pale, a message passing between them. 'I need to take this somewhere private.'

Liv stiffened, her indrawn breath harsh. 'Oh dear.'

Kieran watched as Fen hiked down the verandah, her boots heavy against the deck, her voice a low mix of anger and frustration as she snapped replies into the phone.

'I don't like this at all, Liv. You need to give me the truth about what's happening here.' Torn between keeping an eye on Liam and going after Fen, Kieran hesitated.

'I'm afraid that if I do, someone will get hurt. There's been enough harm. Fen doesn't need any more.'

'Then tell me the whole story so I know what we're up against.'

Liv's gaze followed Fen's progress through the vines. 'I don't even know the full story. Fen is trying to protect me from the worst of it. She won't tell me everything.'

Down the hill, Fen reached the first row of vines and

kicked a clod of earth hard down the line with a boot that would make a footballer proud. She shoved her hand into the back pockets of her jeans and flicked her fringe out of her eyes with a toss of her head as she listened to her caller.

'I'll have a chat to her. If she won't tell me what's going on, I'll have to ask Riggs.'

Liv turned to him, a note of relief in her voice. 'Does that mean you'll stay?'

Kieran sighed. 'Outlaws don't play games, Liv. They're not big on letting things go. The two of you alone out here makes you vulnerable. Damn right I'm going to stay.' His mind told him to walk away, that he had Liam to protect from any more violence, but his heart and conscience intervened. 'That man here yesterday? I doubt that's the last you'll see of one of their patched members if they're making good on a threat.'

'Luke warned her to be quiet about it, but Fen didn't want to let him get away with stealing all that money, so she reported it to the police. We didn't take his threats seriously. We figured they were empty words, that he'd disappear into hiding and the law would do its job finding him. But that's when the real trouble started. Cut brake lines on the tractor. Contamination in the wine vats. Tampering with the temperature control in the cellar. Strange phone calls in the middle of the night.'

'I don't like the sound of that. They won't like the

police being involved. Guys like them tend to deliver their own kind of justice.' Justice that would result in them ramping up the danger with every threat. Fen's safety mattered.

He made a note to contact their security company and upgrade their systems as his first point of business on Monday morning. No matter how big the distance between them had grown, he owed it to Fen to keep her and Liv safe if there was trouble ahead.

Chapter Five

Fen collapsed onto the cool bed of rock that overlooked the creek. 'Damn you, Luke. I'm not playing your games anymore. Leave us alone.'

'Be careful of that attitude, Fenella. You know I won't hesitate to teach you a lesson you'll find hard to forget.' His warning had her jaw aching as a reminder of the damage his fists could do.

She drew in long breaths and let them out slowly to calm the rapid beat of her heart. Anger lit a fire in her blood. 'What do you want from me? You've got the money. Isn't that enough without you trying to ruin what's left?'

His laugh rang harshly in her ears. 'Not when I have thousands of dollars still growing down in the back block.'

74

'You're too late. The cops have seized it. They're coming for you, Luke. I won't let you get away with this.'

Fen pushed a hand into the pocket of her apron and hauled out the collection of pebbles she'd picked up along the way. She selected the largest, heaviest pebble, testing its weight between her palms. Curling her fingers around it, she felt the edge dig into her palm before pulling back her arm and letting fly. *Arsehole.* The pebble skipped downstream three times before sinking into the crystal-clear water to join the stone-littered creek bed.

Luke hissed his anger into her ear. 'I warned you not to go to the cops. You're going to pay for that.'

'Did you think sending in your mate would scare me off? It didn't work, Luke. Riggs has a full description of him.'

'Then you're more naïve than I gave you credit for. Back off, Fenella. You don't want anything nasty to happen to your mother now, do you?'

She let the next pebble rip, making it tumble through the air as tightness threatened to close her chest and cut off her breathing. It made a dead drop in the water. She listened to the sound it made as it broke the surface, watched the splash it made at the drop point. *Bastard.*

'If you harm Liv, I'll kill you myself.'

His harsh laugh in response held no humour and bore no resemblance to the one she'd once loved to listen to. 'Brave, empty words from a girl who couldn't even kill a cockroach. Dead girls can't talk, Fenella. Do you have any idea what these guys do to snitches? They cut out their tongues. While they're still breathing.'

A tear slipped down her cheek. She let it fall. An ache gripped her throat as her carefully built wall crumbled and fell. She'd been dumb enough to trust a handsome face and a bewitching smile that had hidden a black heart and a dishonest mind.

'What do you want from me?' The words edged past the ache in her throat.

'Your word.'

'On what?' A shiver gripped her as dark, dirty shadows crept into her mind. 'I don't know what you mean.'

'Those nightmares of yours. You will remember them one day. And when you do, you'd better come to us first or you will regret it.'

Confusion swirled through her mind. The dreams were from a time long before Luke, long before Wongan Creek. But he'd witnessed the fallout from them, sleeping beside her at night. Seen the damage they'd done. 'What game are you playing?'

'I don't play games. Neither do the big fellas. You're a high risk, Fenella. And we're keen on eliminating risks.'

'You bastard! You stole from us. You took our money and contaminated our crop with your filth, and you're threatening me?' She dragged in a breath, squashing down the fear that rose like bile in her throat. 'Screw you.'

'So stupidly sassy.' He laughed, a sound that sent frissons of fear edging over her skin. 'Keep your mouth shut about what you've seen and heard. We'll be watching. Roach knows exactly what to do with girls like you. He's been away for a while and he's a hungry man. Watch your back, Fenella.'

The line went quiet even as the noise in her mind increased. None of it made sense. She hadn't witnessed any of Luke's involvement with the club. Not until she'd seen his cuts and been silenced by his hands. And even then, she knew nothing. What did her dreams have to do with it?

She hated going there. Delving into the darkness where fear held her captive and shadows morphed into monsters. Where hands grabbed at her, bruising her arms and legs, and strangers dragged her from her safe place under the table. Where she tried to see past the half-closed door of a bedroom she knew she should recognise, but her mind refused to. Red and blue flashing lights bouncing off the walls of an apartment she didn't want to remember, and a woman whose name she wanted to forget. *Antoinette is gone. You need to come with us now.*

None of that was tied up to Luke, except that he'd witnessed the after-effects of her dreams. Was all this just a game to him? Something he could use to scare her with? That the twisted dreams of a child with a crackhead prostitute for a mother was something he could use to blackmail her into silence?

The more she thought about it, the more her head hurt and the scars under her wristbands burned. A reminder of the torment those dreams incurred. She'd think about it later, decipher the clues, piece the puzzle together.

Over in Travis Bailey's field, Harry and his dog wandered aimlessly amongst the sheep. The dog making a half-hearted attempt at herding. Sometimes Harry, sometimes the sheep. Fen watched them and let the anger slowly drain away. She needed a clear head to think about it. Remove the emotion and look at the facts. Think the way men like Luke would.

Kieran would have to know what an idiot she'd been, the extent of her stupidity blinded by what she'd thought could be love. Just how far had that bastard, Luke, gone? What other surprises would the police uncover?

Anger building again, Fen flung the last pebble, sending it whistling through the air, missing the water completely and landing at Harry's feet on the opposite bank.

Harry bent to pick it up, his movements slow. He turned the pebble over in his gnarled and twisted fingers. 'Did you break my shed window?'

'Not recently.'

He frowned, tossed the pebble into the water and rubbed his hands together. 'Coulda sworn it was you.'

'That was a long time ago, Harry. I was thirteen.'

'Not that long ago.' Harry and his dog crossed the bridge.

The grumpy old man had withered away, the disease that consumed his mind taking its toll on his body too. Poor Harry. They'd given him such a hard time during those difficult years of finding their place in a town where they didn't belong. Perhaps his Alzheimer's was a blessing at times, so he could forget some things. No matter how angry she and Kieran had made him as two equally angry teenagers, Harry had always found ways to discipline them without making it feel like capital punishment.

Like the time he'd sent them into the paddock with plastic zip-lock bags to collect sheep poo as punishment for breaking his shed window. They'd argued the senselessness of the task. Poo was good fertiliser for the paddock. But, no, he'd needed it for his garden beds, he'd said.

Fen shivered. Even now the thought made her cringe. The sheep had smelled like hay and grass and damp, smelly sweaters left in the washing machine for too long. Not unpleasant until you came across the occasional one who'd rolled in something awful. Those were the things she preferred to remember. Tears pricked behind her eyes and spilled over onto her cheeks again.

The old man settled onto the big rock next to her and she shifted to make space for the dog to crawl into the space between them. Robbie settled his head on her lap and she rubbed his ears, letting the motion soothe her anger away. Below them, the creek bubbled over the pebbles, sunlight sparkling off the water.

'So, you want to talk about it?' Harry handed her his handkerchief, adjusted his hat over his eyes and let his legs swing over the edge of the rock.

Fen sighed as she wiped away the remnants of her tears from her cheeks. Harry would have forgotten all about Luke already. 'It's a long story, Harry. I was lonely. Where else was I going to meet someone special?'

Harry snorted. 'You didn't meet him on one of those bloody internet dating sites, did you? I coulda told you this bloody technology stuff is dangerous. Whatever happened to face-to-face dating? You know, ask a girl to the movies. Show her your moves in the back row. Much more fun than staring at a screen and picking out a photo like some bloody, cheap-arse porn site. You're a pretty girl. Why would you need to go on one of those things anyway?'

'No, not a dating site, Harry. He came into the cellar bar one day and then kept coming back, asking me out until I agreed. I stupidly said yes. It seemed like a good idea at the time.'

'Wouldn't it be nice if hindsight was foresight, pixie face? Then we'd all make the right decisions in life.'

Fen grinned, her heart warming a little. Harry remembered. *How can a girl with such an innocent pixie face be such a little a shit?* Was all this mess with Luke Karma's payback for the trouble she'd caused Liv and Muzz, and even Harry, when she'd first come to town?

'Where were you when I needed your wisdom, Harry.' She looked up at his weathered face.

Harry patted Robbie's flank and laughed as the dog rolled over and stretched out for a tummy rub. 'Right here with my mate. Waiting.' The look in his eyes grew distant. 'Have you seen Eileen? She said she'd meet me here.'

Fen frowned. 'Eileen? I don't know who that is, Harry, sorry.'

'She's gone, I think. Do you have her number?'

Her heart ached for the man with the big heart and grumpy disposition. So sad to see his mind going when Harry had been a keen storyteller and hard worker. So much would be lost with his memory fading. 'I'd better get back and help Liv set up the breakfast tables for the bingo club. Are you coming along to that, Harry?'

Harry chuckled. 'What and hang out with all the old ducks, watching them stuff their handbags and pockets with food wrapped in napkins? No chance. Although,

Marge will be there. She and I had a thing once, you know. Before I met Eileen. Have you seen Marge?' Easing his body around, he pushed off the rock. 'Come on, Robbie. We have to find Marge.'

Fen jumped down and stood in front of Harry. 'Thank you.' She put her arms around his thick waist and hugged him hard.

He patted her back awkwardly. 'Enough of that now, pixie face. You'll make an old fella cry.'

She let him go and hugged Robbie too. 'Would you like me to walk you home, Harry?' If he got lost on the way back to Travis' place, she'd never forgive herself.

'No, I know the way. You go find that Murphy boy. It's about bloody time you two got married.'

A little of the sadness she'd started to shake off returned. 'We're not together. We never were. He married Diane, remember? From Lavender Ridge.'

Harry walked away, calling for Robbie to follow. Halfway to the bridge, he turned around. 'He needs a real woman.'

'I'm done with men.'

'You're done with scoundrels. Real men know how to treat a woman right. Eileen and I are getting married tomorrow. Is it tomorrow?'

Robbie nudged Harry's legs and Fen watched the dog guide his master in the direction of home. She had to face up to the consequences of her choices. It would be dangerous to forget the threat Luke presented to Liv, to the winery, to her and now to Kieran and Liam too.

Kieran straightened the knife on the table, set a breakfast plate between the setting and tried not to watch Fen walk back up through the vines. He'd told her his whole story, yet she'd walked away from him with hers.

Liam edged in between him and the table and placed a red napkin on the plate. 'I'm helping, Daddy.'

Kieran ruffled his curls. 'You sure are, mate. Did you fold that?'

Liam nodded. 'Liv showed me how.'

'Good job.'

Fen brushed past him. He watched her as she went through the ritual of dropping wildflowers into vases and putting them in the centre of the tables, her coping mechanisms engaged. Fen hadn't changed at all. She coped by doing, thinking through things and battling the inner demons as she went. And when she was done, maybe she'd talk to him like they had in the days when they'd only had each other.

'Okay, love?' he heard Liv murmur and noted Fen's nod, her face still obscured by her fringe.

No, she wasn't okay. Not at all. He could see it in

the stiffness of her shoulders and the occasional rub of her wrists.

Liam tugged on his shirt. 'Daddy, is Fen angry with me cos I did it wrong?'

His heart stuttered, his focus now totally on his son as Liam watched Fen put vases down and move the napkins from the centre of the dinner plates to the side plates under the butter knives. Kieran knelt and placed a gentle hand on Liam's shoulder.

'No, mate. You're doing a great job of the tables. I'm sure she'll be very happy with how hard you've worked. You've helped a lot by putting them out and now Fen is arranging things to make them look nice. That's how it's done. She's not angry at you.'

Damn Diane for taking her bad moods out on Liam in the past, for making a kid feel responsible for how her life had turned out. For making *him* feel that everything that went wrong in her life was either Liam's or his fault. That the boy had lost confidence in himself before he even understood what that meant.

Fen stopped beside them, her fingers clutching the neck of the vase, her eyes full of regret as he looked up. Gently, she placed the vase on the table and knelt beside them.

'Liam, I'm not angry at you, mate. You did very well. I always struggle with those awful packages the napkins come in, so you saved me a lot of time not having to fiddle around with them. I'm very proud of you. The thing is, we put them under the butter knife so the napkins don't blow off the table in the draft from the doors. Would you like to help me again when I set up the lunch tables? At lunch, we make different shapes with linen ones, like swans and flowers, and put them in a holder.'

Liam clung to Kieran's side, his thumb firmly in his mouth, a habit Kieran had been trying to get him to break for twelve long months. 'What do you say, mate?' he prompted.

'No.' Liam scrambled into the vee of Kieran's legs and clung to his neck, his little face buried against him.

Kieran's stomach clenched at the thought of what might follow that adamant 'no'. Next to him, the anguish on Fen's face suggested she'd been thinking the same thing. He reached out a hand to squeeze hers then stood, gathering Liam up in his arms, bracing himself for a tantrum.

Fen stood too. 'That's okay, mate, but if you change your mind, let me know, okay?' She set the vase in the middle of the table and moved the napkin under the butter knife. 'I've been practising making lizards, but I'm not so good at it, so I could use some help.'

Liam made no response except to bury his face in Kieran's shoulder. He let the muscles in his neck and back relax. No need to brace himself this time. For once the storm passed without incident.

'Everything okay, Fen?' He had to ask. To hear it from her.

Her shoulders dipped as she straightened a fork. 'It will be. It has to be.'

'If I can help with anything …'

'There's not much anyone can do. I have to be patient and let the police do their job.' She adjusted the order of the glasses on the table. Swapped the juice glass with the water glass. Touched her wrist and twisted the leather wrapped around them.

Kieran's gaze fell on her wrists as the sleeves of her jacket shifted with the movement. His mind retreated to the first time he'd met her, when those leather strips had covered raw new wounds no young girl should have. A girl tormented by the past, trying to cope in a strange new world. Trying to replace emotional pain and pressure with physical pain, to see if she was still capable of feeling. A girl with a tortured mind. A girl just like Diane. Had the monsters driven her back to self-harming?

Adjusting Liam's weight to his hip, he reached out and lifted Fen's hand, waiting for her to look at him. When she did, he raised a questioning eyebrow, not ready to voice the fear that clogged his throat.

Fen shook her head and tugged her hand from his. 'It's not what you think. I haven't gone there again.'

'I needed to make sure of that, Fen. You've come

too far to let trouble drag you back. Liv's filled me in a little on what's going on. Let me help you.'

She pulled her sleeves down and gripped the edges with her fingers. 'After that call, I'm not even sure it's safe for you to be here. You have something so precious to take care of in Liam and I have Liv. I'm not sure it's safe for her to be here either. I need to find a way to fix this mess before someone gets hurt.'

'Wait, what do you mean it's not safe? Who was that on the phone?' A chill shivered up his spine. 'Have they threatened you again?'

Noise erupted at the doorway to the café. 'The guests have arrived. I must go. Can we talk about this later?' Fen turned away to welcome the breakfast party forming a queue at the counter, a smile plastered to her lips that didn't quite reach her eyes.

Marge Everett made her way towards him. 'Well look what the big bird in the sky brought home from the east coast. And I see you've brought me another passenger for the school bus.' She patted Kieran's arm. 'When will this handsome young man be joining us at school?'

As soon as he could persuade Liam he had to go without engaging in a battle that would leave them both emotionally exhausted. 'When I bring him in for a visit and orientation as soon as we're settled.'

'That's great. A handsome young man just like his father. No spray cans on my bus, okay?'

Kieran grinned. 'It was just that once, Ms Everett.'

'Once was enough. It took ages to scrub the windows.'

'I know. My arm still aches decades later.' He hitched Liam up higher. 'Say hello to Ms Everett, mate. She drives the school bus.'

Liam stayed silent, but Kieran felt his head shift under his chin as the little boy took a quick peek.

'And what's your name, young man?' Marge peered at Liam over her sparkly glasses, her eyes blue and twinkling with laughter.

'Liam.' The whisper was so quiet that Marge had to lean closer to catch it.

Over her head, Liam caught the look Fen cast his way. Sad. Lost. Before she put her game face back on and got on with the job of showing her guests to their tables. Liam, surprisingly, became engaged in a conversation with Marge over how big the wheels of a bus needed to be to go around and around. Kieran let him slide to the floor. Marge took his son's hand and led him to the closest chair where they proceeded to sing the song.

Warmth flowed through him. Yes, he'd made the right decision to come home. The day Marge had made him clean the windows of the bus with a nail brush after his painting spree had changed his life. He'd learned that discipline didn't necessarily mean pain — except

for the ache in the muscles of his fingers and forearm —
and that doing something constructive and proactive
came with its own reward.

And now it looked like his son would have the same
support he'd had from the surrogate mums and grannies
at the CWA. Out here, Liam would have no shortage of
support, if Kieran could keep him safe from the threat
that dogged the winery.

The ladies filtered to the table one by one, and soon
Liam was showing them his sheep and talking favourite
stories. Kieran saw Fen move towards the café door into
the cellar to set up for the first tour group. With a quick
word to Liam to let him know where he'd be, he
followed her. Standing around doing nothing drove him
nuts. The least he could do was offer a hand to help set
up the bar. And maybe Fen would open to him a little if
he did.

'Need a hand?' He waited, hands in pockets while
she hid behind her fringe. With each wipe of the cloth,
her sleeves pulled back to reveal the broad leather bands
hugging them.

With a sigh, she tossed the cloth into the spill basin
and wiped her hands on a towel. 'You want to know
about the wristbands.'

She'd stopped wearing them long before he and
Diane had left town. Seeing her driven to wearing them
again tore at his soul. 'I want to know that you're okay.

That what's happened with Luke and Beyond Hell's Reach hasn't sent you back into hell. I care, Fen. About you. The years between us since will never change that.' He leaned on the bar, arms folded as he watched her take glasses off the shelf and arrange them in neat rows on the counter.

She stopped to look at him, her eyes stormy grey. 'I wear them to remind me of how far I've come and where I never want to be again. Because I'm human and some days, when things go pear-shaped like they have lately, I doubt myself.' Slowly Fen unclipped the fasteners on the leather bracelets. She turned her wrists up and held them out. 'See?'

Kieran studied the long-healed blemishes, stark ridges faded white against her skin. He remembered them red-raw, raised and bleeding, as angry and hurt as the girl who'd worn them all those years ago. Unfolding his arms, he reached for her hands, his thumbs grazing the raised skin over those scars. Her skin around them was silky smooth, pale against his. 'I don't like seeing you angry.' And damn it, she had been angry earlier. Angry, upset, hurting and in trouble.

Fen pulled her hands out of his and busied them with setting up the bar. 'I've made a mess of things, Kieran. I'd give anything to go back and change the decisions I made, but I can't. And Luke isn't the kind of trouble I wanted to bring to Liv's door. Not after all she's done for me.'

The thought of her being in trouble made him shiver. He toyed with the leather bracelets and tried not to pay attention to the scenarios flickering through his mind. Of Fen being in a situation she couldn't be rescued from. 'Then let me help you find a way to make it right.'

'I'm worried about the consequences of that too. Good doesn't always triumph over evil. I've researched Luke's club. They live up to their name and reputation and it scares me to think how far they'd go to get what they want.' She placed her hand over his and stopped his fingers worrying the leather. 'I want to tell you everything, but I can't do that with guests about to arrive. Can we talk later?'

Kieran shifted his hands from under hers because the sensations her touch was sending through his blood were ones he shouldn't be feeling. Not now when their lives were a mess and fear backlit the regret in her eyes. Maybe never because his first concern was his son's safety and welfare. 'Sounds good. How about you come up to the cottage when Liam has gone to bed?' He handed her the leather bracelets and watched her secure them around her wrists, hiding her external scars, knowing the internal ones bled again.

'Thanks. Yes, that sounds good. What time?'

'About seven-thirty?'

'Perfect.' She pulled a list out from under the counter and handed it to him. 'If you want to help, grab those from the storeroom for me. I need to stock up. Our first guests are reps from a national chain of both discount and boutique liquor stores. It's going to get competitive and I want them all to place an order.'

Kieran offered her a mock salute and a grin. 'Yes, boss.' And if he kept his feelings for her on that same level, he wouldn't fail her as he had his wife.

Chapter Six

Fen pushed the thought of an evening chat with Kieran and the trouble she was in from her mind as she welcomed the first guests to arrive. Telling him about the threat to the business would be easy, confessing to her own gullibility was something else entirely.

How could she tell him she'd lost everything to a man she'd thought she'd fallen in love with? No, not the man. The charm. Luke had made her feel loved and wanted, not abandoned and forgotten. And she'd been sucked right in, blinded to reality by her need to be accepted.

As she handed out the tasting glasses, the scars under her wristbands itched; tempting, taunting, daring her to act, testing her limits of resistance. All the demons, past and present, mocking her weakness on a tide of doubt and what ifs.

She turned from the guests and squeezed her eyes shut. What if she dropped the charges against Luke? What if that didn't stop him from carrying out his threat? What if Liv got taken from her too. Like Antoinette. Behind the door that wouldn't open more than a crack and the silhouettes that had played on the wall in the lamplight. The ones she couldn't see because her mind had blanked them out, yet they continued to taunt her dreams, now more than ever before.

Snapping open her eyes, she pulled a bottle of water from the bar fridge under the counter and turned back to her guests. She refused to give in to the shadows that crept into the sun-filled room, the unidentifiable shapes that lurked beyond that hiding place of long ago, the taunts of that voice that echoed in her head, re-awakened by Luke's threats on the phone.

Pushing back the darkness, she smiled until her cheeks ached, served until every drop had been consumed and crates of Cranky Lizard were being loaded into cars to the sound of a satisfying *ding* of the cash register totalling up a good day at the cellar door. All she had to do now was stop Luke from carrying out his threats and find out what he thought it was she knew.

Fen began the task of clearing up as Kieran disappeared to restock the storeroom. He'd helped — washed glasses, kept the bottles coming, done all the legwork — fitting in again as if he'd never left. Having him home felt surreal. As if he'd disappear back into her past as quickly as he'd reappeared. How to tell him what a fool she'd been? A tug on her sleeve had her looking down.

'Can I have a drink, please?' Beside her, Liam clutched his sheep and stared at her with a serious gaze.

'Of course you can. Water?'

'Nah.' He shook his head, making his curls bounce. 'Grumpy Lizard.'

Should she wait for Kieran to come back and ask if it was okay? Kid protocol. 'Okay, how about I give you some water now and we wait for your dad to come back to ask if you can have a Grumpy Lizard?'

Liam's lower lip quivered.

Shit. 'Look ...' Fen put a glass under the filter tap and filled it. 'I'm going to have some water first.'

'K. I'll have water too.'

Fen smiled. 'Awesome.' She filled a lizard cup with water and handed it to Liam. 'Here you go.'

He smiled, an adorable, innocent cherub smile that touched her heart and warmed the chill from it. 'Thanks.'

Fen returned his smile and held up a hand for a high five, thrilled when Liam returned it. She led him outside to the playground as he clutched the plastic cup.

'Would you like to sit here on the bench while I

check the playground? By the time we're finished your dad should be back.'

She thanked the gods of the creek that Marge Everett and the oldies had hung around longer this morning to keep Liam occupied while Kieran had helped her through the rush. Highly likely it was curiosity that had kept them there, but still, they'd done well keeping the boy entertained. And Liam, it seemed, had liked them too, because a little of his shyness had slipped away.

'Can I help?'

'Of course you can, mate. First though, let me make sure there's no glass lying around, okay? Sometimes people carry glasses in here even when we ask them not to, and they break. I don't want you to cut yourself on anything.'

'K. I sit here.' He patted the wooden slats on the space next to him.

'Perfect. When I'm done checking. We're going to take the bucket over there and put some water in it to wash everything down, okay?'

'K.'

Glass check complete, Fen filled the red bucket with water and a dash of disinfectant. She handed Liam a sponge and he put his cup down on the bench. It caught on the edge and toppled over, spilling water all over the rubber soft-fall. His eyes flew to meet hers, filled with a sudden fear she couldn't understand. In an instant, he'd curled into a ball and cowered under the bench.

Fen's heart clenched, reminding her of a little girl, a lifetime ago, who had also hidden under things, terrified of being too loud, too naughty, too much in the way, too *alive*. 'Liam, it's okay, mate. It was an accident.'

His skinny shoulders shuddered. 'S … sorry.' He kept his head buried in his arms, tightly coiled, his back turned to her.

Fen knew that fear. Recognised it in Liam. How many times had she cowered under a bed, a table or in a cupboard at his age. Kieran? No, he'd never harm a child. Diane then? A shiver crept through her, leaving her cold.

She went down on her knees and peered at him under the bench. 'It's okay. I'm not angry.'

A muffled sob answered her reassurances. Desperate, Fen looked around for Kieran. Still no sign of him. Her gaze fell on the bucket. Reaching out, she tipped it over. 'Oops! Silly me.' She watched the water run across the floor away from them. 'See, I messed too. Can you help me clean it up?'

'Will you get in trouble?' His voice was so small, quiet and afraid, it made her heart clench.

'No, sweetheart. Here we don't get into trouble for accidents.' She held out a hand to him. What the hell had happened to make him so afraid of something so normal? 'Come on out.'

He edged closer and she waited, afraid to touch him in case he thought she was going to hurt him.

'Think you can handle a broom to clean up the mess we've made? I've got a special one you can use.' Pretty useless with its toy-sized soft nylon bristles, but if it made him look less afraid, she'd be happy. Messes could always be cleaned, but damaged kids were marred forever.

'I think so.' He placed his hand hesitantly in hers.

Fen let her fingers curl gently around his. 'Come on then.' Rising to her feet, he stood with her. 'See over there against the wall? The yellow broom with the blue bristles and red handle? Why don't you go and get that and start sweeping the water away onto the grass? I'll take the big broom and help. And guess what?'

A little of the fear in his eyes was replaced by curiosity. 'What?'

'We won't have to wash the floor now because the water we messed will help clean it anyway.'

He grinned, the resemblance to Kieran making her heart stutter. 'K.'

Fen followed him across the rubber mat to retrieve her broom and together they swept the water away. She leaned on the broom handle. 'Look at that. What a team we make.'

His bright, broad smile was reward enough, the fear gone from his eyes for just an instant before it was replaced with sadness again. 'My mummy used to shout at me a lot.'

Fen's heart stalled. A selfish part of her didn't want to know about Diane. 'Did she, mate?'

'I was very naughty. That's why my mummy died.' He pressed the toy broom flat with his boot.

Fen dropped the broom and went down on her haunches to his height. 'That's not true, mate. Your mum died because she was sick. It's not your fault.'

'It was!' He stamped his foot down on the broom head.

Tension brought a thumping ache to her frontal lobe. Was this the trigger for his tantrums? Wearing blame on his shoulders the way she had every time Antoinette had turned on her. The same guilt she'd worn feeling responsible for Antoinette's death. That somehow her mother's life being taken that night had been her fault. That there'd been more to it than the overdose Martha Wallace and later, the police reports, had told her it had been.

She reached for Liam's hand. 'Why do you think it's your fault?'

'Because she told me all the time. Naughty, naughty Liam.' He twisted the handle of the broom.

Fen frowned. 'You're just a boy doing boy stuff. Sometimes mums get angry and say things they don't mean. I'm sure she loved you, Liam.'

He shook his head and screwed up his face. 'No. Woolley didn't want to go in the car. Woolley was scared. Mummy said she wished I'd never been borned.'

'Oh, sweetheart!' Fen pulled him into her arms and hugged him close as he cried into her shoulder. 'I'm sure your mummy didn't mean that.'

Cruel words Liam had been old enough to understand, words that revealed too much about the day the accident happened. Barbs that stung her as hard as they had him because they echoed words uttered by another mother in a drug-induced hatred a long time ago.

She soothed the curly head against her shoulder and pressed a kiss to his silky hair, cuddling him until his cries eased and his shoulders stopped shaking. Over the top of Liam's head, she caught sight of the pain in Kieran's eyes.

Kieran turned and walked back inside. It hurt to watch, to hear Diane's careless words repeated from his son's lips. He bit back on the anger the memories raised. He was done being angry. That wouldn't help Liam at all. He busied himself packing away glasses, getting ready for the next round of guests.

'Come on, mate, let's go and have a Grumpy Lizard together. I think we've both earned one. You've done a great job helping me out,' he heard Fen say before she appeared in the doorway with Liam in her arms.

Not once in all Liam's four years had Diane ever

picked him up to comfort him. Not even as a baby. He shouldn't have agreed to the IVF. He could have tried harder to talk her out of it, realised that a child could never fix what was broken inside her. But damn it, Liam was here, and he had to find a way to make it up to his son because he loved him.

He reached for his child, but Liam clung to Fen. She cast him an apologetic glance and he tried not to let the rejection hurt. He should be happy that his son had reached out to someone else who cared. The same way he'd reached out to Marge and her friends. His boy was making progress already.

'How do I make a Grumpy Lizard?' he asked around the lump in his throat.

Fen gave him instructions as she sat at the bar with Liam on her lap. She kept her eyes on his hands, refusing to meet his gaze. In a way, he was glad. He didn't want her to see his thoughts. Fen had always been too damn good at reading them and interpreting them correctly. Instead he listened to Fen talk Liam down.

Kieran handed the Grumpy Lizard to Liam, shrugging off the warmth of the picture they made, reminding himself that Fen was out of bounds. He had to put Liam first. Fen was damaged goods, just like Diane, and he'd be putting his son at risk again if he ventured down a road that led to more than friendship. Liam had to be his focus. Healing, forgetting, making new, happier memories together.

'Daddy? Can I go play in the playground now?'

Kieran looked up from polishing a wine glass to see Fen allow Liam to slide off her lap. 'Of course. Stay where I can see you, okay, mate?'

'Yes, Daddy.' Liam turned to hand Fen his cup and straw. 'Thank you.'

Fen ruffled his hair. 'You're welcome.'

They watched Liam scamper off before Fen slipped off the chair. 'I'll finish up here. Go and spend some time with Liam. You're still off duty until Monday.'

'I need to keep busy.'

'Then be busy with your son, Kieran. Next week you'll be busy enough with the vineyard. He needs you.'

'He didn't need me then.' And now he was torn between thankful and disappointed.

Fen sighed. 'I was there. I took care of it. That doesn't mean he doesn't need his father.' She reached over the bar counter to touch his hand. 'Please tell me Diane didn't really tell him she wished he'd never been born?'

Kieran turned his hand palm up and closed his fingers around hers. 'I wish I could.' And God knows, he knew the world of hurt it would have caused Fen to hear those words spoken. Words her own mother had used on her. Words he'd thought himself at times about Liam for reasons so different from Diane's.

'*Jesus*, Kieran. How is it grown-ups can do so much damage to their children?'

He squeezed her fingers and let her hand slip from his. 'I don't know.' He turned away from her. She didn't need to see the pain the memory caused, or the helplessness it kept alive in his gut. 'I'm hoping he'll grow and forget those awful words.'

As long as he didn't let those words slip from his tongue ever. The last thing he wanted was for his son to be the lost boy Kieran had been. No matter how hard single-parenting had been to date, no matter what challenges it provided in the future, his life had to be for his son. So, the feel of Fen's hand under his, the care in her eyes and her perfume that enveloped him when she was near — none of that could mean anything. Friendship was all he had to offer.

'It must have been hard for you.'

Fen walked around the bar to stand in front of him, making him take his eyes off the view of the vineyard through the window and bring his gaze to her face. The smile in her eyes had been replaced with sadness, turning the grey stormy. Her lips pinched closed, the chance of laughter silenced by the weight of his confession.

He lifted a hand to brush away the fringe of hair that fell over her face and let his fingers run through the silky softness of her hair, the feel of it soothing. 'As hard as it was for you.'

And it felt like the most natural yet dangerous thing in the world to place his hands on her hips and draw her closer, to wrap his arms around her and hold her close. Just for a minute. Just for comfort.

'You should go.' The curl of her arms around his waist negated her words, her voice muffled against his heart, the movement of her lips against his chest sending his thoughts in an unwanted direction.

He'd let her go. In a minute. They stood, the sounds of the vineyard around them, Liam's chatter as he played filtering through the doorway and the quiet beat of their hearts keeping track with their thoughts, neither speaking, only feeling. And when he felt too much, he stepped away.

'I'll see you later at the cottage tonight for that chat.'

Her hands slid away to her sides and she widened the gap between them. 'Yes. I'll be there.'

He tipped up her chin, the urge to lean in and kiss her almost too strong to resist. But he would. 'Thanks. For taking care of Liam.'

She nodded, avoiding his eyes, an elastic band of tension keeping them together. He broke it and walked away while he still had resistance left in him.

Outside, Liam played captain of the pirate ship on the platform, his spyglass aimed at the horizon. Excitement rippled through his voice as he turned to Kieran, hurtful words, salty tears and ugly memories forgotten. 'Look, Daddy! I see pirates. Over there!'

Kieran climbed the kid-sized ladder onto the deck. 'Load the canons.'

While Liam made all the sounds of readying the imaginary canons for firing, Kieran looked through the spyglass, having only a moment to register it was a genuine one before the reality of what his son had seen struck.

A pack of Harleys buzzed into sight like an angry swarm of wasps in the distance, a plume of dust kicked up by thick tyres spinning circles in the back block, churning up sand, soil, turf and crop. A flash of orange and a river of fire ran down the rows between the vines, catching quickly. Sickening fear gripped Kieran's gut as a wall of fire cut his line of vision on the herd of bikers. He left the spyglass spinning as he jumped off the platform, swept Liam up in his arms and ran inside with him.

'We've got a fire in the back block.'

Fen looked up from polishing glasses, caught the look on his face and reached for her phone, calling and running all at once. She flew out the door, her boots hitting the ground hard.

'What's happening, Daddy?' Liam's eyes grew round and fearful. 'Are they real pirates?'

'Something close, Liam. Liv!' He rushed through to the café as the sprinklers outside activated in the blocks closest to the buildings. He doubted it would stop the inferno from building if the bastards had fuelled it.

Liv came running, her arms already out. 'I'll take Liam. You help Fen. There's a water tanker full of recycled water in Muzz's shed. Keys are in the ignition. Kevlar jackets and breathing apparatus on the hook behind the front seats.'

'Stay with Liv, okay?' He leaned his son towards Liv's arms.

Liam resisted. 'No! I want to come with you, Daddy.'

Oh God, Liam, please not now. The words rolled through his mind and tore at his heart. His boy would be confused, terrified. 'It's safe here with Liv, I promise.'

And he would be if those bastards on the bikes had left. He doubted they'd stay around to watch. Their message had been delivered. Mission accomplished. The next bank of irrigation initiated, sending a mist of water into the air.

Liv lifted Liam's weight from his arms and dealt with the resistance, screams and tears, hugging him close and whispering soothing words. She looked at Kieran. *Go*, she mouthed, turning away to provide a distraction. Torn, he hesitated. But Fen couldn't fight a fire alone.

Outside the flames caught the draft, fingers of fire licking the sky above the vines. With one last touch to his son's curls, he took off towards the shed. Fen was there, jackets out, the engine running. She handed him one before climbing into the driver's seat.

'Get in,' she urged, her hand already releasing the

park brake and slamming the tanker into gear. 'I've got Fire and Rescue on the way.'

Kieran hauled himself into the tanker, slamming the door and dragging on his seatbelt only seconds before she took off over the uneven terrain into the vineyard blocks. His kidneys protested each bone-cracking bump and dip as she negotiated the way down the fire break as fast as she could without rolling the truck. She rattled off instructions he already knew by heart, but listened to again anyway, and when they arrived at the fire front, he had to take a step back at the fierceness of its heat.

'We won't make much difference with the tanker, but we can keep it wet until the firies get here,' Fen shouted over the roar, coughing against a lungful of acrid smoke.

She hooked her oxygen mask on over her head and tightened the strap. He did the same, making his way to the back of the tanker and opening the valves as Fen unravelled the hose. The force of the water pumping through the hose had her taking a step back under the pressure. He steadied her until she got her balance before grabbing the second hose. Together they battled against the roar of dragon-fire, water and ash raining down on them, until the wail of sirens brought relief.

Chapter Seven

Filthy, exhausted and reeking of smoke, Fen leaned her back against the backboard on the tanker. Beside her, Kieran's eyes were closed.

Riggs' bulk cast a shadow across them, blocking out the sun that lay low in the sky, veiled in a cloak of smoke. 'Ready to make a statement?'

Fen looked at Kieran's profile, his jaw set tight as his eyes flickered open to meet hers. Doubt edged into her thoughts. Would making a report of arson only make it worse? What if they targeted the house or the cellar next?

Riggs sighed and scratched his head under his police issue cap. 'The empty fuel containers thrown around between the vines tell their own story.' He waved a hand towards where firefighters trailed spot fires in the wake of the beast. 'That and the body in the garbage bag.'

Beside her, alert now, Kieran shot to his feet. 'Say what?'

'Female, age to be determined. Not much left to go on. We're keeping it quiet until we know what we're dealing with.'

Horror kept Fen's back glued to the truck, bile burning her already dry throat. '*Jesus.*' How had this escalated from fraud to murder on the eve of a wedding where the bride and groom had both dealt with losses from fire?

Her mind spun through the months of planning for the Baker-Chalmers wedding, most of which Luke had been present for. He'd known about that, about the body in the suitcase ... but, no, she was reaching for a connection between those incidents and this one. Trying to make sense of something that made no sense at all. But there'd been so much happening that was wrong since Luke had taken off.

She pushed to her feet, her muscles beginning to ache. She'd give her left arm for a soak in the tub and peace in her head from the turmoil. They'd been so busy beating back the fire front that she hadn't had time to ask Kieran if he'd seen how it started.

She listened to the deep baritone of his voice, his account of what happened surreal when, only a handful of hours ago, peace had rested in the valley of vines and the only trauma they'd had to deal with was making a little boy feel loved. And now a woman was dead. She could be a wife, a mother, a friend, a girlfriend. Instead, she was a stranger, dumped in a fire like discarded trash.

Trash. The shadows crept in from the corners of her mind, pushing her towards the door in her nightmares and the angry voice shouting behind it. *You're trash. Common kitchen garbage. And we like to take out the trash.* Hadn't Luke said something similar? Or was it the man who'd come to the tasting session?

She swayed against exhaustion and fought off the monster that forced its way to the front of her memories, her mind stepping on the brakes to cut it off before it opened that door to reveal the horrors behind it. Her seven-year-old self scurrying back to the dark corner under the table like an abused puppy.

Her shoulder bumped against Kieran's bicep, and his arm came around her, holding her close. She let her head rest against the wall of his chest under the bulk of his Kevlar jacket and tried hard to shut out reality. It touched her on the shoulder.

Riggs squeezed her arm. 'Fen, you need to know.'

She turned to look at him, her skin tight under the soot and grime. 'Know what?'

'They've reopened your mother's case. The cold case squad got a tip-off from an anonymous source and they're re-examining evidence and reports.'

She shook her head to clear the fuzz. 'It was suicide. A drug overdose.'

Riggs stood, feet apart, hands on his hips, notepad

and pen clutched in his fingers. 'A recent department crime and corruption investigation has turned up evidence that there might have been a cover-up by a handful of cops on the take at the time. Seems they were in the bikies' pockets. I can tell you that because it's no secret in the city. The media are all over it.'

'What if I don't want her case reopened? Can I stop it?'

Riggs scratched an itch between his shoulder blades with his pen. 'The Department of Child Protection and Family Support spent a lot of time and effort making sure you didn't exist. If you try to stop this, the wrong people will start asking questions. If you let it happen quietly, there's a good chance your whereabouts and identity can remain confidential.'

Confusion furrowed her brow. 'I don't understand. I was an orphan in foster care. Why would that need to be a secret?'

'You were placed in witness protection, given a new identity and lost in the system. Martha Wallace made sure of it when someone started threatening your carers and she realised the police report didn't quite match your case.'

A small piece of the puzzle fell into place. 'You knew. That's why she brought me here.'

'I knew your name and that you were in witness protection. I knew she'd brought you here because she could trust me, the town, and the Watermans.' He blew out a long breath. 'Fen, the owner of the brothel your mother worked in was the president of Beyond Hell's Reach.'

Coincidence. It had to be. Still, the little girl in her hid from the crack in the door. Her scars itched, bared to the rough seams of the Kevlar jacket, the protection of her wristbands removed to fight the fire.

Kieran's hold tightened around her shoulders. 'That doesn't make sense, Sarge. Why would they place Fen in witness protection if it was suicide?'

She wanted to clamp her hands over her ears, drown out the shouts of the firefighters, the drone of truck engines and the noise of the pump as it spewed water over the remains of their livelihood. Fen curled her hands to catch a lump of Kieran's jacket in her fist. She squeezed her eyes shut, willing the visions to recede, but she couldn't block out Riggs' next words.

'Because there is new conflicting evidence on the case that suggests it was more than an overdose that killed Antoinette.'

Memories came crashing in on an unwelcome tide. Jumbled, mixed up, terrifying visions of shadows dancing on walls and screams that blistered and tore at her mind. Terror so cold it froze her spine, chilled her belly and closed her throat. Still, she couldn't look into the face of the man in the room, nor watch the morph of the silhouettes on the wall. Fear clawing at her, she slammed shut the door and retreated to darkness.

The smell of damp ash, soil and scorched earth drifted in over the coppery taste of blood, and reality returned. 'I want to go home. To Liv.' She pulled out of Kieran's hold.

'You know we'll need to talk, Fen.' The sarge's words were quiet, his touch comforting.

'Not now.' Not with the visions still raw in her memory and her scars needing soothing from the heat and strain of fighting the fire. Not when her mind was defenceless, and her body was too exhausted to keep the demons out.

'Tomorrow then,' Riggs agreed.

'I have a wedding to host and I won't let them down.'

'Then the day after that. You can't hide from it anymore, Fenella. They won't let you.'

'I know. I'll come in, Sarge. Just not tomorrow. I want to go home now.' She rubbed a hand over her face, tired, drained, empty.

'I'll take you.' Kieran steered her towards the passenger door of the water truck, lifted her up into the seat, his hands around her waist strong and comforting.

They drove in silence, Fen curled into the corner against the truck door, the blocks of vines passing by, merging from black and charred to autumn colours. The distance from the back block to the cellar building further, taking longer than ever before. Relief flooded her as Liv came into view, Liam in her arms. Fen leaped out of the truck as soon as Kieran engaged the park brake. Liv saw her coming, read the look on her face, said something to Liam before she lowered him from her hip to the grass, and opened her arms.

Fen crashed into them, the terror coiled inside her releasing on gut-wrenching sobs as she sank into the warmth and security of her mum's embrace and let go the horror from her mind. She didn't see Kieran leave with Liam, but she knew he was gone. The same way she knew the events today had cracked open the door a little wider, making the nightmare real again, and this time she wouldn't be able to bury it in the past.

'Let's get you cleaned up, honey.' Liv's hand soothed her back. 'We'll have a nice cup of tea. Chamomile, I think. And a nice long soak in a warm bubble bath.'

'Stay with me, Mum.'

Liv grounded her, chased the fear away, the way she always had on the dark, cold nights when dreams turned to nightmares. But now the nightmare had become reality to threaten everything she'd worked so hard to forget, the life she'd built with a family who cared for her. She'd succumb to the relief of tea and warm baths and the love of a real mother. She'd make sure Liv was safe from the reaches of the monsters who threatened them. And when she had her feet back under her and her facts straight, Fen would fight this.

Lights shone warmly from the windows as Fen made her way up the path to Kieran's cottage later that night. The vineyard lay silent in the distance, the fire extinguished, the crew gone until morning when an investigation would begin.

She'd phoned Harley and Tameka, told them about the fire but not about the body, not when Riggs had specifically said they weren't making any statements yet. She would have cancelled the wedding, refunded them, taken the loss if they'd requested it. Instead, they'd agreed it was too late to cancel and reassured her she and Liv would have the community's ongoing support and assistance to repair the damage to their vines.

Fen's thoughts turned to the woman they'd found. She shivered. Who was she? A threat, a warning, a reminder of what Luke and his club were capable of. She refused to let that happen to Liv.

She'd fired off an email to the security company, requesting the installation of more cameras, more motion detectors and movement activated spotlights, and debated between guard dogs or security patrols. Her mum understood the threat, accepted the consequences it could bring, and ignored Fen's urging her to go away somewhere safe, take a cruise, a holiday away until the threat had passed. Liv had only shaken her head, planted her feet stubbornly on the floor and argued against it until she thought Fen had given up and accepted she was staying.

Fen stepped up onto the verandah and tapped on the door with her knuckles. She tucked her hands back into the sleeves of her jumper and waited, wrapping her arms tightly against her belly to ward off the flutter of nerves. With the risks running higher than ever, she'd give him the choice to take his son out of harm's way and leave.

The door to the cottage opened and Kieran appeared in the doorway, shadowed by the light. 'Hey, you okay?'

He'd filled out in the years he'd been gone, grown into his height, his legs no longer long and skinny, but strong and solid in denim that wrapped them like a lover's hands. Fen shrugged off the thoughts. She didn't want a picture of Kieran in or out of his denims in her head. Or remember how safe she'd felt in his arms with a firestorm at her back and a threat to her future. It could only bring trouble.

'I'm okay. You?'

Shivering against the cold, she stamped the wet grass from her rubber soles onto the coir mat. He stepped back for her to cross the threshold into the hallway and closed the door behind her. Kneeling, she undid the laces and pulled off her boots. Coming back to her feet, she realised how close he stood, how warm the heat was he generated.

'Yeah. Come through. Liam's asleep.' Kieran waved her towards the archway where the warmth from the wood fire filled the living area. 'I didn't think you'd come over after today.'

The narrow hallway felt even smaller with him standing so close, all broad shoulders, hard chest and firm, comforting arms. 'We need to talk about … things. It's nice and toasty in here. Has Liam settled in okay?'

'Yes, thank you. He's not quite ready to be alone in his own room yet, but we'll get there. Thank you for dressing it up the way you did. He loves it. He's fascinated by the lizards.'

Fen allowed her smile to light her eyes. Liam deserved to be happy, to have a normal childhood rather than to be another lost soul and unwanted child. 'I'll have to introduce him to Lucky then.'

'Lucky?' Kieran closed the door against the cold air.

'My bearded dragon.'

Kieran chuckled, the sound sending trickles of pleasure down her spine all the way to her toes. 'I should have guessed. No cats or puppies. Too tame for you.'

'Lucky is a survivor. He was dumped at the vet in Perth with a dislocated shoulder. The vet was a client of mine and when he mentioned it to me, I offered to take care of Lucky. He had to have his leg amputated in the end because of an infection, but he's adapted.'

'Ah, Fen.' He put an arm around her shoulder and led her into the lounge room where the fire blazed merrily in the old wood-fuelled heater. 'Always rescuing lost and damaged souls.'

Not anymore. Not since the last lost soul had turned out to be a scumbag thief and a dirty, rotten, scheming bastard. 'Thank you for today. I couldn't have held off that fire without you.'

'Fire, I can handle. Arson and murder … well, that's a whole other story.'

Fen shivered. 'That poor woman. No-one deserves to die that way. I can only believe she was already dead when they put her in that bag.' Another horror to haunt her nightmares.

He squeezed her arm. 'We'll find out who she is, and when we do, we'll do something nice for her.'

'How did it get this bad? Maybe I shouldn't have gone to the police. I should have let it go, started afresh.'

Kieran blew out a breath. 'If you'd let it slide, he and his friends still would have come back for more. You did the right thing.'

'Except now everyone is in danger. You, Liam, Liv …' She shivered in the heat of the room. 'I'll understand if you don't want to stay on.'

He stepped closer and eased his arms around her. 'I'll tell you the same as I've already told Liv. I won't leave you alone here, unprotected. I don't care what it takes, but we'll make sure everyone is safe until this is over. If that means putting twenty-four-hour security in place, that's what we'll do.'

She sank into the warmth of his embrace and solid wall of his body, accepting his comfort and reassurance, because Kieran was a friend and even if things could never be romantic between them, she'd at least have his warmth and strength by her side through this.

'Promise me that if it gets too dangerous, you'll take Liam and go. He's been through enough.'

'I promise you we'll do everything we can to make sure that won't be necessary. I won't let anyone hurt him again.' He eased his arms from around her and stepped back. 'Make yourself comfortable while I get the coffee then we'll talk it through.'

Fen watched until he disappeared into the kitchen at the back of the cottage, then she snuggled into the corner of the sofa opposite the fire, legs tucked up on the cushions and the rug over her feet. The cottage glowed warmly in the light of the fire and low wattage globes that cast a soft light through the room. At any other time and with anyone else, she might have considered it romantic. But romance wasn't something she could afford to think about with threats, theft and property damage dogging the future.

Alone in the room, watching the flickering flames that reminded her of the fire in the vineyard, an edginess settled over her. A fire started by men on motorcycles. Deliberate, dangerous, fuelled to spread at maximum strength. And then they'd added a murder. A clear threat to destroy everything she loved if she didn't keep her silence. Who'd had to die for them to get that message across?

Kieran came back with the steaming coffee mugs and placed them on the table in front of them. He settled into the opposite corner of the sofa. 'Spill it, Fen. I can hear your thoughts churning.'

Fen sighed. 'I'm such an idiot. You'd think I'd have known better.'

'We're humans, not robots. We make mistakes.'

'True, but this …' The tight grip of guilt closed around her throat. She drew in a deep breath and blew it out. 'This is all my fault.'

Kieran leaned forward and rested his elbows on his thighs, hands clasped, his thumbs rubbing at the frown on his forehead. 'How is it your fault?'

'I fell in love with a man, trusted him with too much and lost everything. I'm not sure if I'm a victim or an accomplice. I know I was blind enough not to ask questions until it was too late.' The words left her lips in a rush as if the quicker she spat them out, the less it would hurt.

His hands stilled, his lips pursed for a second before he blew out a breath. 'I think you need to start at the beginning. Tell me how this all started, so I understand what we're up against here. Don't leave anything out, even if it doesn't seem important.'

She crept further into the corner, drew her legs up and pulled the blanket up to her chin, her fingers clenched around it. 'Luke was the man I'd thought I'd marry. I trusted him with so much and I never got the impression he was anything but honest. Maybe I was too busy to notice. My mistake.'

Kieran stood and began to pace the area between the sofa and the fire, his long legs making short work of the distance. 'You're too smart to make mistakes. He's a con used to telling lies to lure unsuspecting marks.'

Fen sighed. 'Lies I should have been able to see through.'

A half-smile twisted his lips. 'You're tough, resilient, a fighter, but you're not psychic. If he was good at it, you'd never know. You're nobody's fool, Fen.'

Warmth bloomed inside her heart. She hoped he'd still think so later. 'Mum and I were so busy keeping the business running after Muzz died. She was worried for me, thought I needed to get out, away from things once in a while, but I've never been good at making friends and Wongan Creek is a small place. Almost everyone here was paired up already. I didn't want to be a third wheel.'

'Phone a friend?' Kieran picked up his mug off the table and took a long sip.

'Name one.' The only one she'd trusted had been so

far away he might as well have been on another planet. An endless highway and a marriage away.

Fen watched him as he walked back to the fire and leaned on the mantelpiece above it. In days gone by the fire would have been set in the hearth where the flames would be drawn up by the draft from the old chimney. Now the flames were contained behind a heavy glass door in an old-fashioned wood burner built into the empty space left by modernisation.

Kieran sighed. 'I tried to stay in touch. It was … difficult.'

'I know. I understand. I'm not blaming you. I'm just saying you were the only one I trusted, the only real friend I had. Until the day Luke came into the winery with his mates from the mine. He stayed long after they left. All afternoon he hounded me for a date. He came back every day in his lunch break, sold me his story about how unhappy he was in his job. How he needed a change. Made me believe he cared about me.'

She stood, her arms crossed tightly, hugging herself against the chill that crept through her blood despite the heat from the fire, watching him pace, her gaze following the movements.

Placing his mug on the mantle, he walked over and put his hands on her shoulders, his palms cupping the roundness over her black jumper, the warmth seeping through her. 'Fen, you're a beautiful, intelligent, independent woman. It wouldn't have been hard for him to pretend.'

She wrapped the warmth of his compliment around her heart and held it there for comfort. 'Luke seemed like exactly what I was looking for. I was impressed as much by his knowledge of finances and account-keeping as I was by his smile and charm. With Muzz gone, we needed a manager, he had the skills. I got a two-for-one deal. I fell hard in so many ways.'

Kieran's hands dropped away from her shoulders and he shoved them into the front pockets of his jeans. 'Did you ever suspect you were being set up?'

'Not once.' Fen walked around him to the fire, the cold that had crept into her bones seeking warmth. Comfort would be a long time coming. 'Luke was so charming, so believable. Good looking, strong, athletic if a little nerdy. Exactly as you'd expect from an accountant. So convincing, I didn't bother to check his references with the mine's Human Resources department. If I had, I would have known he was only one step away from being fired for misappropriating funds.'

'He must have been damn good.'

She laughed, a bitter sound even to her own ears. 'One day, I was cleaning out our room and I found this box under the bed. Inside was a leather vest decorated with patches. His club name was Spider and he'd been using the winery to launder money, and then he stole a good chunk of the takings.'

'He used you, Fen. It's not your fault.'

She felt his warmth at her back. Not touching. Just there. A solid show of the support she hadn't had until now, an added backbone to give hers the relief it deserved. Fighting this alone for so long had ground away at her resolve to stay strong. No-one, not even Luke, had been able to fill the size fourteens of the only friend she'd ever been able to open to.

'If I'd been paying attention, I would have noticed that all the vines on the far northern boundary had been cleared to make way for a crop of cannabis. I left all that up to Luke while Liv and I got the new liqueur brand up and running. I don't have the head for figures. None of the numbers made any sense to me, except for the bottom line on the bank balance. Then that didn't make sense anymore either and I started asking questions.'

Questions that were brushed aside with a logical explanation. Luke had been a master at making things seem plausible, do-able. And for a while she'd thought she'd found the next best thing to Kieran. She'd even believed she could love him the same way.

'I'm guessing you didn't get the answers you wanted?'

Fen shook her head. 'The day I found his vest, I must have asked too many questions. Or maybe it was the right question that hit too close to the mark. He hit me so hard, I thought he'd broken my jaw.'

'*Jesus.*'

'Liv called the police. By the time they got here, he'd taken off with his Harley and a million dollars of our money he'd been stashing into an offshore bank account, leaving me a mess to deal with and a mature cannabis crop to explain to Riggs. They're still looking for him.'

Kieran grimaced. 'And the phone call today?'

'From him. A follow up on the warning I received yesterday. The man at the bar. Luke thinks I know more than I do and that's the part I don't understand. None of what happened seems serious enough for threats. So, what if he's a member of Beyond Hell's Reach. They ride with their colours, shout it to the world who they are, raise hell wherever they go. It's not like they're a secret group. I couldn't think what it is I've seen or heard that makes him think all this is necessary. Until Riggs mentioned them opening the cold case on my birth mother today.'

'You think it might have something to do with your mother's death?'

'I wish I knew for sure. It's too much of a coincidence that the club president was the owner of the brothel at the time of her death. I've always believed my mother died of an overdose, but I have repressed memories of the night she died. Usually, I have flashbacks in the form of nightmares. I dream of a door I can't see past because what's happening behind it is too real, too confronting, too scary to remember.' She looked at Kieran, his jaw set and a muscle twitching in his cheek. 'I love this place, Kieran. I wish with all my heart that I'd never met Luke. But I can't undo what's happened. All I can do is find out what it is he thinks I know.'

Kieran tugged her close and wrapped his arms around her, securing her firmly against him. 'I'm so sorry, Fen. You know I'll do everything I can to help you solve this mystery. First, we need a plan to protect Liv, Liam and the winery.'

Fen allowed her body to relax into his warmth. Kieran was here. Everything would be okay again. But he was a man dealing with his own problems. She still needed to fight the battle herself even when the future stretched ahead of her littered with the bones of Luke's crimes. How long before hell ascended in Wongan Creek again? She couldn't let that happen.

Chapter Eight

Morning dawned bright and sunny if not a little cold. Organised chaos descended on the vineyard as Liv called for all hands on deck in preparation for the Baker-Chalmers wedding. Tables, cloths and drapes went out and up in record time. A florist's van overflowing with flower arrangements arrived to fill the air with the scent of fresh gardenias, roses, lilies and lavender in a sea of colour. And Fen, stunning out of her usual black.

On his haunches, Kieran paused in the middle of packing the white wine into the fridge to cool and looked. So damn hauntingly beautiful in a fitted silk dress with a Mandarin collar that ended above her knees. The Monet-style print of pink waterlilies and shades of blue emphasised the midnight black of her hair. He didn't need to see her eyes to know that those colours would bring out the blue in them. The whole package stealing his breath in a way it shouldn't.

He found himself thinking how her legs would look when she swapped the ballet flats for high heels. Then his gaze fell on his son and he remembered why he shouldn't see her that way at all. Fen was in the kind of trouble he couldn't afford to get Liam involved in, but he could do whatever it took to get her out of it.

He sighed and unloaded the last of the wine, closing the door and checking the reading on the temperature control panel. They'd be perfectly chilled in time for the reception.

'Daddy?' Liam tapped his shoulder.

'Yeah, mate?'

'Look what I made. I'm helping. Fen showed me how.' Liam held out an origami boat, a little rough around the edges.

'Great effort, mate. Are those for the tables?' Kieran took the boat from him and studied it. He'd forgotten Fen's penchant for origami. Anything to keep her hands busy and her mind off whatever inner battle she was fighting. In the early days, they'd littered her space as she worked through the changes and challenges of settling into a small town and a new family.

Liam nodded. 'Yep. I gotta make more. Red and blue ones. Did I do good?'

He held up his fist for a bump, his heart swelling with pride. 'Really good.'

'We're going to put sugar almonds in them. Pink and blue and white ones. Fen says it's a tra ... dition?'

'That's right. It is.'

'Why?'

Kieran smiled. He loved it when Liam asked questions. For so long his little boy had been silent. 'There should be five in each boat. One each for health, wealth, happiness, fertility, and long life.' Elaine had insisted on sugar almonds at his and Diane's wedding, even though Diane had poo-pooed them as old-fashioned. She'd wanted more modern bonbonnieres.

Liam nodded, his eyes serious as he thought on each one. 'What does fer-til-ity mean?'

'It means they'll have babies.' Kieran handed him back the paper boat.

'Will you have more babies, Daddy?'

Kieran pushed to his feet and swept his son up. 'I'm not sure. Maybe one day. But not now. We have each other for now. That's okay, isn't it?'

A part of him wanted desperately to have a brother or sister for Liam, but after Diane ... He let his gaze slide across the room to where Fen dressed the tables. Did Fen want children? She'd been so kind and patient with Liam so far. But no, there was no point wondering. He never wanted to be that vulnerable again. So far under a woman's spell that he couldn't see the signs that would do his son harm. He had to put Liam first. When the time was right, he'd find someone who would love

Liam like he was her own. But Fen was a friend and off limits.

Liam shrugged. 'I suppose.' He wriggled to be freed. 'I gotta go finish my boats. Fen says we have *hundreds* to make.'

Kieran set him down on his feet. 'Off you go then.'

'You can help too.'

He ruffled Liam's hair. 'I'm sure Fen has other duties for me.' He flexed his muscles and knelt for Liam to feel them. 'I'm the brawn, you're the brains. Together we're the M-Team.'

'I've got muscles too.' Liam flexed his and Kieran gave them a squeeze.

'You need more Weetbix. They're growing nicely. Come on, mate, let's get some work done.'

He followed Liam back to where Fen alternately checked the staff setting up the tables and the watch strapped to her wrist. The broad black band with its over-sized watch face had replaced the leather cuff on her arm. It should have looked too modern for her outfit, yet it suited her. A perfect contrast for the unique personality that symbolised who she was.

'Nice dress.'

She smiled up at him briefly, her concentration clearly on setting up the room. 'Tameka wanted a theme that would reflect both her and Harley's heritages. So, we've planned a mixed of Vietnamese and Australian traditions.'

'Sounds like a lot of planning.'

She smiled again, and he let his gaze linger on her lips. A shiny coating of gloss made those lips so damn kissable. 'No more so than any other wedding. And Tameka deserves something special after the year she's had.'

'How's she recovering?'

'The burns are healing well. But the emotional wounds take a lot longer.'

Damn it, he knew that better than anyone. Liam would grow up and hopefully not remember much of the trauma Diane had caused. He, on the other hand, would remember it for a long time to come. 'Good thing then she has Harley and his family.'

Fen finished folding the last origami boat and dropped it into a basket on the preparation table. 'Yes. She's a lucky girl to have escaped that fire alive. If Harley hadn't seen the flames ...' She shivered. 'Ready to fill these boats with the almonds, Liam?'

Liam nodded enthusiastically.

'Okay then.' She held out her hand. 'Shall we go and wash our hands over there at the basin first?'

He looked up at Kieran who ruffled his hair. 'Off you go, mate. I'll be right here taking care of the boats until you come back.'

At Kieran's nod and after another moment's hesitation, Liam slipped his hand into Fen's.

'Kieran, could you please keep an eye out for the

groom and his party? They'll be arriving any minute now. Liv's set up the guest room at the main house for them to get ready in. If you can show them to it, that would be awesome. Then you can come back and help put the boats on the table.'

'Yes, ma'am.' His dry tone didn't escape her, and she shot him an amused look.

'Might as well get used to it. We're booked out for weddings all through the winter and the better part of spring. No-one escapes wedding fever at The Cranky Lizard.'

And because that put thoughts of Fen walking down the aisle towards him into his mind, he turned his gaze to the driveway where the dust trail on the unsealed road indicated the arrival of one half of the wedding party.

Time sped by in a rush of activity. Only ten minutes late, the bride arrived, stunning in a traditional Vietnamese wedding dress that covered the ravages of the fire that had left her scarred and the town of Wongan Creek shocked at the events that had followed. He'd heard about it, read about it online and watched the news that had reached Sydney channels through disbelief at the cruelty of her case. It had made him so much more thankful that Liam had survived the car crash with Diane almost completely uninjured.

He watched Fen move in her high heels and allowed himself a little smile of appreciation. She really did look hot in stilettos. Although he had no doubt they'd be kicked off as soon as the ceremony was over, and the rush of the reception began.

Liam smiled and whispered to Liv from his spot at the back of the rows of chairs. Perched on a chair so he could see, Liv held him securely to stop him from toppling off. Kieran's heart warmed a little more. Here there was so much to occupy his son and take his mind off the past. And on a day as magical as this one, he could almost forget about the blackened scar in the vineyard and the threat that hung over it like a dark cloud waiting to rain down hell on them.

The celebrant welcomed the couple and the crowd. Oh, good Lord, whoever would have imagined Virginia Turner, the dragon lady of Wongan Creek's school, would be the one blessing the unions of her past students. Kieran smiled at the irony of it. Hell-bent on keeping boys and girls from kissing behind the bicycle shed, here she was years later conducting marriage ceremonies.

'Quite the sight, isn't she?'

Fen's warmth at his side, hand on his arm and whisper that drifted quietly to his ears, had him looking down. Even in heels, she barely reached his shoulder. From deep inside him, the need to throw an arm around her shoulders and draw her closer called, a hug from one friend to another, but he knew it would be more than that. He was proud of what she'd achieved, of how far she'd come. And to have that torn from her the way it had been was unacceptable. He placed a hand over hers and squeezed her fingers.

'The bride or Ms Turner?'

Fen grinned up at him. 'Both.'

'The bride is beautiful. Ms Turner is a puzzle I'll forever be trying to figure out. You've done a great job here today, Fen.'

'I didn't do it alone. Liv is a powerhouse. Speaking of which, could you put those muscles to use for me? I need the champagne brought out of the cool room to be ready for the toasts. We've got a window of about an hour before the reception starts.'

'Of course.' He placed his hand in the small of her back, feeling the curve under his palm. A perfect fit. Too perfect. But when she didn't object to it being there, he left his hand where it was as they walked towards the café, not quite a hug but a connection that made him feel better knowing he could be beside her to help with whatever she needed.

In the kitchen, he watched as she gathered the wait staff and gave them a run-down of the schedule for the reception. Some of the faces he recognised — older now, they'd been primary school age when he'd left Wongan Creek. The unfamiliar faces were either backpackers or new in town since he'd been gone.

In the group, a middle-aged man studied Fen closely. Long hair tied back, his catering company kitchen staff uniform neat if not a little too big. Rugged features that might appeal to a woman who liked the look of a man who'd lived a hard life. Untidy hair concealed by a bandana and teardrop sunglasses with reflective lenses hiding his eyes. As if he'd forgotten he was wearing them, and they were a part of his everyday uniform.

Kieran's senses hit high alert. Not the same guy who'd come to the cellar on his first day here. This guy was taller, older, scrappier, but no less suspicious. He'd keep an eye on him, make sure the man stayed at his post. He made his way to the storeroom to get the stock of drinks, moving quickly so he wouldn't lose sight of the kitchen hand.

Fen stepped out the back door of the kitchen onto the narrow decking, ticking off the checklist in her mind as she headed for the freezer room out the back. If all had run to plan, the supplier should have delivered the bags of ice for the bar.

A movement behind her had her turning. She pasted her I'm-okay smile on her face, expecting it to be Kieran or Liv who'd followed her out. It froze in place as a stranger invaded her space, so close she could smell his lack of cologne and the remaining stench of stale cigarette smoke.

The man's hand closed around her arm, his fingers digging into her flesh, his breath on her face and his words threatening in her ear as he propelled her down the stairs and onto the gravel path. Adrenaline raced through her veins, chasing down the terror as her instinct for fight or flight kicked in.

'Let me go!' She pulled against his grip, knowing his fingers would leave bruises, the pressure of them reminding her of hands that had grasped and hurt before. A long time ago.

'I'll let you go when I'm bloody good and ready.'

'What do you want from me? Did Luke send you?' She looked over her shoulder to the cellar building, panic setting in as he half ran, half walked her down the path. Where was Riggs? She could see the guests in the tasting hall, their backs turned to the windows, no-one facing the grounds. Kieran. He'd been in the kitchen. Had he seen the man come after her? She tugged against his hand again, but the fingers holding her were strong. She could scream, attract attention. She opened her mouth and took a breath.

His nails bit into her skin. 'Not a sound. Don't make me kill you before we've had some fun. Takes all the pleasure out of it. You didn't think you could hide forever, did you?'

'I don't know what you're talking about. Who are you? Why won't you leave us alone?'

'It doesn't matter who I am. You won't live long enough for it to matter. I don't like loose ends, you see. They tend to earn a man a cell in prison.' He pushed the sunglasses up on his head and Fen got a look into eyes so dark they were almost black. Empty eyes with a teardrop tattoo. 'We have unfinished business, you and I … *Rosa.*'

The emphasis he placed on the name had her skin crawling with goosebumps. Recognition flitted in and out of reach. A voice calling her. A name she'd forgotten because she hadn't been called it since the day she turned seven. 'My name is Fenella Waterman. You have the wrong person.'

He rubbed a thumb over her wrist. 'Don't play dumb with me, girl. It would be a shame if people thought you'd taken to cutting yourself again. This time you might succeed. The way your mother did.'

'I don't know what you're talking about.'

The grip on her wrist tightened, pinching her skin. 'Your foster mother is looking well. Maybe I should let you watch me make her suffer. Jog your memory. Before I do exactly the same to you. Do you have any idea how much that appeals to me? Nothing more satisfying than the slice of a knife against skin. But you know all about that, don't you, Rosa?'

Cold terror gripped her spine. 'You leave her alone.' Fen swallowed the fear that rose to claim her words. She'd fight until her last breath to keep Liv safe.

His grip tightened some more. 'Maybe I'll leave her to my friends. You're more my type. I like a feisty girl.

A good fight. If you're lucky when I'm done with you, I'll leave something over for them to play with.'

Fen let her arm relax in his grip. She looked him right in the eye. 'Fuck you.'

Kieran's shout reached her ears, the thud of his feet pounding out a rhythm on the gravel. 'Oi!'

The man's hold on her fell away. 'Make it easy on yourself. Call off the cops, let me deal with this my way, and maybe I'll let you live.' He walked away as Kieran reached her.

'You okay?'

She nodded. 'Fine.' Kieran made to go after the man, but she held him back with a hand on his arm. 'Let him go.'

'What? Fen, are you crazy? That didn't look like a friendly visit.'

'It wasn't. Liv needs to go away for a while. Somewhere safe where they can't harm her.'

Riggs raced across the lawn, reaching them as the sound of a Harley engine disappeared up the drive towards the main road. 'Trouble, Fenella?'

'An unwelcome guest.'

Riggs patted his pocket as he watched the dust settle on the road. 'Lucky I got his rego number then. I don't like what's happening here. If there's anything you need to tell me, now's a good time. Did you recognise him?'

'No. I've never seen him before.'

'Right, I'll run the rego for the records, but I think I

know exactly where it will lead me. Think you can ID him if I show you some photographs?'

Adrenaline seeped out to let fear creep in. 'I'm scared, Sarge. After the fire yesterday and now this ...'

'I can get you protection.'

Anger chased the fear. 'I'm already in protection. *You* told me that. That makes me wonder if I can trust you because Beyond Hell's Reach found me, and I don't even know why I'm their target. You told me they'd reopened my mother's case. You told me it was murder. And you've always known where I came from. Is that a coincidence, *Sarge*? Or are you on the take along with those same cops who filed a false report on my mother's death?'

'Fen ...' Kieran squeezed her shoulders with a gentle warning.

'No, I have a right to be asking.' Fen stepped out of the protection of Kieran's warmth. 'All I have is questions and no answers.'

Riggs folded his notepad and tucked it away in his pocket. His eyes searched hers then held, his gaze direct and full of meaning. 'The only way I can give you all the answers is if you come into the station and give me a positive ID. One answer I can give you with absolute clarity is that I am not on the take. Muzz Waterman was a mate. A good mate. And I won't let anything happen to his wife or the girl he considered his daughter, his flesh and blood, even when blood had nothing to do with it. I kept your secret from the day Martha Wallace came into my office to tell me she was bringing you here and why. When you're ready to confront the truth, Fenella, you know where to find me. In the meantime, I'll make sure I have back up from the anti-gang task force in this town by nightfall because things are about to get ugly.'

His words smashed at her heart. She wanted to believe the honesty in his eyes, wanted to be sure she had the law on her side. The time had come to crawl out of the shadows and face what lay behind that bedroom door. 'I'll come in, but first I have a wedding to wrap up and a bride to keep happy. I won't let any of this spoil Tameka's big day.'

Liam's wail flowed across the lawns. 'Daddy!'

The panic in his cry made Fen's heart ache. The speed with which Kieran turned and ran towards his son cemented how precious he was to his father. The way he swept the little boy up in his arms and comforted him against his chest made her wish she could do the same. And the reality of it all made her realise all the reasons she needed to make Kieran go back to Sydney where both he and Liam would be safe too. Safe and untouched by the dark forces that currently ruled her life and had the potential to harm them.

'He couldn't see you anywhere, love, and he panicked.' Marge Everett's tone was apologetic as she patted Liam's back.

'Thanks for bringing him to me, Mrs Everett.'

Minutes earlier and Liam would have witnessed what happened. Damn it, he could have been bait if the man sent to threaten her had chosen to make him so. Anger shot through her as Fen made her way across the grassy patch and past the roses still in full bloom. Kieran and Liam had suffered enough, and they were no longer close enough to be dragged into her nightmares. Not like when they were kids and their situations had been similar. Kieran had pulled himself out of that life. She'd succeeded in doing the same until Luke had dragged her back there again. Neither Liv nor Kieran deserved that kind of treatment.

The raised ridges of her scars itched. She rubbed them against the silk of her dress. A long time ago, she would have taken a knife to them to stop the irritation, but she was better than that now.

By the time she reached the café dining room, the guests had started to filter in and Liv was guiding them to tables with the help of the wait staff. Bella's daughter, Janet, waved hello and Fen waved back. John Bannister held court to one side with the mayor and a councilman. Virginia Turner herded a group of children off to one side, doing what she did best.

Fen's heart still pounded, and her mind spun, despite her efforts to refocus her thoughts. She stopped to give Liv a quick hug, ground herself in knowing her mum was okay, still untouched by the ugliness of what had to come.

'Is Liam okay, sweetheart? I heard him crying.'

'He's fine, Mum. He panicked a little when he couldn't find Kieran. We had another visitor.'

'Oh no, Fen!' Worry backlit her eyes as she searched Fen's face. 'What happened?'

'He left quietly when Kieran and Riggs came running. We need to talk, Mum. About the nightmares and how I came to be here.'

'Oh, honey, of course we can. I'm not sure how much I can help though. All we were told is that your behaviour was partly due to long-term trauma and repressed memory. I don't know much more than you do. But we'll work through it together the way we've always done.'

'I love you, Mum.'

Liv touched her cheek. 'And I love you too, Fen. We'll get through this, I promise.'

'While we work through it, I want you to go somewhere safe until it's over.'

Liv's soft blue eyes flashed. 'I will not. We fight whatever this is together. Murray left the winery to us. You and me. Equal shares. I didn't abandon you at your worst times, darling, and I have no intention of abandoning you now. Riggs will make sure we're safe.'

Doubt niggled again. 'Can we truly trust him? Can we trust anyone?'

'I have complete faith in Riggs. Murray trusted him, the town trusts him. He doesn't give up until he finds justice. If you need proof of that, talk to Travis Bailey or Harley Baker or even our bride, Tameka.'

She didn't need to. She'd witnessed the cases, watched them unfold, listened to the gossip around the tables at the high teas they'd hosted. But until she could find the trigger to release the memories of what happened behind Antoinette's bedroom door that day, she'd question everything.

Fen kissed her mum's cheek. 'Let's get this reception on the go. Tameka and Harley deserve our focus today. Tomorrow, I'll do as Riggs has asked. It's past time to lay the ghosts to rest.'

'You're a brave soul, my darling girl. I wish it hadn't come to this. But together we'll find out why it has and fix it.' Liv hugged her hard. 'Take over, would you love? I need to go and check in with the chef. It was so kind of John Bannister to lend us the mine site kitchen staff.'

Fen agreed. 'And the cleaning staff who will come in later to help. I think he has a soft spot for you, Mum.'

Liv blushed, her palms to her cheeks to cool them. 'Don't be silly, sweetheart. Good Lord, he's almost twenty years older than me.'

'Old but not dead yet.' She hugged Liv tight. 'And you're gorgeous. Who doesn't love you?'

Liv smiled and handed her the list of table numbers and guest placements. 'Stop it.' She pressed a kiss to

Fen's cheek. 'You look so beautiful in that dress, Fen. I'm so proud of you. And in case you hadn't noticed, Kieran can't keep his eyes off you.'

If only Liv knew the real reason he stood looking at her now with his son at his side and the little boy's hand securely in his. 'Not me, Liv. Janet.'

Fen watched as Bella's daughter snagged Kieran's attention. Stunning in a red velvet dress that ended mid-thigh and complemented her long, dark hair and Italian heritage, the pre-school teacher re-introduced herself to Kieran and made her acquaintance with Liam. Fen pushed back the stab of jealousy. Janet was a lovely girl and far better suited for Kieran than she was. Stable, loved kids, single with no backstory or baggage, a great cook and an active CWA member, she'd be the perfect wife and mother.

Turning her attention back to the guests and the seating arrangements, she blocked out the peripheral scene of the two laughing together, rekindling an old acquaintance that had the potential and freedom to lead to more. If it didn't hurt so much, Fen would cheer them on and encourage it.

'She's not for him, pixie face. You are.' Harry Murchison's gnarled hand lifted the pen from her hand and he ticked his own name off the list against table two.

'You're the only man for me, Harry.'

'Bullshit. But if I was a hundred years younger …'

'You wouldn't be born.' She took back her pen. 'Behave yourself. Do I need to show you to your table?'

'Can find it myself.' He looked at her, his eyes watery, old and confused. 'I know a good match when I see one. Janine and Murphy aren't it.'

'Janet,' she reminded him. Sometimes it was hard to believe he had Alzheimer's. Other times, when his look grew vacant and his thoughts muddled, she wished she'd known Harry in his youth. That she could go back and change whatever it was in his genes that brought the disease with it.

'Janine, Janet … doesn't matter. Only name he needs to know is yours.'

And with that, he hobbled away as the next guests stepped up to take his place, their knowing smiles proving that they'd heard every word.

Travis Bailey grinned down at her from his six-foot-plus height from under the shock of white fringe that contrasted his blond hair. 'Never argue with Harry. The old bugger has a gift for it.'

'He has a gift for something, that's for sure.' Fen met the warm brown eyes of Travis' wife. 'Hi, Heather. I hope you're keeping this beast tamed.'

'I'm giving it my shot.' She winked.

Fen smiled. Heather Bailey was a lot nicer, warmer than her predecessor, Martha Wallace, who'd been colder than an arctic wind. 'Good to hear.'

'Maybe when this is all over, we can catch up for a coffee?'

'That would be lovely, thank you. You're on table two with Harry. Enjoy.'

As they walked away and she welcomed the next guests, Fen wished more than ever that life could be normal and hell didn't wait in the wings to wreak havoc on the town if she couldn't bring Luke to justice.

Chapter Nine

Fen looked up from her clipboard as the last of the guests made their way to their seats. He couldn't begin to imagine how shaken she must be after her run-in with that arsehole outside. He tried to concentrate on his conversation with Janet and not think about what might have happened if he hadn't followed Fen out the door.

'Thanks, Janet. I'll bring Liam by one morning next week to see how he goes.'

Kieran shook the school teacher's hand and hoped that kindy would be as good for Liam as she hoped. Liam's eyes had lit up at the mention of Benji and Casey, two of the kids closest to his age. Both were here today, as Janet had pointed out, and no doubt by the end of the evening Liam would have met them at least once.

Kids could be cruel and Kieran wasn't convinced

that Liam was ready for the schoolyard just yet. He'd considered home-schooling as an option but juggling a day job and school duties would be difficult when it came to meeting departmental requirements.

And sooner or later, Liam would have to learn to socialise again. He'd been doing so well at playgroups and day-care back in Sydney. Until life as they'd known it had ended up in a cold and swollen river.

How would the kids at school cope with Liam's volatile behaviour, tantrums triggered by a fear only he could see? Who would hold him close and bring him down if he wasn't there to do it? It wouldn't be fair to lay that responsibility at Janet's feet in a classroom that consisted of children of mixed ages as most small-town schools did. She'd have enough on her hands.

Liam tugged on his hand. 'Don't wanna go to stupid school.'

And the quiver of his lip suggested he hadn't recovered fully from his earlier meltdown, so Kieran searched for a distraction. 'Would you like to see if Fen needs help with anything?'

'K.' Liam's face brightened.

Together they crossed the room. This close, he could see the shadows forming under Fen's eyes that spoke of the troubled thoughts churning behind her smile. No doubt about it, the incident outside had her unsettled. Jesus, it had him in knots.

If he hadn't spotted that idiot … Damn it, the

outcome could have been very different. God only knew what the man was capable of or what exactly he'd had in mind to do with Fen.

Too many witnesses though. He'd have been an idiot to try anything more serious than deliver his message. At least the colour had come back into her face now. He couldn't afford to think about his own reaction to seeing her manhandled like that. If he did, he'd have to admit that he still cared for her. More than he should. More than he deserved to.

Kieran stepped closer to Fen. 'Need help with anything? Liam and I appear to be at a loose end now all the guests are seated.'

Fen placed her clipboard on the table near the door. 'The wedding party will be coming in soon. We have a table near the kitchen where I can keep an eye on things. Why don't you two take a seat. Liv is supervising in the kitchen and it will be chaos in there, so not a good place to be in case there are accidents.' She looked down at Liam and then up at Kieran. A smile of understanding crossed her lips and he thought it was the most beautiful thing he'd seen all day. 'I know what you can do for me. I'm going to be stuck here for a while before I can take a break and Lucky will be getting hungry.'

'Who's Lucky?' Liam's face lit with curiosity, all fears forgotten.

'Lucky is my bearded dragon. Do you know what that is?'

'Uh-huh. It's a big lizard with spiky things on its head.' Liam demonstrated with his hands.

'That's right. He's only a baby so he needs to eat a lot while he's growing. Do you think you could feed him some crickets for me?'

Enthusiasm had Liam hopping from foot to foot. 'Yeah! Live crickets?'

Fen nodded. 'You've got to be quick though otherwise the crickets will hop away.'

And she'd be chasing them around her room trying to recapture them all if he wasn't. Kieran grimaced.

'Think you can do that?' Fen held out her hand to shake on it.

'Yeah! How many crickets?' Liam shook her hand with vigorous enthusiasm.

'Can you count to ten?'

'Of course I can!' He held up both hands, fingers stretched out.

'Lucky will be very happy. If you talk to him while you feed him, he might show you his beard.'

'Does he bite?' Uncertainty niggled at Kieran. Trusting Liam to make paper boats was one thing. Trusting him with your pet lizard was another mission entirely. He had visions of punctured fingers, a trip to Wongan Creek's emergency department and tetanus injections.

'No, he's very docile.'

'What's docile mean?' Liam tugged on Fen's dress.

'Harmless, gentle. You can give him some carrots and cabbage too. Just a little bit.'

'Why?'

'Because he's only a baby and he needs more insects than veggies right now.'

'K. Can we go now, Daddy?'

'Sure can, mate. Are you sure about this, Fen?' Kieran hoped he sounded convincing. How much trouble could a baby bearded dragon be?

'Of course. His food is next to his enclosure in my room.'

'Your bedroom?' Jesus, the last time he'd been in that room they were fifteen and he'd been wrapping bandages around her wrists to stop the bleeding.

Fen straightened to look at him. 'Yes. Something wrong with that?'

'Isn't it unhealthy?'

'His enclosure is cleaner than most houses. It has to be that way.'

Kieran shivered. 'What if he escapes during the night?' Waking up to a lizard crawling across his face wasn't his idea of fun.

Liam laughed, a sound that warmed Kieran's heart. 'Are you afraid of Lucky, Daddy?'

'You know, I think your dad might be.' Fen's eyes twinkled with mischief and it gave his heart a whole new exercise regime. 'You might have to hold his hand while you're feeding Lucky, okay? I'd hate for him to scare my dragon.'

'I'll look after him and the dragon, Fen. I promise. Come on, Daddy. We don't want Lucky to get too hungry.'

Kieran wasted another few moments watching Fen walk away, catching the smile before she turned her head and focused on the tasks ahead. He was about to get a whole new look into the life of the girl who'd once hidden behind bandages and over-sized black hoodies.

Liam tugged at his hand. 'Don't worry, Daddy. You'll be safe with me.'

He tore his gaze away from Fen and focused on his son. 'Of course I will, mate. Let's go.'

Together they headed for the main house. Built on top of the gentle slope that ran up from the cellar building, the house had the advantage of a three-hundred-and-sixty-degree view. Kieran took a moment to run his hands across the hand-crafted kaolinitic sandstone with a nod to the skill of the stonemasons. No-one built houses like this anymore.

The wraparound verandah cast shade around the house, shielding it from the baking heat of the sun. The old tin roof had been restored recently, providing a fresh grey backdrop for the row of three dormer windows facing the vines and the shadowy shapes of the Whispering Hills.

The middle window was Fen's room. He

remembered when they'd first arrived in town, how many times she'd escaped through that window and slipped down the roof, away and into the night. The frantic calls for help from Liv and Muzz because Kieran was the only one who could talk her out of running away again.

But all that had changed, and she'd settled down, as he had, into life in Wongan Creek. She'd no longer needed him to bandage her wrists or rub salve on the welts on her arms or rescue her in the middle of the night out on a road somewhere in the dark. Instead, Diane had needed him more. The boy from the Brabham housing project, who'd never been needed before, had been torn between the two girls he loved.

In the end, he'd been forced to make the choice and he'd chosen the weakest of the two, knowing full well Fen would survive. But it hadn't made him love her any less, something that hadn't gone unnoticed by Diane. A flaw she'd raised at every opportunity, using Fen as an excuse to drive a wedge between them. To drive herself to the edge and over. And the blame lay squarely with him. For that he'd never forgive himself. Because if he hadn't weakened and started that email to Fen, Diane would never have found it and she might still be alive.

'Is it okay to go inside, Daddy?' Liam placed a hand on the jarrah hardwood front door with the polished brass knocker and handle.

'Of course it is, mate. We have permission from Fen, remember?'

'Do you know which room hers is?'

'Up the stairs in the corner, to the left and it's the second door you come to.'

They pushed open the front door and stepped inside. The first thing that struck Kieran was that everything was the same. Nothing had changed in the years he'd been away. A vase of fresh flowers still adorned the nineteenth-century hall table. The house still smelled like vanilla and cinnamon and freshly squeezed lemons.

The warm, welcoming feel still hung in the air and no doubt, the fire in the lounge room hearth would still be burning softly, ready to be stoked up when Fen and Liv came home after a long day at work. The only one missing was Muzz, the lack of television noise and weekend football a silence that echoed down the hallway.

Kieran reflected for a moment on the twinge of regret that he'd never got to say goodbye to the man who'd been a stoic force behind his rehabilitation from troubled teen to responsible husband and father. So much yet so little had changed here. He turned his attention back to his son.

Liam climbed the stairs cautiously, stopping to check that Kieran was right behind him. A boy heading into an unknown adventure, full of expectation and excitement. Exactly what he wanted to see more of in his son. To recapture the adventurous spirit he'd once been.

They found her room and Liam raced to the corner where Lucky lounged on a rock inside his glass enclosure next to Fen's desk. In the plastic tub next to it, crickets chirped and leaped about, trying to escape their fate. Time to show his son how to catch a cricket.

'Look, Daddy! His beard is out.'

True enough, Lucky's beard spread wide, his mouth open in expectation. Or warning. Crickets he could handle. Bearded dragons? The jury was still out on that one. 'Okay, so how did Fen say we do this again?'

'Pick up a tube from the tub. There'll be crickets inside.'

'Right. And shake it into the enclosure, right?'

'Right. Can I do it?'

'We have to be quick or they might escape.' The thought made Kieran shudder.

'We've got this, Dad.'

And suddenly his four-year-old sounded a lot more grown-up than he did. Kieran smiled as he lifted the lid on the tub and Liam reached in for a cardboard tube filled with creatures that made his skin crawl. The transfer took place thankfully without incident and Liam watched, fascinated, as Lucky began to hunt and catch his dinner.

Kieran's gaze fell on a folder lying on the desk next to the tub of crickets. Stapled to the front was a business card with a police case number scribbled on it, a harsh reminder of the trouble that dogged Fen. A reality that had the potential to touch them all, do damage, threaten lives. Like the woman whose body had been dumped in the fire, her identity and the reason she'd been there still a mystery.

A damn good reason for him to take his son somewhere safe and out of harm's way. Motivation to stay and fight alongside the friend who'd been there for him over and over, long before he'd married Diane. A dilemma that would keep him awake while he watched his son sleep and tried to think of a way to help Fen and Liv without putting his child's life and emotional recovery at risk to keep his promise to the girl who'd always owned his heart.

Fen supervised the serving of the entree to the tables and checked her watch for timing. Twenty minutes for the guests to down the alternate seating dishes of Chicken Marsala or marinated beef tips with capsicum and Spanish onion. Then onto the champagne and speeches.

Around her the waiters began their ritual of collecting emptied plates while the drinks staff placed champagne in the ice buckets. All going well. If she kept focused on the routine, she couldn't think about the man and what he would have done to her if Kieran hadn't come to her rescue. That made her think about the body they'd found in the fire. She rubbed the itch of her scars against the cool, soothing silk of her dress.

The safest option would be for Kieran to leave and take Liam back to Sydney where they would be out of harm's way. Hadn't they suffered enough without this added threat that shadowed her? And because the thought of them leaving made her heart ache for things she couldn't have, she picked up a couple of bottles of champagne and busied her hands filling ice buckets.

If none of this had happened — Luke, Diane — they might have rekindled the spark that had simmered between them. Explored the possibilities of a relationship that ran deeper than friendship, but life had changed everything. For as long as the door stayed closed on her past, she'd never move on, and until she could pinpoint what it was Beyond Hell's Reach thought she knew, she'd never wake from the nightmares in her mind.

Kieran and Liam came back into the dining room, a smile stretched wide across Liam's lips and a frown furrowing Kieran's brow. Her heart stuttered at the likeness between man and boy.

In another dimension, Liam might have been her

son. She wasn't sure she wanted kids. What could she offer a child? Poor genetics, nightmares and a screwed up past? No matter how hard she fought the black dog that gnawed at her heels, it would always be there. Waiting for a weak moment, reminding her with every itch of her scars that it was still there. A shadow in her mind, a secret behind a door she avoided opening to release it.

Fen pushed aside the thoughts that rolled clouds across her sunshine, Liam's happy smile warming the chill in her bones. Seeing that smile light his face was enough to put that black dog right back in its kennel. 'How did you go with Lucky?'

Kieran shrugged. 'He ate.'

'He showed me his beard.' Liam added. 'I talked to him and he liked it.'

She smiled and ruffled the kid's hair. 'Next time I'll let you hold him, if that's okay with your dad?'

Liam's grin spread wider, hopping from one foot to the other. 'Can I, Daddy?'

Fen raised her eyes to Kieran's and noted the frown was still there. He looked at her long and hard before he answered, 'Sure, mate. So long as he doesn't bite. I've seen what he does to crickets.'

Travis Bailey stepped up to them. 'Hey, Kieran. How you doing, mate? Welcome back.'

'Cheers, thanks.' Kieran shook the outstretched hand.

'My niece, Casey, and her friend, Benji, want to know if Liam would like to sit with them at the kids' table?'

Fen looked down to see six-year-old Casey at her uncle's side, already sizing Liam up. Pretty in a pink dress that didn't quite go with her leather work boots, Casey offered a shy smile which Liam returned. Kieran hesitated, and Fen placed a hand on his arm, warm and strong to her touch.

'It's okay, Kieran. We'll be right there to keep an eye out. Liam, would you like to tell Casey and Benji all about how you fed Lucky tonight?'

Liam nodded shyly, his hand securely in Kieran's. Casey held out her hand with the confidence of her added two years senior.

'Come on then. We've got cool stuff on our table. Fen said you made the boats. I can draw, but folding stuff … not so good.' She chatted away as Liam transferred his grip from Kieran's to hers and they moved towards a table full of kids ranging in years.

'Thanks, mate.' Kieran gave Travis' shoulder a man pat.

'No problem. The kids around here tend to take care of each other, irrespective of their age differences. They know Marge Everett will tan their hides if they don't. Figuratively speaking, of course.' Travis grinned. 'I'd better get back and supervise. Join us later for a drink?'

'Will do, thanks.' They waited until Travis had

walked away before Kieran turned to Fen. 'Everything okay?'

She nodded. It had to be. 'Fine. We're about to start with the speeches and champagne, and then onto the main course.'

'That's not what I meant.'

He leaned down to say the words in her ear, his breath touching her cheek, the warmth of his hand at her back. She leaned into him a little because, damn it, this was Kieran and she'd missed him, no matter how much she tried to deny it.

'I know. I'm fine.' Tonight, alone in the silence of her bedroom and the darkness that came with it? That would be the test. 'I need to check on the main course.'

She slipped out of his hold, because it would be too easy to stay there, lean on him, need him, ask him to stay with her tonight instead of roping her mum into an all-night movie marathon for distraction from the demons that would dog her sleep.

Kieran's sigh filled the air and his presence warmed her back as he followed her into the kitchen, clearly not ready to let the subject drop. Pots and pans clanged and the sound of plates hitting the stainless-steel bench indicated that the mine chef, Col, had everything under control.

The noise, heat and lack of privacy gave her the cover she'd hoped for, but when the hand at her back guided her to the storeroom, she realised Kieran wasn't about to accept anything less than answers and letting Liam feed Lucky hadn't worked in her plan to distract him.

He pushed the door to the storeroom closed and leaned against it. Fen tried not to remember the last time they'd been in here. When he'd kissed her goodbye. Not the kind of kiss she'd wanted from him, but a gentle sweep of his lips that aimed for her cheek and would have missed her mouth, except she'd turned her head. Cheek kisses were something they'd grown into, something that wouldn't change the dynamics of their friendship when Kieran had belonged to Diane.

But that day, some devil inside her had made her turn her head and capture his lips, knowing he'd be gone the next day, lost to her forever. She'd kissed him with everything in her heart — the sadness, the friendship, her love for him — knowing that, legally and in his heart, he belonged to Diane now and she'd have to be the one to move on.

He'd let her down gently. Easing her away, not saying anything except, 'Goodbye, Fen.' Then he was gone, and she'd slid down the wall and cried until Liv had come to find her.

She'd almost slipped back into old habits that day. It would have been so easy to. Her scars had almost begged her to with an itch that crawled up her arms like fire ants. Her penknife had taunted her from the drawer next to her bed to rid herself of the ache in her soul and replace it with a tangible pain. And if Liv hadn't arrived in time with hot chocolate, Tim Tams and warm hugs to talk her through it, she might have succeeded.

Fen folded her arms and kept her back to Kieran, tears stinging her eyes.

'Fen.' His voice was quiet in the room. 'Look at me.'

She shook her head, not trusting her voice because the tightness in her throat would have her choking on her words. Gentle hands settled on her shoulders and turned her around. She kept her gaze on the floor. How much longer could she keep fighting the demons, real and emotional, so determined to consume her?

He pulled her close and wrapped his arms around her, holding her against the unsteady beat of his heart. She put her hands to his chest, meant them to be a barrier, but no real barrier at all, because the feel of Kieran under her hands made her want to finish what she'd started right here in this poorly lit room all those years ago. To sink into his kiss, his body and everything he personified and push away the real world that snapped at her heels.

He tipped up her chin, his gaze holding hers in the dim light of the storeroom. A flicker of something she couldn't read in the shadows cast by that light, and then his head blocked out what was left of it, and she met him halfway.

The minute his lips touched hers, she was lost in his taste, a flavour she remembered every time she thought of him, but different. Newer, fresher, better. Too good. His hands cupped her face, the thumbs — rough from hard work — rubbing against her jaw, creating a hunger far more desperate than she remembered.

Kieran explored at his own pace and created a fire in her that would take more than a cold shower to cool it. She returned each nip and tease, her hands slipping from his chest and tracing a path to his hips, his body hard, muscled and toned under her palms.

His hands tangled in her hair and drew her closer, deepening the kiss until she melted against him, into him, forgetting all the reasons she shouldn't. He whispered her name against her lips, before releasing her mouth and holding her head against his chest, their hearts beating erratically out of rhythm with each other, bodies radiating warmth off one another, the world outside the storeroom forgotten.

She should stop this before she lost herself in him again, make him go. Make him take Liam far away from the shitstorm to come, from the danger Luke and his damned brotherhood presented. From the mess she'd made of her life and the nightmares she couldn't escape. But she felt so safe in his arms, with him at her back, seeing him every day the way she used to. The anchor in her life that had been missing for too long.

Kieran eased his mouth from hers and resisted the urge to bang his head against the storeroom door. What the hell was he thinking kissing Fen, raising feelings he had no right to explore? Feelings and actions that would hurt them both. And Liam. They stood close, coming down from the high and the feelings neither of them would be ready to give voice to.

'I shouldn't have done that,' he whispered into the silence.

Her hands fell away from his hips and she stepped away. The dim light reflected the tears that welled in her eyes. '*Déjà vu.*'

He rubbed the wry pull of her mouth away with his thumb. 'We've got the timing all wrong again.'

'Was it ever right for us?' She stepped out of reach and he let his hand fall away, the shelves behind her preventing her from retreating completely.

Her warmth still filled the space between them, her hands only inches from his, close enough for him to slip his fingers through hers. But he wouldn't. He couldn't expose his son to another broken woman. One more broken than Diane had ever been. One even more vulnerable because of the past they shared. A girl trapped by dark memories that surfaced in nightmares and had her taking a blade to her skin to ease the pain they caused. He could only ever be a friend to Fen.

'I'm scared, Kieran.'

Her words, too quiet in the room, tore through him. 'What are you afraid of?'

'That the dreams might mean something after all. That somewhere in my mind I'm hiding from something worse than seeing my mother taken away in an ambulance, dead from an overdose.'

He reached for her shoulders because it would anchor them both. 'Which could be true if they're re-opening the investigation into her death. Tell me what you feel.'

She shook her head. 'It's hard to explain. A gut feeling, a niggling, the terror when the dreams happen. There's something important behind that door that I can't open.'

'Have the nightmares got worse?'

She nodded, chewing down on her lip. 'Since I found Luke's cuts.' She raised her eyes to his, deep pools of fear. 'Since I saw the teardrop tattoo on the man's face at the bar. And today when that man grabbed hold of my arm.'

'Repressed memory. Liam's therapist warned me about it after the accident. The trauma makes the mind disassociate with the event, effectively blocking it, until something happens to trigger it.' He nodded. 'With

165

Liam, when a memory manifests itself, it triggers his tantrums because he's too emotionally immature to understand what happened. Tell me what you feel.'

'There is a danger I can feel, touch, smell in those dreams, but I can't unlock that door. Sometimes I know I've seen something different to previous nightmares, but I can't remember what it is, and all I feel is this deep-seated fear. Like an animal being hunted, like I'm hiding from something and if it finds me … I felt that same fear with that man here today. I don't know what it means.' She drew in a long, shuddery breath. 'I can take care of this. Go, Kieran. Take Liam and go back to Sydney. This isn't what you signed up for. As much as I know you'll be good for the winery and help us build it again, I can't let them harm you or Liam. And whatever it is they think I know, has the potential to do that. I need Liv to be somewhere safe too. Somewhere they can't touch her.'

He ran a hand through his hair. Frustration boiled through his gut, his mind divided between taking Liam out of harm's reach and staying to protect the girl who'd always held a large chunk of his heart in her hands. 'We need to find out more.'

'If this gets ugly, Liam will be caught in the middle of it. Is that what you want?'

Straight for the place she knew would hurt. He almost felt the gut punch. 'I don't want any of this for anyone.' If he stayed, he couldn't avoid getting involved. If he left, he'd never forgive himself if something happened to her. Like he'd let something happen to Diane. He'd lost one woman, he couldn't lose Fen too. Not after all they'd survived together.

'I've got to get back to the wedding. I can't let this spoil Tameka's day.' She opened a box of tissues from the shelf behind her and wiped her eyes, blew her nose. 'There's nothing more I can do today. Riggs is on it. I have to trust him to find out what he can.'

He dragged a hand through his hair. 'We will talk this through after.'

Fen shook her head. 'Take Liam and go home, Kieran. Where it's safe. Where neither of you will be in danger.'

His heart slammed against his ribs. No damn way would she make him leave. 'Do you honestly think I'd leave you with this mess? I'm not going anywhere.'

'Then you're an idiot.'

There could even be some truth in that. 'Your guests are waiting. Let's get this wedding out of the way and then we'll talk.' He opened the door to let the noise of the working kitchen flood their space. Light spilled into the room, highlighting the haunted look on her face. He hated seeing her like this ... broken, defeated. 'Are you sure you're okay to go out there? I can cover for you if you need a moment.'

Fen drew her shoulders up, stiffened her spine and walked towards him. 'I'll be fine. If you could supervise the start of serving the next course, I'd appreciate it. I need to stop by the ladies' room to patch up my panda eyes otherwise Liv will be all over it that something's up.'

He reached out to tip up her chin with his forefinger, her skin smooth as the silk of her dress, her whole being as pale and delicate as his mother-in-law's bone china serving plates and just as breakable. 'I'll be waiting.' He couldn't let her be broken. Not by this. Not by anything.

Chapter Ten

The twenty-minute drive into Wongan Creek felt like it took forever. Next to her, Kieran stayed silent as he negotiated the bends and overtook road trains. A crew of police detectives and forensics specialists had arrived soon after eight and entered the taped-off, burnt-out block of tangled vines which had morphed into a crime scene investigation. Only because of their presence on site had she felt safe leaving Liam and Liv alone at The Cranky Lizard when Kieran had insisted in coming with her to see Riggs.

Somewhere in this mess there had to be a common denominator, a trigger. A reason Luke had chosen her and the winery to carry out his illegal activities. Perhaps it was the seclusion of the property, the size of the land. She hadn't been a random pick off a dating site or the girl he'd taken a liking to behind the bar of a winery, she'd been a carefully researched target. Her mind whirled.

The tattoo that looked like Luke's, the same as the man in the bar and the one who'd shown up at the wedding. She'd Googled it, found out it symbolised murder, and in Luke's case of a colourless one, attempted murder. She'd slept with a man who'd tried to take a life.

What was it they thought she knew? A memory, a flicker like an old black and white movie on a screen, hovered around the edges of her subconscious. She pushed it away automatically, habitually, the same way she'd done since she was seven, trapped under a table in the dark with screams and shouts and thumps ringing in her ears.

Kieran steered the SUV into a parking spot outside the Wongan Creek Police Station. 'Ready?'

'Ready as I'll ever be.'

He cut the engine and released his seatbelt. 'You've got this, Fen.' His fingers squeezed hers where they lay in her lap.

She blew out a breath. 'What if I can't remember? What if I can't identify these men? What if doing this escalates the threats? One victim won't be enough for them, Kieran.'

'Then we need to stop them. We need to find the key to put them away.' He leaned across and released her seatbelt from the buckle. 'We're going to go in there and Riggs will help us put it all together. One step at a time.'

Unease crawled in her belly, a trickle of fear sparking in her mind. She'd be okay. Kieran was there. The way he'd been in the car from Armadale and in her room when her wrists had bled. 'I want it to be over.'

'Then let's do this.' He got out of the SUV and closed the door.

She shivered against the chill in her spine and reached for the door handle. Kieran was there, his hand out to take hers, his fingers strong and warm as they closed around her cold ones. Together they walked into the station.

Riggs stood behind the desk, his usual smile drawn down in a grim drag of his mouth. 'Fenella, Murphy.' His greeting was short and sharp. 'Come around into my office.' He turned to the pretty police constable beside him. 'Haines, you're it. Hold all calls unless it's urgent. And by urgent, I don't mean Mavis calling to say someone stole her cookie jar or the neighbour's cat drank all her milk again.'

Merryn Haines smiled. 'Got it, Sarge.'

Fen tightened her hold on Kieran's hand as they followed Riggs into his office. He stood aside as they passed then closed the door behind them.

'Sit. Can I get you a coffee? Although you might want water instead. The coffee hasn't improved any. Still tastes like hundred-year-old mud.'

Fen shook her head. 'I'm fine.' Irritation skittered along her nerve-endings. *Get to the point*.

Riggs dragged a binder off the pile on the edge of his desk as he sat. 'We'll start with some photographs to see if you can ID any of the men you've seen come to the winery. Relax, take your time. Look hard.' He pushed the binder towards her.

She opened it and looked, turning each page face down until she stopped. 'This guy. He was the one at the bar.' She looked at Kieran for confirmation.

He nodded. 'Yeah, that's him.'

Riggs turned the photograph towards him. 'Mario Marino, also known as Turtle. Road captain of Beyond Hell's Reach with a string of assault charges, one resulting in grievous bodily harm upgraded to manslaughter when the victim died from a brain haemorrhage.' He stood and pinned the photograph to his whiteboard with a magnet.

Kieran moved his chair closer to hers, the touch of his leg comforting, the weight of his arm on the backrest behind her reassuring. Her belly crawled with nerves and a knot of fear squeezed at her throat. She flipped through the rest of the photographs, studying each one. Her fingers hovered over one, recognition crawling through her mind, triggering a long-forgotten memory. Good looking, a kind smile, a harsh voice, but never harsh with her. Or Antoinette. He'd always had lollies for her in a white paper bag or a sandwich she'd eat

172

under the table, in her dark corner, away from the noises behind the door.

Riggs turned the page for her. 'Luciano Romano, recently deceased. He was the president of the club and the owner of the brothel Antoinette worked and lived in. I'll spare you from the details of how he died.'

Fen nodded, her belly churning. She turned another page. The face leaped out at her in recognition, making her shift back in her chair, icy fingers raking her spine. 'This is the man at the wedding.'

'Bingo.' Riggs leaned back in his chair. 'A man who's spent half his life in jail and the other half on the streets. Luke's father, Ray Sampson, accurately nicknamed Roach, fresh out of a fifteen-year sentence on drug dealing charges. A man who murders for money, who sells anything he can get his hands on in the black market, who has friends with nicknames like Slasher and reputations that make some of the most hardened criminals on file steer clear of their clubhouse. The new president of Beyond Hell's Reach.'

Kieran shifted closer, leaning forward to study the photo. 'The fact that Luke contacted Fen is no coincidence, is it?'

Riggs shook his head. 'Nothing with these guys is a coincidence. I know the how, I don't know the why and what they want. If it was only money and a place to launder it, they wouldn't still be hanging around. There are plenty of small towns in the area they could start up new business in. What concerns me is how they found you, Fenella.'

She rubbed at the gooseflesh climbing her skin and flicked over the page, not wanting to see that face or the tattoo under his eye. 'How?'

'When Luke Sampson was employed at the mine, he became mates with Zac Bannister. That part is the only coincidence. The question is how Sampson made the connection between Fenella Rose-Waterman and Rosa De Lucio.' With a look at Kieran, he added, 'Bannister was arrested a year ago for murder and assault with intent to cause grievous bodily harm. The boy had very loose lips. Still has. He didn't mind telling the detectives how he came to know these boys. Less of a coincidence was how he ended up sharing a cell with Roach Sampson. Bannister bragged about all the girls he'd wanted to "do".' He looked back at Fen and continued. 'Your name came up, he told them about the foster care, how you came to be here with Martha Wallace and how trash like you needed to be taken out.'

Fen shivered. Trash. The word bounced off the walls to echo in her head. Shadows playing in the lamplight. Raised voices. Harsh words. She stiffened against the memory and Kieran's hand covered hers, the visions and sounds receding as she turned her hand palm up and curled her fingers around his.

'And then you were on Sampson's list. He put the sums together and realised where they'd hidden you when the Department of Child Protection and Family Support "lost" you in the system after Antoinette's death. What we still don't know is why it's so important he needed to find her daughter.'

'How did he know about me?'

'Club members had free entry to the bar at *La Paloma Negra*, all they had to pay for was services rendered. Before he went to jail, Roach was vice-president at Beyond Hell's Reach. He knew Antoinette, had been a client, but she was off limits after Romano took her off the table and labelled her his property.' Riggs leaned forward in his seat. 'Fen, it's important you try to remember what happened that day. With your mother's case reopened, the investigation team will be asking you a lot of questions.' Regret edged its way into his voice. 'Especially now their informant is dead.'

Fen raised her head from focusing on the strength of Kieran's hand on hers. 'The woman in the garbage bag?'

Riggs nodded. 'When Martha Wallace heard Roach had served his sentence and was being released, she contacted the police with her suspicions about Antoinette's death and the anomalies she's found in the reports at the time. She wanted to make sure he couldn't find you. Except she chose the wrong cop to talk to. Now she's dead.'

'Oh my God, that's ...' Words formed a lump that lodged in Fen's throat. Martha Wallace hadn't deserved to die to protect her.

'She was fiercely committed to her job and her charges, but she wouldn't have done herself any favours by becoming too emotionally attached to them. Her coldness was self-preservation. She cared for every single child she put through the system. If she hadn't, she wouldn't have gone to such great lengths to keep you hidden from Beyond Hell's Reach all this time.'

'But they still found me.'

'My theory is that once he knew where you were, Roach coached his son, Luke, to stay close to you until his release so he could find out how much you remember of that night your mother died.'

'I don't remember anything except being terrified and hiding in the dark under a table.' Fen shrank against the backrest. 'Why would he do that?'

'Because we think he had something to do with it.'

'It was an overdose.'

'Sampson was Antoinette's supplier. The police reports were too clean, too cut-and-dried. A high that resulted in hallucinations, causing the victim to self-inflict life-threatening wounds. Martha wasn't convinced that the trauma you suffered was consistent with accidental death. It was enough for her to lose you on the grid.' His voice turned gentle. 'I need you to remember, Fen, so we can stop this nightmare before someone else dies. I don't want outlaws in my town. I don't want people dying at their hands.'

'Repressed memories aren't always retrievable and

even if they are, they're not reliable. The things I remember come in nightmares or at moments I least expect them. I don't know what the triggers are. I don't know if what I see is real or made up. Most of the time, I don't remember the dreams. I was seven.' Her hands turned cold and the scars on her wrist began a fiery crawl.

'I'm going to ask you to do something for me, okay?'

She nodded. 'If it will stop these threats and the damage they're doing, I'll do it.'

'Good girl. I need you to go back to *La Paloma Negra*, to the rooms you lived in. Maybe seeing it, retracing your steps that night from what you do remember will trigger what followed.'

Kieran released his hold on her hand and sat up in the chair, his spine stiff, his tone angry. 'That's insane, Sarge. You're throwing her under the bus sending her into their territory.'

'It's not their territory anymore. Romano gave the business to one of his girls after Antoinette's death and club members have been banned from the premises ever since.'

'I want guarantees that Fen will be safe going there.'

Riggs looked hard at him. 'She'll have protection. Mine. Her visit will be off the records.'

'No, I'll go with her.'

'Kieran, no. You need to stay with Liam. I don't

want him and Liv alone.' She placed her hand on his arm, the muscles tense under her fingers. 'Please.'

He turned to her, taking her face between his palms. 'I can't let you face that alone.' Those warm green eyes turned haunted. 'I won't abandon you when you'll need me most.'

His unspoken words and the weight of regret lay between them. Like he thought he'd abandoned Diane when she'd needed him. That if he'd stayed with her that day, she might still be alive, and his son wouldn't be experiencing the same repressed trauma Fen was. In setting her demons free, he'd be releasing some of his own. Then maybe they'd both be free. Away from harm, uncontrolled by guilt, permitted to move on from the past.

She held his gaze, anchored by it. 'Only if Riggs can promise Liv and Liam will be safe.'

'I'll see to it myself. I've got back up coming in, forensics are still processing the scene, the detectives investigating Martha's death will be here for a few days. There's enough of a police presence to keep the club out of town for a while.'

'It won't stop guys like Roach Sampson from sneaking in alone.' Kieran dropped his hands from Fen's face to the arm of her chair, his knuckles brushing her wrist.

'Constable Haines is good with kids. She has a horde of nieces and nephews. She's also a crack shot with a taser. And a gun. I've seen her wield a police baton, and trust me, you don't want to get in her way. She's not as harmless and sweet as she looks when it comes to the job. I'll play bodyguard to Liv for the day. She won't like having me under her feet in the café, but I'll find a way to convince her.'

'Then all that's left is when.' Fen rubbed at the crawl of terror in her belly.

'It can't wait. Once we release the statement about Martha's death in that fire, the hell these boys are known for creating will explode. They're already edgy about the cold case investigation into Antoinette's death. The cops still taking payment under the table will be volatile under the pressure of being exposed.' He pushed a sticky note towards her. 'That's the name of *La Paloma Negra's* owner and her number. She's expecting me to call and arrange it.'

'How do we know we can trust her?' What if they were walking into a setup? Fen shivered.

'She was in the club the night your mother died. Someone paid her to change her statement and buy her silence. She's come forward to the crime and corruption commission voluntarily and is willing to make a statement in the cold case investigation. She's done living with the nightmares too. But we need other witnesses. And you were there, Fen. In the room.'

Nausea rose in waves. She reached for a water glass, sipped and swallowed it down. She didn't want to think about the demons a visit to the past would unleash, or the consequences if the black dog turned on her and she picked up a blade again. The time had come to set that dog free and slash the demons instead of her skin, to take full control of her life instead of hiding from the truth in the shadows. To claim justice for her lost childhood and freedom from the chains of the past. To bring peace and safety back to the vineyard again.

'I'll do it.'

'Good. Now go home while I arrange my schedule and make a date for you to go and see Cherish.'

They stood and Kieran guided her out the door with a hand at her waist, leaving Riggs with a pile of paperwork on his desk and two positively identified criminals on his board. Out in the sunlight, Fen shaded her eyes with a shaky hand.

'Remember when we first arrived in town and we used to go to Mama Bella's because sitting there, sipping milkshakes made us feel invisible and part of the crowd?'

Kieran grinned and turned her to face him. 'I remember. Bella would always throw in a plate of cookies for free.'

'Can we do that before we go home?' She wrinkled her nose at him, standing in the shelter of his strength. 'Before reality tears away that magic cloak of invisibility and brings all the bad memories screaming to the surface?'

'My treat.' He leaned down to whisper in her ear. 'I've got you, Fen. I won't let you go through this alone. You mean too much to me.'

The words shot heat straight up from the soles of her feet into her heart, warming everything through on its way up. But she shouldn't be reading too much into those words, even when his eyes blazed hot on hers with promise. Her gaze dropped to his lips where his teeth teased the bottom one. Her toes itched for her to step up and kiss him, except that would have the town talking for weeks. She stepped away instead.

'There's a lot of distance still between us, Kieran. So much to still sort through. Liam. Me. This mess with Luke, outlaw motorcycle clubs, fires, threats … Having you by my side to fight it, means more to me than you'll ever know.'

That and having him home again with a kid who, every day, stole another piece of her heart. It would make it so much harder to send them away if she couldn't stop Luke and Roach from destroying their lives.

Kieran took her hand and tugged her into step beside him. 'One step at a time and we'll work through it. I'm not going anywhere, Fen. I promised myself I'd give Liam a fresh start, but I know now that unless he faces his fears, his repressed memories will always dog his future. He wasn't young enough to fall into the bracket from birth to three when the mind holds no consciously retrievable memories. So, at some stage in his life, we're going to have to deal with that.'

She stopped walking and her fingers slipped from his grip.

He turned and frowned, then took a step back towards her. 'What's up?'

She stepped into him and his arms closed around her automatically. 'Maybe if I find the key to unlock my memories, I can help Liam unlock his.'

'You'd do that for him?'

'For him. For you. For Diane.'

'Then you're a lot more forgiving of her than I am. I'm still angry at her, Fen. She had no right to try to take Liam with her.' He stood stiff and solid against her.

'Being broken makes people do irrational things. Antoinette was broken too. I didn't understand that as a seven-year-old. I didn't understand why some days she hated me so much when on the days she was sober and straight, she'd tell me how much she loved me before she'd say she didn't want me anymore. Then Liv came into my life and became that mother who loved me and taught me that sometimes when people are that broken, you can't fix them, and that's not your fault.'

She slipped her arms around him and his hands settled at her waist as he drew her against him. He held her gaze for a long moment, took her silence and the narrowing of the gap between them as consent, then he kissed her until she forgot they were in the middle of Main Street with half the town looking on.

She kissed him back until the heat level threatened to melt the light frost on the grass in Memorial Park and steam up the windows of the shops that lined the street where she knew an audience would have gathered. And because it was too late to salvage any pride, she kissed him back with everything she had in her heart. Because damn it, she loved him against all the odds.

Kieran held her close, so close she could feel every hard edge and ridge, the heat that rose off him, and the need for comfort in each other that had always bound them together. Then his head lifted, his hands fell away and he retreated enough to allow a sliver of ice-cold wind to come between them. 'We should go.'

Fen nodded. Like her faded memories, and with emotions running high between them, they couldn't possibly tell the difference between real and fantasy in that kiss. She opened her eyes to meet his gaze, warmth flooding her cheeks.

He smiled that smile that tripped the circuit breaker on her heart and made her believe things would be okay. 'It's a step, Fen. A small one towards beating this.'

Chapter Eleven

Fen's mind swirled with the events of the morning as she clicked on the icon for an eight-week cruise to Canada and Alaska. The knowledge that she had to go back to that dark and dingy place in her past had brought reality crashing down, stealing the comfort from sweet kisses and double thick milkshakes.

'This one looks awesome, Mum. It includes a train trip. You've always said you wanted to see the Rockies.'

No matter what Riggs promised, the need to keep her mum safe niggled. An urgent, gnawing demand she couldn't find a reason for. As if something awful would happen to Liv if she didn't hide her away under that table that featured so often in her nightmares.

Her safe zone, where no-one could see her or hear her. Where they didn't know she breathed as quietly as she could, where the clawing hands and rough grasps couldn't reach.

'For the last time, I'm not leaving you, Fenella. And anyway, that one is too far and too long. If I were to go on a cruise, I'd try a short one first. Like the one that goes from Fremantle to Albany.'

'Then go on that one. It's the perfect time. You know things slow down over winter. When was the last time you took time off?'

Liv's warm, gentle hand came to rest on her shoulder as Fen clicked through the photographs of glass-topped trains travelling across bridges with forests of firs flashing by. 'I know what you're trying to do, and it won't work.'

With a sigh, Fen closed the browser on her laptop and covered Liv's hand with hers. 'I'm scared, Liv. If I hadn't given in to him, let him move in ...'

'He would still have found a way in. Those men know exactly what they're doing. Do you really think going back to that awful place will help?'

'If I don't try, the nightmares won't stop.' Fen squeezed her mum's fingers. 'If I don't find out what it is they're looking for, they'll keep terrorising us until I do, or until they destroy everything.'

Liv squeezed back. 'What if you remember?'

'I'm a target whether I remember or not. I can only trust that Riggs knows what he's doing and can protect us from it. I'm afraid of what will happen if I remember.

I'm terrified of what will happen to you and Kieran and Liam if I don't.'

Fen stood, Liv's hand slipping from her shoulder, and walked over to the window. Outside on the lawn, Kieran played ball with Liam, enjoying his last day off before work in the morning.

The little boy's smile stretched wide, his infectious laugh melting the ice around her heart. She could really like the kid. Be the same person for him that Liv had been for her back when she'd been a motherless, lost child. If things were different.

Her gaze cut to Kieran, rugged up against the crisp, cold air in a sheepskin jacket, a scarf around his neck and a black beanie warming his ears. He unbuttoned the jacket and tossed it onto the grass, closely followed by his beanie. The sweater he'd worn underneath clung to his torso, highlighting his broad shoulders and solid strength.

Liv came to stand at her side. 'You've always loved him.'

She could deny it, argue against it, but what was the point of that? 'Always. That's why I need to send him away too, Liv. He has Liam to take care of, nightmares of his own to deal with. We can't be more than friends. Every day they're here, I grow more attached to Liam. What if I put everyone here in more danger than we already are by proceeding with these charges against Luke and his thugs? Whatever it is that's locked away in my mind … what happens if it's so terrible, I can't deal with it? What if I'm too emotionally and mentally scarred, like Diane? That's no role model for a child who has already experienced rejection. I have no right to add my problems to Kieran's.'

Liv slipped her arm around Fen. 'If Kieran didn't care about you, he wouldn't have committed to going back to that awful place with you.'

'That's my point, Mum. He's already been to a dark place with his wife. I don't have the right to drag him and his son into another nightmare.'

'He loves you, Fen. He's just not ready for you yet. He will be, when the time is right and you've both dealt with the past. This trauma in your mind, you've lived with it since you were seven. Maybe it's not as bad if, or when, you remember what happened. Repressed memories can be exaggerated by time and emotion. But if you don't face it, you'll never heal completely.'

'What if facing it and bringing it to the surface puts us all in danger? It's clear that Luke and Beyond Hell's Reach think I'm a threat to them, that I know more than I do.'

The link was there, buried deep inside her mind, dragging it to the surface by Antoinette's association with the club.

Martha Wallace had believed Fen was in danger, enough to change her name and make her disappear into the system, and now she was dead. Brutally murdered and dumped, left to burn in a fire on their property because she'd known something.

'What if you don't? You owe it to yourself, to Martha, to Antoinette, to remember what happened that night. It's time to let go of the nightmares and grow another new tail, Fen. Kieran came back here for a reason, not just because he needed a job, or to heal, or for the familiarity of the place where he was at his happiest. He could have got a job anywhere in the world, far away from Wongan Creek, yet he chose to come here. I believe he came back for you. Maybe he doesn't realise that yet, but he will.'

'You're wrong. He's thinking of his boy's future and rightly so. We can be friends, that's all.' But damn it, that kiss had promised so much more yesterday. 'I'm not the girl for him.'

'Why not?'

'Because I'm as toxic to him as Diane was. Look at me, Mum.' She held out her wrists, the scars pink from where she's worried them with her thoughts. 'I'm as unbalanced as Diane was. Kieran deserves better.'

'Darling, you're far from being unbalanced. You're the most together girl I know. Look how far you've come. The outer scars are long healed. You won't go back there again. I have faith that you won't. It's the emotional scars that are still hurting. Sometimes in life a situation has to get worse so it can get better.'

'It's dangerous. Someone else could die.' And the consequences of that would be unbearable.

'Riggs won't let that happen. And Kieran will have your back. He's always been there for you, Fen, except for a moment in time when he couldn't be because his wife and child needed him. He did the right thing. He's an honourable man. And when time heals him and Liam, he'll be free to love you again.'

Fen rubbed at her wrists. She needed to put her cuffs back on. To stop the itch, to curb the temptation. 'I'm still damaged goods.'

'That never stopped him loving you.'

Fen's hands stilled. Had he loved her? 'He didn't love me. We had a close friendship, a bond.' She sighed.

If he had loved her, it would have been the way a brother loved a sister. It hadn't stopped her from loving him, but that was before another damaged woman broke his heart and stole his happiness.

The cycle had to end with Diane. The right woman for him would carry no baggage, have no questionable past. A woman like Janet who came from a stable family background, adored kids and had a steady, reliable job.

'Lucky's looking a bit pale. Take him out into the sunshine. I'm sure Liam would love to see him outside.' Liv held out Lucky's leash.

'Lucky is pale. It's his skin tone. You just want to stop me pressing the book-now button on that cruise.'

Liv smiled. 'That too. But, honey, out there is a man

189

who is your friend and he needs you as much as you need him. Don't waste time not making the best of having him here.'

'I've got so much to do.'

'Go on. Go out there while I get a batch of cookies on the go.' Liv took hold of Fen's hand, placed the leash in her palm and closed her fingers around it. 'Take your dragon for a walk. The sunshine will do you both good.'

With a sigh, Fen turned from the window towards Lucky's enclosure. She lifted him out and held the bulk of his body in the palm of her hand while his tail curled around her arm.

For a second, he allowed her to stroke the tip of her finger down his back then Lucky turned and crawled up her arm to settle on her shoulder, his head buried against the warmth of her neck.

She walked down the stairs, outside and across the lawn to where Liam and Kieran had engaged in a play tackle and were rolling around on the grass. They sat up at her approach, Liam's eyes widened at the sight of Lucky on her shoulder. He got to his feet and came over to stroke the dragon's tail.

'He can come outside?'

She knelt so he could tickle Lucky's back. 'Bearded dragon's need sunshine just like people.'

'Why does he live inside then?'

'See how he only has three legs?'

'Uh-huh.'

'He's a rescue dragon. He was found on the side of the road and he was very sick, so we had to fix him up and nurse him back to health.' Fen eased Lucky from her shoulder and placed him in her upturned palm. The dragon's front foot closed around her fingers for balance. She slipped on his leash and let him slide down onto the grass. 'Would you like to take him for a walk?'

Excitement lit the boy's eyes. He did a little happy dance and Fen felt her heart lurch against her ribs. God, she couldn't allow affection for the kid to take hold.

'Can I? Can I?' He looked at Kieran who nodded.

'Of course you can, squirt. Just be careful with him, okay?'

Fen slipped the end of the leash over his wrist and showed him how to hold it. 'Let him lead you where he wants to go and try not to tug on the leash if he stops. He gets tired really quickly so he'll go a little slowly.' She pointed towards the neatly trimmed hedges of Muzz's mini maze. 'Take him to the hedge over there then bring him back, okay? When you turn around, he'll follow you.'

'K. Come, Lucky.'

She stood next to Kieran and watched the pair make slow progress across the lawn. Kieran nudged her shoulder, his warmth cutting the chill around her.

'He won't bite, will he?'

She looked up and caught his frown. 'He might sneak in a lick or two.'

'Ew.' He shuddered.

Liam and Lucky turned around at the maze and began their slow trek back across the lawn. Roach's warning on the day of the wedding rang in her ears. *Cute kid. Be a shame if something happens to him.*

'Are you sure you want to visit the past with me?' The words drifted between them, a dark cloud crossing the sun.

Kieran sighed. 'I want your nightmares to end, the threats to go away. The same way you do.'

'It's dangerous when I don't know what it will uncover or what the fallout will be.'

'It's dangerous already. I won't let you deal with this alone. I've seen the damage your past has done before.' He turned his head to catch her gaze. 'I've rescued you off rooftops and from hitchhiking down lonely country roads. I did that because I wanted to, not because I needed to. I want to help you now.'

'I wish you'd go home, Kieran. Where it's safe for you and Liam.'

'I am home.'

Fen turned away from watching Liam and Lucky to face him. 'You spent more years in Sydney than you did here. How can this be home for you?'

His eyes held hers for a long time before he

answered, 'Because home will always be here in Wongan Creek where I found a purpose for life, a reason to change and a friendship that goes so much deeper than that. You're my anchor, Fen.'

The words left his lips and he knew there was no taking them back. Nor did he want to. He'd meant every word of the email to her he'd never hit the send button on. The one that had tipped Diane into a downward spiral she hadn't come back from. The one he had no intention of sending, but it had helped to write anyway. Because it set him free from the confines in which he'd found himself, and that made him the world's biggest Grade A arsehole. Because it would have been the equivalent of cheating on his wife. And he wasn't a cheater.

God damn it, he hadn't physically cheated, but his mind had often wandered to Fen over the years, and that was bad enough. Long, cold, dark nights alone with his thoughts, pacing the floor with a teething, feverish baby while Diane slept out a prescription of sedatives or lay crippled by depression, held captive by the dark demons that haunted her. Torn between the two women he loved. Differently. All while Fen had fought her own demons — real live danger — on the other side of the country. Alone.

Her eyes flashed a fiery warning. 'Don't.'

'It is what it is.'

'I'm not who you need, Kieran. I'll only end up hurting you and Liam.'

And damned if he wasn't afraid of exactly that. He couldn't do that to his son again. But when he'd held her, kissed her … The timing sucked for it to feel like the best thing he'd ever done. The right thing. Just not the right time.

'Look, Daddy, Lucky likes me.' Liam crouched next to the lizard and tickled his back. 'Come and touch him.'

Kieran shivered. 'Maybe later.'

'He's not as squishy as he looks. But he feels cool.'

Fen moved away and the chill in the air filled the gap where she'd been. 'I think he might need to go back into his enclosure now. He'll need warming up a little.'

And there she was, running again. Shutting him out. He watched her walk away. How deep was he getting himself in and would he simply be repeating his mistakes of the past?

'Daddy? Can I go play in the maze?'

He looked down at Liam tugging on the leg of his denims. 'Of course, mate. Let's go. I'll follow you.'

'I need a map.'

'I've got GPS on the phone.'

'That's cheating.'

Kieran grinned. 'Okay, we'll only use it if we get lost. Deal?'

'Deal!' Liam scampered away to the entrance of the maze.

Kieran followed more slowly, his legs long enough to close the distance between them if Liam's mood shifted suddenly and his boy became the lost and confused child he'd been for most of his life.

Liam led Kieran through the maze, each section opening new adventures until exhausted, the little boy dragged his feet out the other side too tired to chat about what he'd seen. Kieran smiled. Perhaps for once Liam would be too exhausted by his adventures to be plagued by nightmares, and that at last both might get a good night's sleep.

'Why don't we see if we can get some lunch at the café, mate? Are you hungry?'

'Can I have Vegemite and cheese sandwiches?'

'Plenty of B vitamins in that, so yes, why not?'

'And a milkshake?'

'Let's see what we can get Liv to rustle up for you.'

'K, Daddy.' Liam's shoulders slouched and his feet dragged. 'Can you carry me? My feet are hurting.'

'Piggyback?'

Liam nodded, his curls bobbing. Kieran knelt and let him scramble aboard, tiny arms forming a choke-hold on his neck. 'Let's go, Daddy. I'm thirsty too.'

Kieran strode back across the lawn towards the

winery buildings, his thoughts a little lighter. The country air and exercise was proving good for his little mate's appetite. A niggle of hunger tickled at his own stomach. Food until now had been a necessity to stay alive, but with delicious smells drifting out the doors of the café as he stepped onto the verandah, he felt real hunger for the first time in months.

Chapter Twelve

F en dealt with the flood of emails and weeded out the junk mail from ones that came from legitimate suppliers and clients. If she got one more survey, offer of a hardware store voucher or invitation from a potential Russian bride, she'd toss the damn laptop out the window. The same window through which she could see Kieran strolling through the rows with Liam, marking out which of the fire-damaged vines outside the cordoned-off block where Martha had been found would need to be uprooted and replaced.

When the investigation was over and crew moved to clear the land ravaged by the flames, Liam would have to be kept out of the way. A dilemma considering he was nowhere near ready to spend the day or even a full week with the other kids at the school in town.

Heather had promised to come in to spend time with him while they worked in the field, but that had Kieran on edge for reasons she could understand. Not that he needed to worry. Heather was already a fan. No way in hell would she find anything lacking in Kieran's parenting skills. But she understood his reluctance. While Liam had settled in quickly, the hesitance and wariness remained in his eyes and body language at times.

Fen smiled. If only their circumstances could be different. She'd never imagined how much fun it would be to have a kid that age around, and her range of kids' drinks was fast expanding thanks to having him to taste-test.

In the distance, Kieran showed Liam how to spray a cross on a vine with the can of orange paint. Liv had laughed when a couple of the vines to go had been marked with graffiti reminiscent of their teenage days. How easily they'd all slipped back into the habits of the happiest days in Wongan Creek. Back before adulthood had changed them again and delivered reminders of what a bitch reality could be. Her phone rang, and apprehension had her checking the caller ID. If it was Luke calling again, it would mean more trouble on the way. Her mouth drew down in a grimace as she read the name on her screen.

'Hey, Sarge. What have you got for me?'

'A date for a meeting with Cherish, the owner of *La Paloma Negra,* on a day that she's closed for business so there'll be no-one to see you coming or going.'

Nerves twisted in her belly. 'What if someone follows us there?'

'I've arranged for an unmarked car to stay close and keep an eye out for anything suspicious. The detectives on the case had no problem with that.'

His reassurance did little to settle the moths of apprehension trying to beat their way out through her throat. She hadn't been in that place for a long time, and the last person to carry her out of those dingy hallways was dead. Trust. She had to trust Riggs, trust the detectives when the only people she was certain of were her mum and Kieran.

'When?'

'Day after tomorrow. Not before noon. Since it's a couple of hours drive to Perth, I'll be at yours around ten to stay with Liv.'

'Thank you.' The reality of what she was about to do struck with the force of a cricket bat cracking the ball past the boundary lines. She'd had no reason to face the past before, happy to leave the bad memories where they belonged, but now lives depended on her remembering what happened in the room the night Antoinette died. 'What if what I remember isn't relevant? What if I don't remember anything, Sarge?'

'What if you do? If it's not relevant, you get to let the ghosts rest and we explore new avenues of investigation. If it is relevant, you get answers and we can put Roach Sampson and his offspring back in jail before they create any more havoc in this town.' He sighed, the sound weighing heavily down the line. 'And if you don't remember anything, we go to Plan B.'

'Which is?'

'Find something else on the bastards and make it stick while the detectives working the cold case rehash the evidence. What we have on them, the arson and fraud, it's not enough. The maximum penalty is ten to fifteen. With a good lawyer, they'll be out in five. I don't want any more bodies showing up in bags in this town, especially not Liv's. Or yours.'

'Fen? Heather's here!' Liv's call drifted through the office door.

'I've got to go, Sarge. I'll see you in a couple of days then.'

'Good girl. The detectives will want to debrief you after, whether you remember anything or not.'

'Got it.' The thought of unleashing the horror of her past made her skin crawl with goosebumps.

'And, Fenella? You be careful, okay. Don't take any risks. After burying Muzz, Liv wouldn't want to lose you too. You're everything to her. I don't think I can handle bringing her that kind of bad news again.'

'No risks, I promise.' The memory of the day Riggs

had come to deliver the news that Muzz had collapsed outside the hardware store remained etched in her memory. She never wanted Liv to be that broken again. Fen hung up and pushed away from the desk as Heather appeared in the doorway. 'Goodness, I think that baby will make his or her appearance any day now.'

Heather groaned and leaned back against the door frame. 'Tell me about it. I think I'm carrying a future Olympic gymnast.' She patted her belly.

'Are you sure you'll be okay with Liam today? I'm sure you'd rather have your feet up.'

Heather waved a hand at her. 'Oh God no! I'd go crazy. Besides, exercise is good. It will help this little monkey find his way to the door out of here. Where is the young man?'

'He's out amongst the vines with his dad.' Fen shuffled papers on the desk into neat piles and tried to push away the trepidation that came with the thought of her upcoming excursion. 'I'll let Kieran know you're here.'

'Everything okay, hun? You look a little stressed.'

Fen looked at Heather with her bulging belly, thought of Harry who remembered little yet still played such a big part in the community, of Tameka and what she'd been through. This town didn't deserve more trouble. And that's what it would get if she couldn't bring Luke and his father to justice. She forced a smile to her lips.

'All good. Just some business I need to take care of in the city. I've put it off for far too long.' Fen shrugged.

'Anything I can help you with?'

That feeling of knowing something awful was about to happen clawed at her belly. She shook her head. 'No-one can. I'll only be free if I can unlock the truth of lost memories. I'm terrified, Heather. I don't know what I'll find when I do. It's like a secret I've kept for so long I don't know if it's the truth or a lie anymore.'

Heather lowered herself gingerly into a chair in front of the desk. 'You know as well as I do that it won't be the first time a secret has surfaced in this town. Riggs told me about Martha and some of the trouble you're dealing with. It's comforting to know she had a heart after all, but darn it, no-one deserves to die like that.'

She shivered and rubbed circles over her belly. 'I'm here for you, Fen. As a friend, a counsellor, a confidante, if you need one. Kieran and Liam aren't the only ones who need help. You do too. And I can assure I will stand behind you every step of the way. Repressed memories are usually the result of something terribly traumatic and facing those nightmares without a support group could have you rocking in a corner. I don't want to see that happen to you.'

Rocking silently in a corner in the shadows under a table with a knife. Been there. 'Thank you. What happens next depends on the presence of triggers. For years, my therapist has advised against consciously looking for those triggers, and now I'm forced to find them anyway. I wonder how much of what's happened with Luke could have been avoided if I'd gone looking to settle the past sooner?'

'Wouldn't it be nice if we had all the answers? So much in life could be avoided. The thing is we don't and who says the outcome would have been any different? I don't know your whole story, but I'm here if you need me to help.'

'Thank you.' Fen sighed. 'Baby steps, Heather. Let's start with Liam. I've set up a corner in the playground where you'll be sheltered from the wind and cold. There is paper, crayons, paint and some other stuff there to keep him occupied. If you need anything else, Liv will sort it for you. The cellar and café are closed for business today, so Liv will be around doing some book work, clean up and stock take. I'll be out there amongst the vines getting my hands dirty, but please yell out if it gets too much for you and I'll take over.'

'I'll be fine, hun, and so will you. You won't be alone this time.' Heather nodded towards the window. 'That's some serious manpower you have out there. The girls can't wait for summer to see what's under that jumper and how much the skinny rebel kid has filled out.'

Fen glanced in the same direction and caught sight of the exposed skin and muscle between the waistband of Kieran's denims and the hem of the bloody jumper in question as he lifted Liam into the air. Jealousy pinged through Fen like another email landing in her inbox. She sent it straight to the recycle bin. Kieran didn't belong exclusively to her. It might be he never would. 'Then they'd better dust off their gloves because they'll be picking grapes while they do it.'

Heather grinned. 'If I was you, I'd padlock the gate for the whole summer to keep them out.'

'Kieran and I are friends. That's all. If he wants to date anyone in town, he can.' Each one of the single girls were welcome to take their best shot at getting a date with him. That thought shouldn't hurt so much or make her see green when she had so much more to worry about. She stepped around the desk. Physical work would help take her mind off how much she stood to lose. 'Let's get this party started.'

Kieran watched Fen and Heather walk out onto the deck of the café. 'C'mon, mate, we've got to go up now.' He pointed to where the digger reversed off a truck bed and mentally crossed his fingers that Liam wouldn't resist. 'The machines are coming in to help pull out the old vines and we need to keep you safe.'

'But, Daddy, I want to see.'

'You'll be able to see it from the playground, mate.'

'It's too far.'

Fen skipped down the stairs and walked towards them as Liam planted his booted feet in the mud, resisting the tug of Kieran's hand. Damn it, he'd thought that after yesterday, Liam would have had a good night. But instead of sleep, exhaustion had brought more of the same haunted dreams and broken rest, and this morning both their moods edged on volatile. Liam's lip pouted, his face set to stubborn and his weight dragged at Kieran's arm.

'Hey, guys,' Fen called. From behind her back she pulled out a yellow hard hat and waved it towards them. 'Look what I've got for you, Liam.'

The drag on his arm released as Liam's attention focused on the hat. 'For me?'

Fen reached them and dropped the hat on Liam's head with a quick pat. 'Yes, for you. You're our supervisor today. See, Heather has one too.' She pointed to where Heather waved from the deck.

Liam released Kieran's hand to touch the hat. 'Why?'

Fen smiled. 'Because you need to watch from the playground to make sure we're taking out the right vines. If you see us taking out the wrong ones, you need to tell Heather.'

'Is it a 'portant job?' Liam took the hat off, studied it a moment and put it back on again.

'A very important job. So important that even Lucky is on duty. He's in his cage in the playground. He'd love it if you could give him some morning tea later? His food is in a tub on the table.'

'O-kay.' Liam drew out the word on a sigh. 'I guess.'

Fen held out a hand for a fist bump. 'Thanks, mate. Off you go then.'

Kieran caught Fen's gaze as she straightened. Damn it, he could sweep her up and kiss her stupid for averting another crisis. Instead, he watched his son take off at a run with one hand keeping the hat in place, the other pumping at his side. 'That was clever thinking.'

Fen shrugged. 'Not really. I figured he might need an incentive. How's he doing?'

He watched Liam climb the stairs and give Heather a shy high five, but Liv was there too and then Liam was skipping between them towards the playground. 'I thought yesterday would tire him out enough.'

She reached out to touch his arm, the wool of his sweater no barrier against the feel of it. 'It will take time. Give him a chance.'

He placed his hand over hers. 'I know. It's just sometimes I wish … God, I don't know what I wish anymore. If Diane had lived … things would only have got worse. There'd be more damage, more fall out.'

'You're doing fine with him. He's young enough for some of those unpleasant memories to fade completely and leave no scars. I wasn't there to see how things were between you and Diane, so I can't say what is right or wrong. But I know that you would have given her everything she needed, everything you had to give. You don't know any other way to give. Her death was not your fault.' She slipped her arm through his and tugged him to take a step forward with her. 'There are no losers, no winners. Only survival and a future for Liam.'

'We've got through worse.' He hugged her close, loving the strength and warmth she brought with her. God, he'd missed that. He'd missed everything Fenella — her perfume, her humour, her hugs, the way she worked through things even at her lowest, most difficult to deal with moments. Nothing at all like Diane. Fen was a survivor. Her leather wrist guards and dark clothing were no longer the symbol of a girl on the edge, but that of a woman on a mission not to fall back on the past. He could do this. With Fen by his side, he could handle it. Together they could handle anything. Hadn't that always been the way?

'And there's still more to come. We'll get through that too.' She leaned her head against his bicep for a moment.

It would be so easy to turn and take her in his arms. Kiss her until the last flicker of Diane's memory between them faded, until only the good memories of Liam's mother remained. But they weren't quite there yet. Not when Fen's demons still roamed amongst the tangle of her life in the city.

She tugged on a pair of leather work gloves. 'So

Riggs has set up a meeting with Cherish for the day after tomorrow. Will you be okay with that?'

Tension pulled his muscles into a knot between his shoulder blades. 'That was quick.'

'He's keen to get this over with.'

She looked at him and the uncertainty in her eyes tugged at his chest. She was nothing like Diane and everything like him and Liam. A child who'd lost a birth mother, a girl affected by the trauma humans inflicted on one another, a survivor who deserved to be free of her past and untouched by the harm of the present. How they handled the future would depend on the depth of their bond.

'Then come over tonight and we'll go over the logistics of how we'll deal with this when we get there. If Liam goes alright with Heather today, maybe she can convince him to start kindy. He'll be safe with the other kids and plenty of people around him.'

'If not, he'll be fine with Liv and Riggs. There's a lot to distract him here. He might get overwhelmed if he goes to school and we'll be too far away to get back to him quickly.'

His heart warmed. He loved that she cared about his boy the same way he did. If her world imploded though, would it be enough? If bad memories returned to eat at her mind, would she be strong enough to stop herself from picking up a knife again or would she be tipped over the edge the same way Diane had been? The answer had to be yes to being strong enough because he couldn't bear it if Liam became a witness to another tragedy, nor would he lose Fen when he'd only just found her friendship again. When the scars had finally begun to heal, and his son was on the road to being a normal, happy, well-adjusted little boy.

Chapter Thirteen

F en stretched against the tug of tired and taut muscles as she walked up the path to the cottage. A long soak in the tub after a hard day of physical labour had gone a long way to ease some of the stiffness from her back and the tension created by the thought of having to go back into the city. She'd never wanted to go back to that place or wanted to remember the things that had happened there, but Antoinette's case deserved closure, whatever the truth that came out. And she'd make sure Martha Wallace's killers received the justice they deserved.

Lights blazed at full wattage inside the cottage. Liam's sobs reached out through the gap in the open window and wrapped around Fen's heart in a tight grip. Torn between turning away or stepping up to the door to offer help, she stood with one foot on the bottom step leading up to the verandah.

Tomorrow Kieran would be at her side when she walked into the unknown, taking time away from his son to support her. The least she could do was find a way to help him out tonight. Surely Liam would stay with her for a while, so Kieran could get some sleep. Fen rolled the tension from her shoulders under her warm jacket, shrugged off the doubts and climbed the remaining steps. As a friend, she could reach out a hand to help.

With Lucky as a buffer, the little boy was slowly beginning to trust her. Trust that was slowly developing into a bond. She was starting to like the kid.

She knocked on the door and pushed it open. Liam's cries echoed down the hallway. Tired, helpless, forlorn cries that reached in and made her own eyes tear up and a lump of sadness lodge in her throat. Kieran murmured soft reassurances, the floorboards creaking under his feet as he paced. Fen stepped into the lounge room of the little cottage, leaning a shoulder against the door frame. Over Liam's head, she caught Kieran's gaze. He smiled, a weary tug to his lips.

'Sorry. I thought he'd be settled by now.' His apology came out softly against Liam's little head tucked into his shoulder.

'Bad dream?' Fen pushed away from the door.

'Not asleep yet. I'm not even sure what's triggered this.'

The raw ache of desperation in his voice made the lump in her throat grow. 'How can I help?'

'I don't know.' His hand moved soothingly over Liam's back as the cries turned to hiccupping sobs, the volume decreasing, muffled by Kieran's flannel shirt.

Fen stepped closer, her hand on Kieran's arm, his warmth easing the chill from her fingers. 'Hey, Liam.'

The little boy angled his head to look at her, eyes bright green with tears, his thumb finding its way into his mouth. Behind them, the hands on the clock on the mantelpiece moved to eight o'clock. Way past a four-year-old's bedtime. And by the look of the fatigue on Kieran's face, way past his too.

Fen held out her arms to Liam. 'Would you like me to tell you a story while your dad makes you some hot chocolate?'

'No.' Liam buried his face in Kieran's shirt, his little fists bunching into the material.

'It's Lucky's favourite story. He likes to hear it before he goes to sleep.'

Green eyes so like his father's found hers. 'What's it 'bout?' A little hiccup followed the question.

'It's the story of how a lizard was rescued and found his forever home. Would you like to hear it?'

'Daddy wants to hear it.'

Fen dropped her arms and pushed her hands into the

pockets of her jacket. 'Okay, how about I go make the hot chocolate and some popcorn then. We can have a picnic in front of the fire and tell stories until we all fall asleep. Is that a good idea?'

'Maybe.' Liam pushed a little away from Kieran's chest. 'Can I bring my blankie and Woolly?'

'I'm sure Woolly would love to hear the story too.'

'K.' He looked up at his father, his tiny hand reaching up to touch the beard along Kieran's jawline. 'Is it okay, Daddy?'

Relief eased the lines of fatigue on Kieran's face. 'Of course it is.' He set a wriggling Liam down on his feet. 'I'll set up the picnic spot while you go and get Woolly.'

Liam disappeared up the hallway to the bedrooms in a flurry of socks and cartoon pyjamas. Fen slipped out of her jacket, Kieran's hands there to take it from her. He leaned in and pressed his warm cheek to her cold one. A small gesture, a simple thank you that shouldn't make her heart race, but it did.

'Thank you.' He whispered the words against her ear, his hand squeezing hers. A simple action that shouldn't feel so damn intimate. That shouldn't make her want to curl around him and absorb all the pain he carried inside.

Fen stepped away. 'I'll make that hot chocolate now.'

'Sure.' Kieran moved, dropped her jacket over the

back of a chair then moved to the sofa and tossed cushions onto the floor in front of the fire. He dragged a throw rug off the backrest and spread it out on the carpet.

Fen turned and made her way into the kitchen. She filled the kettle with water and flicked the switch, reached up and pulled mugs from the cupboard, and focused on the task at hand. To help Liam fall asleep and let Kieran get some rest.

While she waited for the kettle to boil, she turned off the overhead lights and turned on the softer glow of the small lamps around the house, all while trying to push the intimacy of flickering firelight, subdued lighting and being alone with Kieran from her mind. This was for Liam.

Hot chocolate and popcorn ready, she carried the tray back into the lounge room. Kieran and Liam were snuggled together on the floor under the throw, propped up on cushions and pillows. Fen placed the tray on the floor.

'You come under the blanket too, Fen.' Liam held up the corner of the throw.

Firelight flickered over the features of father and son. So alike, so damaged. What the hell was she doing falling in deeper when tomorrow lay ahead full of the horrors of the past? Her stomach churned at the thought, a timely reminder of the reason she'd come over tonight.

A story, a mug of hot chocolate, and when Liam and

Kieran were asleep, she'd sneak back home to Lucky for company. And tomorrow, she'd face the past alone while Kieran stayed to take care of his son. That was the safest option. The only choice. She slipped in next to Liam and tucked the blanket under her thigh.

Liam snuggled down between them, tears and tantrums forgotten, the only sign of his distress the dried tracks on his pink cheeks. 'What is the lizard's story name, Fen? Is it Lucky?'

Fen smiled and snuggled down beside him. 'Oh no. Not Lucky. This is another lizard who grew up here.' She lowered her voice to tell the story Liv had told her when she'd arrived in Wongan Creek, an older child as damaged by life as the little boy and man beside her.

Liam curled into a ball against her, his long eyelashes feathering down onto his cheeks as he listened, the warm comfort, serenity and flicker of flames in the soft light soothing him to sleep. He sighed softly and Fen's heart melted into a puddle. How could she possibly resist the sweet-faced kid, asleep with a soft smile on his lips, and not fall a little in love? He snuggled closer. She ran her hand over his curls, baby-soft under her touch, and smiled.

Fen looked up to find Kieran watching her. He lay on his side, his hands tucked under his face, the blanket drawn high over his shoulder.

'What?' She tucked Woolly under Liam's arm.

'You're so good with him.'

'He's a good kid. Glad I could help settle him down.'

Kieran reached over and ran a finger down her cheek. 'Thank you.'

She covered his hand with hers and pressed it to her face. Just for a moment. To feel the press of his skin against hers. To hold the memory close when he was gone. 'You need to sleep too.'

'Will you stay?'

'For a while. To make sure you do get some rest.'

'It's been tough, Fen. Diane never did what you did tonight. Not even on her good days.'

Fen laced her fingers through Kieran's and rested their hands on the bump of Liam's body under the blanket. 'I'm sure she loved him as much as you do. Some people just have difficulty dealing with parenthood.'

'You'd be a good mum, Fen.'

Unease etched its way up her spine, an uncomfortable ache out of character with the peaceful pop of wood on the fire. She pulled her hand from his and tucked it back under the blanket.

'I'm not sure I would be. A child needs a stable home, a safe and loving environment. I don't know that I can provide that when there is so much about my past I can't be sure of. What if I'm no better than Diane was because of my mental health?'

'The difference is that you're facing your demons,

216

dealing with them so you can heal and grow. You're so much stronger than she was, Fen.'

'Am I? I think tomorrow will be a big test of my strengths. You should get some rest. We have a long drive tomorrow. Will you be okay leaving Liam after tonight? I can go alone.'

'I'm not letting you go alone. He'll be okay tomorrow. No doubt Liv will find many ways to distract him.'

'You're leaving him here?' Fen smiled. 'I think you've made the right choice. Mum has that magic touch with kids. I wish I could catch it and bottle it.'

Liam burrowed closer and Fen hugged him in, the movement reflexive as the sleeping child sought comfort from his dreams. She ignored the tug of love as another brick in her carefully constructed wall slipped out and shattered.

Kieran smiled, slow and sexy. The kind of smile that would have melted her last attempt at resistance if not for the fact that his son lay between them. He leaned across Liam, his breath light on her cheek. 'Fen?'

She looked up, a small part of her knowing it was a trap. 'Yeah?'

'I think you have that same magic touch.' Then he kissed her in a way that had her awake long after he'd turned away and the soft sounds of his breathing evened out in sleep.

Kieran woke to the thin red hue of dawn on the horizon. Another clear and cool autumn day ahead. The fire had died to grey coals, the residual heat still warming the room. He stretched out the kinks from a night spent on the floor. Beside him, Liam lay sleeping in the comfort of Fen's arms, spooned against her protectively. She'd stayed, and he'd had the best night's sleep in forever.

So beautiful. So tender and giving. So completely wrong for him. Even though the scene before him said otherwise. He took her hand in his and turned it wrist-up. The damage of the past lay pearly white against her pale skin. A constant reminder of what she'd survived. He lifted her hand and pressed his lips to her pulse. She stirred in her sleep. Beautiful Fen. In trouble, again.

Kieran released her hand and pulled the blanket up over them as he eased out of the makeshift bed. They'd sleep on while he got breakfast underway and his emotions under control.

On the kitchen bench, his phone vibrated. With a quick glance at the screen, he tapped the answer icon.

'It's sparrow's fart. You're up early for a country cop.' Kieran pushed the kitchen door closed and kept his voice low.

'Big week ahead. I wanted to make sure you had things covered for the visit to Perth.' Riggs offered up a satisfied sigh before saying, 'Best thing I invested in off the internet.'

'What's that?'

'A coffee machine and six month's supply of pods. No more trench mud.' Paper rustled, followed by a slurp, and another satisfied sigh. 'That's good stuff. I hope you're prepared for what might happen on the day.'

'I've got it covered.'

'Depending on what she remembers, it could be quite confronting. I have a copy of the original coroner's report in front of me. It's not a pretty picture. I can't pass on the details for a few reasons, one because it's fanned the fire under the internal investigation and two, we don't want to contaminate Fen's memories with the information. She needs to remember it as she saw it. If she remembers at all.'

'I get it. No prompting.'

'Yep, no prompting, but be warned that if there is a trigger present, it could turn to shit really quickly and we have no idea what her reaction will be.' The tinkle of a spoon against the cup formed an image of Riggs stirring his new coffee. 'If that happens, there'll be two detectives in an unmarked car downstairs, waiting. I'll text you a contact number. They'll take her to a station where she'll be placed in the care of a psych and receive access to every available resource the department can provide.'

'I don't like the sound of that.' The thought of Fen knowing something that would break her again, gripped his throat and squeezed.

'I don't either. I'm praying to whichever god is listening that she won't need it. I just needed to know that you'll be there with her all the way through it, otherwise I need to take her in myself, and that would be a little too conspicuous.'

'You almost have me believing you care.' Kieran dropped instant coffee into the mugs he'd taken down from the cupboard and wished he had some of Riggs' pods. Strong ones.

'I do care. No-one needed to witness what that girl has, any of it, and I'm going to make sure we nail those bastards to the wall for it. But since she was the only one in the room at the time, hers is the only witness account that will stand up in court.'

'She was a minor at the time. Will her testimony make a difference? Childhood memories can be unreliable.'

Riggs blew out a breath that whistled down the line. 'Not if her account matches the photographs that landed on the investigating officer's desk this morning, and no-one alive has seen those, except the detectives on the case. Not even me.'

'How's that?'

'They turned up a few years too late. Martha Wallace, God rest her soul, reached out beyond the grave. It looks like she had them sent to the department not long before someone caught up with her, trashed her office and set it alight. Someone's running scared.'

Kieran dragged a hand through his hair, the chill stealing up his spine spreading in a shiver. 'I hope to hell you've got us covered from all angles, because if anything happens —'

'The one thing I am sure of, Murphy, is that there is more protective manpower on this case than the boys at the top would like, but that's too bad, because they're going to be too busy looking for rats in their department to have the time to care.'

'What if she doesn't remember anything?'

'Then they'll have to go with the lesser charges of fraud, arson and cultivating commercial quantities of cannabis while I keep pushing and the whole lot of you go into witness protection. They're not going to stop, Murphy. Not if she knows something they don't want made public. Alive, she's a risk to someone out there and I want to know why.'

He didn't want to ask the question that rang in his head. 'They've proved they're not afraid to remove witnesses, so why are they still playing games with Fen?'

'They're hunters, Murphy. Where's the fun in fishing if there's no catch and release before you hook the big one? I'll be out there soon. You take care of that girl, okay? Liv will have my hide if something happens to her.'

'That's the one thing you can be sure of, Sarge. And I expect the same of you.'

Riggs chuckled. 'I wouldn't have it any other way, son.'

Kieran hung up and stirred the milk into the coffee. Behind him the door inched open. He turned to see Fen halfway into the kitchen, her hand on the door. 'You're awake. I was talking to Riggs.' He let his gaze travel over her sleep-tousled hair and the pink glow of warmth in her cheeks. His arms itched to pull her in for a hug and hold her there. 'Toast for breakfast?'

'I should go home.' She tugged on the sleeves of her black woollen jumper. 'Liam's still asleep. I've put the telly on softly so he doesn't wake up to silence and no-one there. The cartoons should distract him until you're done with his breakfast.'

And there it was again, the difference between Fen and Diane. Diane's first thought would have been for herself. But then Diane would never have spent the night on a blanket on the floor, comforting a child who wasn't hers. Hell, she hadn't even wanted to comfort her own son.

An ache formed in his chest at the thought and he reminded himself that Diane had been ill. Her actions couldn't be justified the way a person with a healthy mind could. Still, here was Fen with a boatload of trouble on her doorstep, her own inner turmoil, putting his son first.

Lying there next to her last night had felt so perfect, so right. He'd watched them sleep when instinct to check on Liam had woken him somewhere around three in the morning. Liam with one hand under his cheek and the other wrapped in Fen's, her arm around him, hugging his little boy close. He'd thought he'd be torn apart by resentment that his son had found sleep and comfort in her arms, yet instead he'd felt relief and a love for Fen so overwhelming, it had scared the shit out of him. Because now he wanted to wake up to that scene every morning.

'I made you coffee. At least have that before you go.' He placed the mug an arm's length down the benchtop.

She moved closer and wrapped her hands around the mug, the sleeves of her jumper pulled down over her hands to protect them from the heat of the ceramic. 'Thanks.'

Kieran hauled the loaf of bread towards him, plugged in the toaster and fed two slices into the slots. He pressed the lever and watched the toast disappear between the red-hot coils. 'Thank you for staying last night.'

'Did you at least get some sleep?' Fen leaned back and sipped her coffee before putting the mug back down on the benchtop.

'Yes.' He wanted to ask her to stay again tonight, because after Thursday's excursion into the unknown, she would be the one needing to be held. Because, damn it, he wanted to hold her like she'd held Liam. The way he'd held her all those years ago when the relentless demons of their past had threatened the possibility of a peaceful future. Only when their pasts were laid to rest, could their true healing begin. Then he'd have an even better night's sleep.

'Good.' She pushed her fringe out of her face. 'He's a good kid. I'm glad he got some sleep.'

Kieran braced his arms on either side of the toaster, his hands curled into fists. 'Me too.'

Her hand covered his, so small and pale against his skin. 'If you need help with him again, shout.'

He turned his hand up and laced his fingers through hers. 'He likes you. I've never seen him respond to anyone the way he does to you.' Unable to resist any longer, he tugged her to his side, stood back and wrapped her in his arms. 'You have a magic touch for making people heal, Fen.'

Her hands came to rest at his waist, her cheek against his heart. 'Then why can't I heal myself?'

'You've come a long way. This is just a bump in the road. We'll get through it, Fen. We've survived worse.' He pressed a kiss against her crown then tipped her face up. 'I won't leave you to deal with it alone.'

'I'm afraid that what I need to do will make things

worse. I'll never forgive myself if something happened to you, Liam or Liv because of me.'

'Nothing will happen. We won't let it.' He held her tighter because having her in his arms felt so damn good he didn't want to let her go.

Her arms slipped around his waist and she hugged him hard. 'I've missed you, Kieran.' Her eyes captured his, the blue-grey depths a pool he wanted to lose himself in. 'For so many reasons.'

Then she stood on tiptoe to kiss him, a soft touch of her lips that might have been his imagination were it not for the reality of her breath mingling with his and the press of her breasts against his chest. He tightened his arms around her and kissed her back, every minute of missing her in each sweep, nip and hold, until his head spun from the taste of Fen.

Her arms reached around his neck as she burrowed into his body, the clothes between them a barrier. As if only without them, flesh on flesh, could they believe each other real and present. With her hands in his hair and the gentle massage of her fingers on his scalp, Kieran let go of everything he'd ever felt and put it into the kiss. His friend, his confidante, the girl he'd abandoned for another, regretted it, hated himself for it, and couldn't forgive himself for still loving while he'd been bound to his wife.

And so, just like the ping of the toaster, Diane slipped between them again.

Chapter Fourteen

Fen walked through the morning chores and tried to forget the moment Kieran's eyes had turned sad and the wall had gone up between them again. As if kissing her had made him feel guilty. Her phone pinged and a message popped up from an unknown number. She wanted to ignore the threat, but the photograph of Liam walking Lucky in the garden told her she couldn't.

Back off or someone gets hurt. And you won't know who until it's too late.

Liv's smile glowed up at her from the screen of her phone, taken on the day of Harley and Tameka's wedding.

You look exactly like your mother.

And the ugly face of the past reared its head. The broken, empty soul that peered through lifeless, vacant

226

eyes. Antoinette — prostitute, drug addict, slave to the underworld — the woman who'd often forgotten her daughter existed. The girl alone in her dark corner, dressed in op shop clothing, hiding behind her fringe, misunderstood and difficult to handle.

Why won't you co-operate, Fenella? You're making my job damn hard, you and that Murphy boy. Ms Wallace's words echoed in her mind, uttered before she'd met Kieran. She'd felt for the boy who'd appeared to be as misplaced as she was. Fen shook herself free of the dark thoughts. She wouldn't let the past drag her back down into that bottomless pit where physical pain erased the ache, blades were sharp against her skin, a canvas etched in nightmares.

Fen stabbed at the share icon on her phone and forwarded the texts and photos to Riggs. There was too much she didn't understand, too many questions she might never know the answer to. In her dreams, she avoided opening that door. If she didn't open it and step into the nightmare, the threats wouldn't stop, and she would never know the reason behind them or why Martha Wallace had to die protecting her secrets.

'Excuse me?'

Liam's loud whisper sounded beside her and his tug at the edge of her jacket drew her out of her thoughts. 'Hi, Liam. Have you come to visit Lucky?'

His curls bounced as he shook his head. 'No. I camed to see you.'

Fen ignored the warmth of affection that flooded her at his words. She couldn't afford to become too attached to the kid. But how could she resist such an angelic face? 'Oh, okay. Did you want me to read you a story?'

Liam shook his head again. 'Nuh-uh. I need help.'

'What kind of help, buddy?'

'It's my daddy's birthday tomorrow and I want to make him a surprise.'

She hadn't forgotten. The calendar on her laptop reminded her every year. Only this year, she could wish him in person rather than whisper her happy birthday to the universe. 'What a great idea.'

'Yeah. My daddy always makes me feel special on my birthday. But no-one makes my daddy feel special on his birthday.'

'Hmm, that's a bit sad, isn't it?' Yet another clue as to how alone he'd been since leaving Wongan Creek. And how much she'd missed sharing their respective birthdays in the ritual they'd developed since arriving in town together, neither of them ever having had the usual birthday parties most kids were accustomed to having. 'What did you have in mind, buddy?'

'I drewed some pictures with Heather. She helped me. But I want to make something else special.'

'I'm listening.'

'Will you help me carve a lizard like Lucky? Heather says I can do it with soap. But I need an adult to help.'

Fen shivered at the thought of herself, only a little older than Liam, using her first knife. 'What if you draw the picture on the soap and I carve it out for you? Will that work?' She'd never forgive herself if the knife slipped and sliced open his flawless, baby-soft skin.

A smile lit his face that had her falling in love with the little boy all over again. 'Thank you, Fen. Can we do it now?'

'Of course we can. How would you like to help me finish the chores first and then we can head up to the house?'

He nodded. 'I can.'

Fen ruffled his curls. 'Awesome, but first, does your daddy know where you are?'

'Uh-huh. I said I was going to help you feed the chooks. He's up there watching me.' Liam turned to wave to Kieran, who waved back before turning to go back inside the cottage.

Fen's heart glowed a little. Liam had taken a big step towards facing his fears, even if he was too young to realise how much he'd achieved by walking out on his own. The clouds crept back in over the light of that glow when she remembered the message on her phone. She had to remember, had to deal with that closed door, so all the bad things happening would go away. So that the dark shadows of her past life wouldn't encroach on brightening Liam and Kieran's future. So that the threat that was Beyond Hell's Reach could be extinguished like the fire they'd set in the vineyard and they'd never hurt anyone again.

~

Birthdays. He tried hard to make Liam's memorable. His own? Forget it. Kieran settled into the chair behind his desk in the manager's office attached to the cottage. Another year older and still the future flickered uncertainly like an old black and white movie fading in and out on the big wide movie screen of life.

The Vincents hadn't believed in celebrating birthdays. Or Christmas. No balloons or candles or presents. No Christmas carols or cookies and milk under the tree. So, for four years he'd celebrated Liam's birthdays and Christmases without them because no kid deserved to miss out on the excitement of tearing the wrapping off a box and finding out what was inside. No kid should ever feel like he wasn't loved or appreciated and not be given a special day to celebrate it.

Would Fen remember? Every year after they'd arrived in Wongan Creek, they'd celebrated their birthdays together. Two kids who'd never had cause or opportunity to celebrate before. The presents had been small. Flowers from Harry's rampant rose garden, a lizard carved from wood, Liv's homemade scones and jam or chocolate cupcakes. Precious moments stolen together. Ones he hadn't appreciated until they were gone.

He opened the winery's reporting system and scrolled through the list of folders until he found the current fermentation lab reports, trying not to worry too much about Liam being with Fen. Would she be able to handle a full-blown tantrum? He shook off the thought. She'd already talked him through two.

A smile tugged at the corner of his mouth. At last, Liam had taken a huge step on his own. He'd asked to go help feed the chooks, refused Kieran's offer to go with him, but agreed that Kieran could watch over him until he reached Fen's side. With increased security being installed today and the forensics crew still on site, the threat of Beyond Hell's Reach or any of its members showing up to cause more trouble would be limited. Liam would be safe. For now.

He clicked to open the report and scanned the figures, making notes, planning the bottling schedule and vat rotations. By morning tea time, his shoulders ached, his neck had a crick in it and he had a plan outlined ready to be uploaded into the software program.

Liam's muffled giggles reached his ears. What was the little tyke up to now? An exaggerated 'shhh' followed footsteps across the verandah. Kieran frowned, dropping the pen onto his notepad. He shut down the computer and tidied his desk. Better go and see what mischief Liam was up to.

'Surprise!'

The dual shout had him looking up. Liam and Fen stood in the doorway with big grins on their faces. Liam clutched an armful of treasure, and whatever Fen had under the red-and-white checkered cloth smelled a hell of a lot better than his Weetbix breakfast.

'Happy Birthday, Daddy,' Liam yelled. He thrust out his arms. 'I made you presents. Fen and Nanna Liv helped me. Here, Daddy, take them.'

Kieran swallowed the lump that formed in his throat and took the armful of rolled paper and small box from his son. 'That's awesome, mate. Thank you.'

'Put them on the table so you can see Fen's present first. Then you can open them while we … oops …' He clamped his hands over his mouth. 'I nearly gave away the surprise. Sorry, Fen.'

'That's okay, little buddy.' She ruffled Liam's hair. 'I'm pretty sure your dad has sniffed out the surprise anyway.' She turned to face him. 'Liv sends you her best wishes. She says she'll see you at lunch for your favourite — barbecue pork ribs. Don't be late or the soufflé will spoil.'

Kieran blinked against the burn in his eyes. 'Cheese and chives?'

Fen nodded. 'And chorizo.' She handed him the

plate in her hands. 'But for now … lemonade scones and homemade strawberry jam. Happy birthday, Kieran.'

He took it, lifted the cloth and sniffed the hot, sweet aroma of freshly baked goods, his eyes closing at the memories that smell brought back. 'You remembered.'

'I've never forgotten.'

He opened his eyes and captured her gaze, the emotion in it punching straight to his gut. Yes, Fen loved him, but not in the way she could. If they went down that path, the bond between them would change, morph into something different. Something tenuous and breakable he wasn't prepared to risk. Fen was broken enough.

Still, he couldn't stop his hand from reaching for her face, had no control over the descent of his head to find her mouth, no will to resist the shot of pure desire that shot through him when his lips found hers in the sweetest, most innocent kiss he could deliver in front of a four-year-old.

'Thank you,' he said when he could find his voice again, his thumb tracing her cheekbone.

'You're welcome.' Her hand covered his for an instant before she stepped back. 'Why don't we go into the kitchen and you can open your presents from Liam while I make coffee?'

And because he couldn't speak past the need to keep

a hold on her, he nodded and clenched his fist around the feel of her skin on his palm. They collected everything and Kieran followed as Liam skipped inside in Fen's wake. In the kitchen, he placed the gifts on the table.

'This one first, Daddy.' Liam pushed a rolled-up poster-sized paper towards him. 'I drawed it myself.'

'Drew,' he corrected automatically as he slipped the rubber band off the roll and opened the drawing. Surprise filtered through him. Never had Liam done more than scribble on paper. Squiggly lines and odd shapes in blues, greens, greys and black. This time, Liam had drawn himself walking Lucky on the bright green lawn. A drawing far advanced for his age. He'd inherited Diane's artistic talent. A talent, perhaps the only one, she'd given her son. 'That's beautiful, Liam. Well done. You have a special gift, you know.'

'I do? What do you mean, Daddy?'

Kieran looked at Fen who'd turned to carry the mugs to the table. She'd know of Diane's talent. The artwork that had once graced the walls of the Wongan Creek's town hall. The happier ones. Not the ones Diane had sketched at the darkest of dark times.

Fen placed a mug of steaming coffee in front of him, before sitting opposite him at the table and wrapping her hands around her own mug, staring into the stirred swirl left by the spoon.

He cleared his throat and looked back at the picture.

'Your mum could draw too. She was quite famous here in Wongan Creek. Many people came to buy her sketches and paintings.'

'Oh,' said Liam. 'But my mummy never showed me her drawings.'

'No, but she shared her gift with you and that's something pretty special.'

And damn it, he'd do everything in his power to encourage his son to use that talent for something good and positive, something that would make him happy. But more than that, it made him happy that Diane had achieved in giving her son something she couldn't give him while she was alive. Her love of art. That at last he had something positive about the mother of his child to share with her son. That the blue and green squiggly lines that had once represented Liam's descent into the darkness of the river had turned to a sunny scene full of colour and happy thoughts. That at last, his child had begun to heal. And that, just maybe, he could start to find forgiveness in his heart for what Diane had done. For what he'd done.

For the first time in a long time, it didn't feel like Diane hovered over them to cast an unhappy stain on the future. Instead, the sun shone through the clouds, casting a cheerful, somewhat watery glow across the kitchen as some of the sadness in his heart shifted and dissolved.

'Did you have a good birthday surprise, Daddy?'

Kieran caught Fen's gaze across the table. Warmth spread through him at the tentative smile she offered. This was where he wanted to be. Here in this kitchen with a happy boy and the girl who was slowly capturing his heart again, in a way that went deeper than the bond of friendship and trust. 'The best ever.'

Liam's smile grew wider. 'I'm happy, Daddy.'

'Then I'm happy too.'

Fen's phone pinged and he looked across as she picked it up, a frown stealing the smile from her lips. 'That's weird.'

'What's up?' A chill curdled the coffee warming his belly.

'Robbie's missing.'

'Harry's dog?'

Fen ran her finger over the screen. 'Yeah. Heather says when Harry got up this morning, Robbie wasn't by his bed. He hasn't been seen all morning.'

The chill turned to unease. 'Maybe he's wandered off and can't find his way back.'

'That's what Heather's thinking. She's asked us to keep an eye out for him. They're out checking his usual spots.' She dropped her phone on the table. 'Robbie never goes anywhere without Harry. My gut says something's not right.'

Kieran agreed. 'We'll ask Liv to keep an eye on Liam and we can help them look.'

'I can go if you want to stay here with him. It's your birthday. You should be here celebrating it.'

'There'll be plenty of time for celebration later when we find Robbie.' He stood and scooped Liam up for a hug. 'Fen and I are going to help look for Harry's dog. Will you stay here and take care of Liv for us?'

Liam placed his warm hands against Kieran's cheeks. 'She said I could call her Nanna Liv. That's okay isn't it, Daddy? Granny Laine won't be cross, will she?'

'If Liv says it's okay, then it's fine.' Warmth flooded him, chasing away some of the chill. With the people of Wongan Creek opening their hearts to him, Liam grew stronger and more confident every day. 'We'll be back soon, okay?'

'Don't worry, Daddy, I'll take care of Nanna Liv.'

Kieran hugged his son a little tighter until he wiggled to get down. He set Liam on his feet and turned to Fen. 'Ready?'

She nodded. 'Yes. I'll let Heather know we're going to cover this side of the creek down to the boundary fence.'

She sent off the message as they closed the cottage door and walked the path to the cellar building. Leaving Liam and Liv to bake blueberry scones for the forensics crew, they hiked down to the creek, calling for Robbie, their shouts echoing those from the Bailey property across the creek.

Kieran fingered the packet of doggy treats in his pocket. Liv had pushed them towards him along with a couple of bottles of water. *He might be hungry and dehydrated if he's been lost for a while.* Kieran hoped that he had simply wandered off and got lost, but the unease that nibbled at his gut wouldn't go away. Too many strange things had happened in the vineyard lately. Rows of vines slashed, root balls damaged, the fire, a murder, and a block of cannabis crop down the far end of the vineyard, grown with the intent to supply, currently being seized by police.

Someone out there wouldn't be happy to lose that kind of money, and he'd bet that person was Luke Sampson. Was that why the club members had been on the property on the day of the fire? Had their intent been to harvest what they could before they destroyed the remaining crop? A convenient way to destroy evidence. Any traces left would be lost when the block was cleared and rejuvenated for a fresh planting of vines.

Ahead of him, Fen searched rows of vines that wouldn't provide much shelter with the leaves withering and falling. If she hadn't been so vigilant cleaning up the dried debris, the fire could have done a lot more damage. His mind turned to the repairs that would be required to the irrigation system, mentally calculating the cost as he searched a row parallel to Fen's.

A whine reached his ears from the row nearest a

hedge that formed the back border of the garden maze he and Liam had explored. 'Got something,' he called and made his way out the row towards the noise.

Kieran stopped to assess the damage. Someone had taken an axe to the underside of the hedge, hacking away the tightly packed branches. The axe that lay abandoned inside the maze.

'Be careful. We don't know if the person who used that is still inside.' He crawled through the gap with Fen close behind him. Straightening up, he checked left and right. Smears of blood stained the bleached river pebbles.

At his back, Fen shivered. 'Oh God, I hope Robbie's not hurt.'

He hoped so too, but the alternative would mean the blood belonged to someone or something else. 'Stay close,' he whispered.

They turned a corner and there, stretched out up against the far wall of hedge, lay Robbie, his fur matted with blood. Fen made to rush to him, but Kieran held her back. He shook his head. Robbie looked up and cried, shivers shaking his sides.

'I need to see him.' Urgency raced through her words.

'I want to make sure there aren't any nasty surprises around the corner first,' he whispered back. 'Come with me. I'm not leaving you here alone.'

She moved with him, each step painfully slow. They reached Robbie and, satisfied there was no danger behind them, he waved her to stay with the dog while he searched the long corridor of the maze ahead. He found where Robbie's attacker had made his exit, pleased to note by the ripped remnants of a bloody black T-shirt, that Robbie had at least had the opportunity to fight back. He turned and walked back to Fen.

'How is he?' Kieran handed her a bottle of water from his jacket pocket.

'Hurt, but he'll be okay. Cuts on his front leg and side.' She poured some water into her cupped palm to let Robbie drink. 'Take my phone and call Heather. It's in my back pocket. We'll need a vet.'

Kieran reached down and pulled her phone from the pocket of her jeans. He pressed on Heather's number from the call register. 'Hey, Heather, it's Kieran. We've found Robbie.'

At his feet, Fen spoke to Harry's dog in soothing tones as she checked him gently for injuries. She rubbed the dog's silky ears, then froze as she lifted Robbie's head to check his chest. 'Jesus.' She sat back, her butt hitting the ground hard, grimy hands clamping over her mouth. 'Tell them to call Riggs.'

He relayed the instructions and hung up, his heart a solid block of ice against his rib cage. 'What is it, Fen?'

She looked up at him, her eyes haunted grey, bright

with tears, her face pale. 'That's my knife in his shoulder. Kieran, I swear to God I'd never hurt Robbie.'

He crouched low beside her, his blue jeans pulling tight across his thighs. 'I know that, honey.'

'That knife has been locked away in a drawer for a long time. How did it get here? Who would do this?'

He drew her to her knees and tugged her closer, his arms closing around her as she lay her cheek against his shoulder. 'I don't know, baby, but we'll find out. I found a T-shirt further into the maze. It's ripped to pieces, so I hope Robbie got a good bite out of him. Maybe Riggs can identify something on it. Blood, DNA, a logo.'

'Why is this happening to us? First Martha, now Robbie …'

'Robbie's going to be fine. Those are flesh wounds, right? Not life-threatening. Otherwise he wouldn't have survived this long.' He stroked the softness of her hair, reassuring himself as much as he was comforting Fen, glad he'd left Liam at home with Liv.

'I don't know about the shoulder wound. I don't want to pull the knife out. We have to wait for the vet.' Her words were muffled against his jacket.

'You don't want to touch it anyway. Hopefully there'll be fingerprints on it Riggs can work with.'

'But, poor Robbie, he must be in such pain.'

'He's tough, aren't you, boy?' Robbie whined a response. 'See? Let's do what we can to make him comfortable until the others get here. We'll feed him treats and water, and tell him what a hero he is, okay?'

She nodded and answered, a small smile in her response, 'Okay. I think Harry would appreciate that. I hope Riggs can stop this, Kieran.'

Her eyes held his, the sadness in them running deep. Damn it, for all their sakes, he hoped this nightmare would end soon.

It felt like a lifetime before the rush of footsteps and calls entered the maze, a place where Liam had played, the place where the peaceful and calming atmosphere Muzz had created had been turned into a vicious scene of senseless cruelty that raised too many unanswerable questions. It had to stop. Before it touched the people he loved most. Before any more unnecessary violence and harm sent them all spiralling back down the void of darkness.

In his arms, Fen watched the vet attend to Robbie after Riggs had given the go-ahead to remove the knife with care not to contaminate any fingerprints on it. He bagged it for evidence as the vet cleaned Robbie's wound.

Fen stepped away to face Riggs. 'This mess ends here. I will remember.'

Riggs sealed the plastic bag and logged it on a sheet on his clipboard. 'Forcing repressed memories to return could be as harmful as they can be unsuccessful. Do the best you can, Fenella. That's all you need to do. We can't force your mind to remember. In some ways, I don't want you to remember what you saw. But I agree this must stop, and anything you remember will help with that. In the meantime, I can work with what I have, the gang squad will keep Beyond Hell's Reach out of town, and Liv and Liam will have all the protection I can muster while you deal with business at *La Paloma Negra* tomorrow. '

Chapter Fifteen

The two-hour drive into Perth had been mostly in silence, her nerves on edge and her scars crawling under her wristbands. Kieran pulled into a parking spot and pressed the screen on his infotainment system to end his handsfree call.

'So, Travis says Robbie's going to be fine. He's out of surgery, awake and not liking the cone around his neck. Harry's with him. He's not happy that Robbie has to stay in for observation for a few days.'

'That's good to hear.' She was glad he'd repeated the news, because her mind had blocked out all white noise as the ugly purple painted exterior of *La Paloma Negra* had come into view.

He turned off the engine and placed his hand on the SUV's door handle. 'You ready?'

Fen let out a steadying breath. 'Ready as I'll ever be.'

'Whatever happens, I'll be right there, okay?'

She nodded, her belly clenching into knots. 'Let's go.'

Together they approached the charcoal-coloured door set in a windowless brick wall beside an inconspicuous, faded signboard. People walked by on their way to life as if the door didn't exist. Those who knew its purpose ignoring it, those who didn't, not intrigued enough by the name to enquire. Exactly the way the owner, past and present, wanted it.

Kieran rang the bell and Fen tightened her grip on his hand as they waited for a response. Under the wristbands, her skin tingled against opening old wounds and unleashing bad memories that would cause anguish far worse than physical pain.

Her mind had churned over the possibilities all night over what today would bring. Beside her, Kieran had been just as restless until they'd given up on sleep and sat at the kitchen table to find comfort in conversation and hot chocolate instead until a dull, grey dawn broke over the vines.

The hollow echo of heels clicking across a wooden floor preceded the twist of the brass knob. The door opened to a tired looking woman, her face void of make-up, ravaged by a profession that paid well but destroyed the soul. She wasted no time on pleasantries.

'You must be Fenella. I don't normally work with cops, but I've made an exception for you. Antoinette was a good friend. Hurry up and come inside. I don't need sticky-beakers peering in.' She waved them in and closed the door, snapping on locks and tapping in a code on the alarm panel on the wall. 'In case someone tampers with the door. Sets off an alarm upstairs.'

'I hope we're not interrupting anything.' Fen shivered at the thought of what lay ahead up the dingy narrow staircase. She remembered being carried down them, clinging to Martha Wallace, terrified.

'We're closed today. Even hookers need a day off, you know. Head on up, I'll be in the office if you need me. Take your time. All the rooms are unattended. The girls have been sent out as per the cops' instructions. If this results in a raid, I'm sending you the bill for damages.'

'I'm not here to cause harm to your business, Cherish. All I want is answers.'

The woman's eyes flickered away from hers, the tug to her lips not unkind but sad. 'It's what happens when you know the answers I'm afraid of. Business hasn't been good since Diablo gave the club to me. It needs a makeover and I can't afford one. Messing around in the past won't encourage new business. And now Diablo's gone … Those bastards should pay for that. It's the only reason I agreed to letting you in here. I hope you realise the danger you've put me in if they find out I'm helping you.'

Anger slipped in over apprehension. 'I appreciate the help. I'm not exactly happy about the harm they're doing to my people and property either. If I ever recover the money Spider stole from me, recoup the loss of income from the vines he ploughed over to grow his cannabis crop, finish paying for the funeral of an innocent woman who didn't deserve to die, or the vet bills for a dog hurt in such a cruel way, I'll make sure you're compensated for your efforts.'

'You think I want compensation?' She laughed, the sound harsh from smoking and abused throat muscles. 'I don't want your money, I want justice. For myself. For Antoinette. For all the girls up there who take the kind of shit we have to take to make a living. It's a vicious circle, honey. The more we take, the more we need. You were lucky to escape that. You were lucky Diablo made sure of it the night your mother died.'

Fen narrowed her eyes. 'You know what happened.'

'I know nothing.' An answer without conviction, eyes that couldn't meet hers and a chilling feeling that Cherish was lying her tired arse off. 'I've given my statement to the cops and that's all you'll get from me. I won't help you with anything more. When Diablo died so did my protection.'

'Who is this Diablo?'

'Luciano Romano. He had you taken away. There were a few children here he arranged homes for. He was a good man, and they killed him.'

'Not that good a man when he's the president of an outlaw motorcycle club, funding prostitution and manufacturing and selling drugs, killing people who don't follow club rules.'

'You don't know anything about him, so don't think you do.' Cherish spat the words between them. 'You had a lucky escape, people looking out for you. Don't let these bastards take that away from you. Don't let them steal your life the way they stole mine. I was a girl with dreams once too. Soliciting the streets of Perth wasn't it. But then dying wasn't on my agenda either. The likelihood of that happening if Roach finds out I let you in here is pretty high, Rosa. And unlike you, I don't have anyone left who cares what happens to me anymore.' She held out an old-fashioned brass key in keeping with the age of the rotting building and Fen took it. 'This is the key to your mother's rooms. Make it count for something.'

Beside Fen, Kieran's muscles tensed. 'We can arrange for protection for you.'

A sneer twisted Cherish's lips. 'With who? The cops? I'm more likely to need protection against them. Who do you think covered this mess up?' She wrapped her worn cardigan around her, covering the daggy track pants, the nail polish on her toes in the heeled slippers chipped and peeling. 'I'm done talking. Go do what it is you have to do. I've got to plan the entertainment for tonight. Assuming the place won't be crawling with cops by sundown.'

She opened a door to the left and disappeared into what looked like an office, closing it behind her. Fen shivered, eyeing the shadowy staircase ahead.

'Well, that was pleasant. Ready?' Beside her, Kieran's warmth and solid strength gave her comfort. 'Let's get this over with so we can go home.'

'Agreed,' he said. 'Do you remember her?'

Fen shook her head. 'No. I thought I might, but I don't remember leaving the room much or seeing anyone other than the men who came inside.'

'Let's see if anything upstairs is familiar.'

His hand at her waist, he squeezed lightly, and they moved to climb the old wooden staircase with the worn carpet that had seen years of traffic. If the walls could talk, she could only imagine their description of the characters who'd climbed these stairs. A shiver climbed her spine in sync with each footfall until she stepped onto the first-floor landing.

Sometimes the answers to our questions are where we least expect to find them. Riggs' words echoed in her ears. Apprehension clawed at her throat chased by determination. She'd hidden from the root of her problems for long enough.

The years hadn't been kind to the place, as Cherish

had pointed out. Since banning Beyond Hell's Reach, business had taken a downturn and a toll on upkeep. The dark, dingy place of horrors stood exactly as the seven-year-old inside her mind remembered, only worse.

Peeling paint on the walls, once a classy shade of vintage rose, now a grimy shade of something unidentifiable. The carpet, threadbare in shades of red and gold exposing scuffed jarrah floorboards, stretched the length of the corridor. Nameplates in tarnished brass on scuffed and splintered doors identified fetishes of choice. The Naughty Room. The Play Room. Mummy's Room.

Fen shivered. 'Bloody hell.'

Beside her Kieran chuckled. 'Interesting choices. God knows what other rooms lie in wait further down. Do you think they have a librarian's room?'

Fen slipped her hand back into his, her fingers cold as memories crept in from the shadows. The Jungle Room? *Oh, dear God.* She stopped opposite it at a door marked "Private. DO NOT ENTER" shouted in the child-like scrawl of someone who hadn't attended school for long. The shiver clinging to her spine crawled along her skin, releasing a churn in her belly.

'This is it. The rooms I grew up in.'

'Looks like they were never used again after you left.' Kieran studied the door, the yellowed warning sign, then pushed the old-fashioned key into the lock. 'You sure you want to do this, Fen?'

She nodded. 'I want this to stop. The nightmares, the threats, the harming. Whatever happened here that night, my memory of Antoinette deserves closure too.'

Kieran turned her to face him, taking her free hand in his too. 'Any time you want to stop, leave, run, you tell me.'

She swallowed and nodded. 'Just hold my hand and don't let go, okay?'

'I can do that. Ready?'

Fen chewed her lip, her hand shaking as she reached for the key, turned it and prayed that the sea of memories behind the door wouldn't drown her. She pushed open the door and with Kieran close, stepped over the threshold into the dim, musty smell of the past.

Silence screamed out of the interior, abandonment riding on the backs of dust particles drifting in the air, disturbed by the draft creeping in from the hallway. Kieran reached for the light switch, but Fen stopped him.

'No. This is how it was. Always dark. No sun in through the windows because the blinds were always closed.'

She edged further into the cramped room, her grip tightening on his hand. In the corner, to her left, the battered fridge, almost always empty, stood silent. On top of it, a small television, so old it had never worked. Beside it, a table and two chairs, covered in dust and a gaudy orange vinyl tablecloth.

'I used to hide under that table when the men came. Right up in the corner against the wall, next to the rat catcher. It wasn't much comfort with the noise from the room next door. The walls were incredibly thin. Even thinner at night.' Her words drifted into the silence as she faced the only refuge she'd had. 'I used to clamp my hands over my ears, squeeze my eyes shut and sing songs in my head until the noises stopped.'

In the corner next to the table, a mattress lay on the floor, the dirty sheets crumpled, a tattered blanket bundled in a heap against the wall. 'That was my bed.' Her hands began to shake, and she reached for her wrists, twisting the leather bands against the itch.

'You're doing fine, Fen. It's okay. I'm here.' Kieran's fingers were warm around hers, taking her hand back in his, his touch almost unbearably hot against the icy chill.

She took a deep breath and turned to face the door in the wall opposite. The door she couldn't open in her dreams. It stood innocently ajar, the way it had that night when she'd approached it, except now there was no light burning inside, no sounds from behind it.

Pleading screams began echoing in her mind. *Stop*. Answered by ugly words tossed out in a deep voice. Vicious shouts that swelled and grew like angry waves in a storm. Her grip on Kieran's hand fell away, her footsteps slow and heavy as she crept closer, the way she had before. 'They were shouting. I thought they were fighting.'

Fear clutched at her throat, the pressure on her windpipe squeezing in a grip around her throat. She reached out her hand to the door and drew it back again quickly, her fingers clutching at the wristbands, trying to tear them off and stop the itch.

'Fen.' Kieran's hands stilled the movement. 'We can do this together, open that door, or we can leave and find another way to fix this mess. You don't have to do this to yourself.'

She shook her head and peered through the opening in the door. 'They wouldn't stop.'

'Who wouldn't stop?'

'Not who. The screams. He hurt her. Did terrible things to her.'

Shadows morphed into silhouettes on the wall, the soft lamplight that had once shone against it, a stark contrast to the harshness it backlit. She pushed the door open with her fingertips and the demons crouching in the shadows raced in to claim the room.

Memories came crashing in, a tangle of terror that rolled over her and pushed her back into the wall of Kieran's chest. Antoinette on the bed, a man over her with a knife in his hand—slashing, stabbing—blood all over the walls and Antoinette's lifeless eyes staring at her where she stood in the doorway.

She'd run. Silently, the way she'd been taught.

Under the table. Into the corner. Tried to make herself smaller than the rat caught in the trap. Listening. Waiting for the man with the teardrop tattoo to find her hiding place and cut her too.

'He didn't know I was there. Another man came running into the room. They shouted at each other.' *I told you to stay away from her. Fuck, man, you killed her! For what?* 'I heard more noises, swearing, like they were punching each other, having a fight. Then the man with the knife ran away.'

'Did you see his face? The man with the knife.'

Fen nodded. 'Yes. It was Ray Sampson. He's older now, lankier, more weathered, but it was him.' Ice crept into her veins, making her shiver.

Kieran closed his arms around her. 'What happened next?'

'The police came. They talked about making the problem go away. No need for a crime scene investigation. She was a prostitute, no-one would care. They'd be taking out the trash. They laughed, like someone had made a joke. Then an ambulance arrived. I was still hiding under the table. When everyone had gone, I was alone. Someone came in and took all the bedding away, cleaned the room. The chemicals made me sneeze. That's when he found me.'

'Who found you?'

'Luciano Romano.' His face as she'd seen it had looked nothing like the one in the police file. His expression had been softer, kinder, changing instantly from angry to concerned when he'd found her curled tightly in the dark corner. A bruise had started to bloom on his cheek and he'd wiped blood away from his split lip with the back of his hand.

Cherish walked into the room. 'Diablo knew you were there, hiding somewhere, but he didn't know if you'd understood what you saw and heard. If Roach had found out you were in the room, he'd have killed you too. That's why Diablo told the social worker to make you disappear.'

Fen shivered, leaning into Kieran's warmth, the walls of the room creeping in closer. 'Why would Diablo do that if he knew I'd seen something? One of his men murdered his property, surely he wouldn't want witnesses?'

'Antoinette had been off the table since she fell pregnant with you. She ran the reception, bookings, events.'

Fen shook her head. 'No, I remember men coming in, going to her room.'

'Only two men. Her dealer and Diablo. She was Diablo's property. It's why she had the only one-bedroomed apartment in the building. All the others are studio rooms. Roach was lucky Diablo let him live after what he did to Antoinette. He should have eliminated that arsehole while he had the chance, but Diablo lived by the code and club brothers don't rat on each other. Fat lot of good that did him. Now he's dead too.'

'I still don't understand why he would let me go. Surely he knew there'd always be a risk that Roach would find out I was there that night?'

Cherish smiled, a movement of her mouth that could have been interpreted as kindness or sadness were it not for the emotionless void in her eyes, destroyed by her work, by the need to make a living and a life that required drug abuse to be tolerable.

'Risk is a challenge we live with every time we open that door downstairs.' Cherish pulled the door to Antoinette's bedroom closed. 'Diablo didn't want that life for you, not when it killed Antoinette. It touched her even though she was his property, under his protection. He made you disappear, made sure you stayed hidden for as long as he could.'

'Why would he care about a skinny kid when Antoinette had never cared about her own child?' Fen shivered, Cherish's words tumbling over each other in her mind in the effort to find sense in it all.

'Because he was your father.'

Fen's stomach bottomed out. If Romano had been more like Roach, she wouldn't have made it out alive, whether she was blood or not. And now there was more blood on her hands, another death resulting from the search for the witness to a murder.

Cherish wrapped her worn cardigan tighter around

her. 'You have what you came for. You need to leave now. The longer you stay here the worse the consequences. Make it end today, Rosa.'

'My name is Fenella, and I intend to.' Fen forced down the nausea that curdled her stomach, walked out into the hallway and away from the horror that tore at her mind.

Chapter Sixteen

Kieran turned fertiliser into the soil around the base of the new vine and watched as Liam copied his movements. He'd worried himself sick all night, waiting to hear if Fen was okay.

Leaving her in the city with the detectives working her mother's case hadn't been something he wanted to do. He'd wanted to stay with her, but he had Liam to think about too, and his son had never spent a night away from him in the four years of his life.

Fen faced a battery of psych interviews, long hours of questioning about her mother's murder, reliving the past over and over. New memories that would taunt her with their darkness, but she'd promised she'd be okay.

He trusted she would. He had to have confidence in her. He had to believe that she wouldn't pick up a knife and take it to her scars, that she wouldn't take her life the way Diane had when things had got too confronting. Fen was tough, a survivor, a different person to Diane.

In his shirt pocket, his phone pinged the arrival of a text message. He dug out the phone and checked the screen.

On my way home.

Smiling, he pulled off his glove and texted back.

See you soon.

Stopping for coffee on the way. Perks of a police escort.

Be safe. He hesitated before sending: *We missed you.*

Too much too soon? His heart stuck in his throat waiting for her response. Damn it, he did miss her. He wanted her home where he could take her in his arms and hold her against him, protect her from everything she faced. And, just for once, the guilty shimmer of Diane's ghost didn't rise to call him out on his thoughts. His phone pinged twice.

Will do.

Missed u 2.

He wanted to call her, to hear her voice, convince himself she was okay. He let his finger hover over the call button for a second. Bugger it. He hit the green icon and waited.

'Hey.' Her voice filled his senses and sent pleasant tingles down his spine.

'Hey yourself. Everything okay? How did it go?'

Her long sigh in his ear made him wish he'd stayed with her after all.

'Hard. A long day and night. I could identify more from the photos they showed me. Some of them were awful, Kieran. What that man did to her …'

'I'm so sorry you had to go through that. I wish I could have stayed.' Guilt flooded him. He hated that Fen had had to face this situation alone, that it had turned out to be far worse than the one she thought she'd left behind as a child.

'It's okay. I'll be okay. They'll catch Roach Sampson and he'll pay. I have faith they will.' Her voice echoed with hollow conviction, as if she couldn't let herself believe that until it happened.

'Riggs will make sure the cops do everything they can to make sure he does.' He had to believe that too. 'Lucky sends his love. Liam asked if he could get a Mrs Lucky for his birthday.'

She laughed, the sound reaching in and tripping his heart. God, he loved the sound of her laugh. 'I think we can arrange that as long as you can handle a dragon occupying space in the cottage.'

He chuckled. 'I might need you to hold my hand if we're catching crickets for dinner.'

'I wish you'd been there last night.' Her voice softened, the words barely above a whisper. 'It's not over yet. Not until they can make an arrest. And until they can put Roach and Luke away, there is still a threat to us all. Are you prepared for that?'

Kieran leaned on the fork. Liam played at his feet, drawing pictures in the soil with a stick. 'If we don't do this, it will never be over for you.'

He wanted it to be over, for all of them. This pain, the memories, the pasts he wanted to box up and put away on a shelf in the dark and close the door on them forever. He wanted his son safe. He wanted Liv and Fen out of danger.

'I'll be home in a couple of hours and I'll fill you in.' She paused. 'Kieran?'

The way she said his name had his stomach contracting and heart pounding in turns. He wanted her home safe, not with a threat still hanging in the air. 'Yeah?'

'Can I stay with you tonight?'

Indecision, confusion, heartache — it was all there in her voice, and he felt every emotion echo hers on its way through him. 'What about Liv? Will she be okay on her own? Riggs stayed over last night to keep an eye on her.'

She hesitated as in the distance the driver of a road train leaned on his horn. 'He told me. He said he'd stay again tonight if I needed him to. Is it selfish of me to want to be with you?'

The last words came out so softly he had to strain to hear them over the roar of blood in his ears. 'Not selfish at all.' Already his arms itched to hold her. All night if she wanted him too. 'Barbecue okay?'

'Perfect. See you soon.' Her voice softened around the words.

Warmth spread through him along with relief. Soon she'd be home safe with him. The words *I love you* played on his tongue, but it was way too soon to say them out loud. Not yet. Not until all the hurdles were down and all the ghosts were laid to rest. 'See you soon.'

'Say hi to Liam for me.'

The warmth morphed to a glow. She really cared about his boy. 'Fen says hi, mate.'

'Hi, Fen. Can I feed Lucky? Can I?'

'Did you hear that?' Kieran laughed.

'I did. Tell him yes, but to make sure Lucky gets some greens as well as crickets, okay?'

'Maybe we can get a dog instead?' He shivered against the personal ring to his words. Like they were in a long-term relationship. But they weren't. Not yet. After tonight? Who knew?

'And miss out on all the fun of watching you squirm over touching innocent creepy crawly creatures? No way.'

'You're a hard woman. Hurry home so you can deal with the crickets. I can handle the greens.' Her chuckle made him think of everything else he'd like to handle that had nothing at all to do with pets and everything to do with bedsheets and soft sighs.

'Toughen up, princess. I'll be home by seven.'

Suddenly, he didn't want to hang up. He wanted this over. For all of them. So they could bury the past and move on to a future. So he could be free to fall in love with Fen again without feeling guilty, without Diane between them, and with the man who'd destroyed Fen's life behind bars so he could never hurt her again.

He wanted to keep her on the phone until the headlights of the police car lit up the access road to The Cranky Lizard. When he could open her door and help her out of the seat, kiss her hello while she stretched out the kinks of the long drive, then wrap her in his arms and keep her close all night.

The unmarked car pulled up in front of the main house a little after seven. Fen breathed a sigh of relief. The ghostly shapes of the bare vines rested in the valley against the star blanket above the Whispering Hills.

If she turned from that view, she'd see the distant glow of the work lights that lit up the 24-hour working compound at Wongan Creek Mining.

Across the road that led north, the construction machinery clearing Harry's block for the new lifestyle village would be parked up for the night, rested until morning. It felt good to be home.

Finally, she'd made progress. A full report to the police about her mother's murder, a promise of protection from Beyond Hell's Reach while the case was being re-investigated, all the bad memories that collected in her mind forever, now released.

Liv opened the front door and walked out onto the verandah with Riggs striding along behind her. She took one look at the car and rushed down the steps. Liv threw open her arms and Fen got out the car to walk into her hug, holding on tight to the woman she'd always considered her mother.

'Darling, you're home. How did it go?' Liv whispered into her hair, her hold firm and strong.

Fen pulled back to kiss her mum's cheek. 'It's been a rough night and day, but it's for the best. I remembered everything. I've got a lot to tell you.' She tried not to glance in the direction of the manager's cottage where light glowed warm in the windows.

Liv smiled and let her go. 'Mmm, I can see you're not going to settle until you've been up to the cottage. I've got some cupcakes freshly baked for young Liam. Kieran's waiting for you. Go to him, darling. I understand you need to. Riggs has commandeered the use of the guest room. He's overseeing the installation of the new security systems and setting up the monitoring while Kieran's busy out in the blocks, so he's staying a few nights. I'll be here when you're ready to talk.'

Her mum had always understood the bond that had bound Fen and Kieran together, and Fen loved her even more for it. Antoinette had given her life, but Liv had made it worth living. Liv, Muzz, Kieran and now Riggs too. With them on her side, she'd always been able to face anything. 'Thanks, Mum. And you too, Sarge.'

Riggs patted her shoulder. 'You did a very brave thing, Fenella, facing the truth and making a statement. I swear to you, we'll catch these bastards.'

'I hope you can do that before they do any more harm, Sarge.'

'I'll make sure of it. I'll have a chat to these boys before they head into town for the night.' He nodded to the two detectives still sitting in the car. They watched him walk to the open window and engage in handshakes and conversation.

'I need to wash away the grime. Going back to that place felt so dirty. Nothing had been touched after the night of the murder.'

'Oh, love, that's awful, but probably for the best if it helped you remember. Are you okay?'

'I'll be fine. The appointed psych talked me through it and the detectives on the case have been amazingly understanding.' Fen wrinkled her nose and sniffed. 'I never realised how much sweeter the air is out in the country compared to the city.'

'Always sweeter and fresher.' Liv hugged her tightly. 'Go now. I'll pack the basket for Liam while you freshen up.'

'Thanks, Mum.'

Liv touched her cheek with soft, gentle fingers. 'It's good to have you home safe, sweetheart. We will get through this.' Her eyes were full of promise and hope.

Fen prayed they would get through it alive as her mum led her up the stairs and into the house. With a mug of warm tea in her hand, she made her way to the bathroom to scrub away the smell of murder, lies and betrayal from her skin.

Half an hour later, Fen made her way up the path to Kieran's door. She tapped lightly on the glass panel that bled light onto the verandah.

He didn't make her wait long. The door swung open. Kieran balanced Liam on his hip with one arm and held the door open with the other.

'Fen!' Liam reached out with both arms and latched them around her neck as he launched himself from Kieran's hold to hers.

'Hey, little guy.' Surprised, she swapped the basket for Liam's weight and hugged him tightly. 'You did a great job feeding Lucky for me. He's a very happy, contented dragon tonight.'

'I love Lucky.' His plump, sticky hands cupped her face. 'He ate three crickets. But I gave him veggies too. Just one.'

'You did good. He's asleep now. In a food coma.' She grinned, whatever it was on Liam's hands making her cheeks feel rubbery as they moved under his touch. Over Liam's head, she looked at Kieran. 'Hey.'

He smiled and her heart skipped a beat. 'Hey. You must be tired after … everything.'

'I'm awake now.' She wanted to step into his arms and be held, but some invisible barrier remained between them. A distance she couldn't quite touch on. Liam yawned loudly. 'Unlike you, little man. It's a little past your bedtime, isn't it?'

'I waited for you.' His curls brushed her cheek as he lay his head on her shoulder and cuddled into her.

She tightened her hold, ignored the warning bells ringing in her mind for her not to get too attached, and hitched him closer. She'd have to be totally emotionless not to have her heart expand with affection for this kid. A child Kieran had raised virtually alone. A child like the one she'd once been, who'd survived trauma to come out the other side okay. More than okay.

'That's very sweet of you.' She pressed a kiss to Liam's baby-soft hair.

Kieran cleared his throat and reached around her to close the door. 'You're letting the heat out, kids. Liam, let's clean up in the kitchen and then we can do a bedtime story, okay?'

'Can Fen come too?' Liam's voice came out on a sleepy sigh, muffled by her woollen jumper where he'd burrowed his face against her. 'You smell nice.'

Fen grinned. 'Thank you, mate. So do you.'

He smelled like honey, bath bubbles and tired little boy, like a bundle she wanted to cuddle every night before bedtime. It made her forget that her early childhood hadn't been sweet. Gave her hope that maybe one day she'd have a baby of her own. With Kieran. And that scared her. Because she hadn't let herself believe she could be the two-point-five-kids-and-a-dog type before.

What if she sucked at being a mother? What if she caused a child of her own the same harm and emotional turmoil Antoinette had caused her? Her wrists itched for the first time since leaving the city.

She realised she'd forgotten to put on the leather strips that soothed them. A step. A big step towards healing the harm caused by dark shadows, dirty corners and men bent on evil.

Kieran's hand at her back warmed her through as he eased her ahead of him up the hallway to the kitchen. 'Of course she can, if she wants to.' He stopped to look at her, a plea in his eyes.

Fen searched his face, his eyes. He wanted her to stay, to be a part of that special time reserved for father and son. She wouldn't trade that opportunity for anything. She wouldn't hurt a boy already damaged by rejection, but she could stay and make him feel safe and loved, so she put that promise in her heart, returning his gaze. 'I'd like that.'

His smile came low and sexy, the last remnants of doubt clearing from his eyes like the clouds after the rain. 'We missed you.'

Liam hummed his agreement against her shoulder. 'Yeah, Fen.'

She turned into Kieran and pressed a hand to the warmth of his grey knitted jumper, holding his gaze and hoping that she conveyed what was in her heart with a good long look. 'I've missed you both too.'

'Let's clean up,' he said, covering her hand with his for a moment. Then he released it to tingle from his touch all the way to the kitchen.

The kitchen table bore the fallout of a pre-bedtime snack. A jar of honey beside a Cranky Lizard logo mug half full of now cold milk. A golden crumpet with tiny toothy bites all around the outside circle lay half eaten on a plate.

Fen smiled. 'And here I was worried about feeding him fairy bread.'

Kieran dropped the basket of cupcakes on a clear spot on the table. 'Thank God he's not the kind of kid who gets hyped up on sugar easily. Marge assures me the honey is at its most natural with no additional sugar added. The crumpets I'm not so sure about.' He pointed to the wrapper. 'Store bought.'

Liam's warm body relaxed against hers and the first sounds of softened breaths filled the space between them. 'Doesn't look like it will keep him awake.'

Kieran pulled out a chair. 'Sit with him while I clear this away. You have a magic touch, Fen. We might not make it to the bedtime story after all.' His hand warmed her shoulder as she sat. 'I think he's in love with you.'

Her heart did a little dance in time with the waltz of butterflies in her stomach. 'He's a cute kid. It's hard not to love him back.'

Shadows of pain crossed his face. 'If only Diane had loved him that way.'

Fen tried not to let the hurt Diane's name caused show. Would Kieran ever let her rest? Would he ever be free to love again? 'She loved him in her own way. Not all mothers love the same. It doesn't mean they love any less.'

Kieran turned away, picked up the washcloth he'd used to clean Liam's face and rinsed it under the warm water of the kitchen tap. He returned to kneel next to her chair. 'You've got sticky cheeks from Liam's fingers.' He wiped the honey streaks from her skin with gentle strokes, his face so close to hers she could see the hazel flecks in his green eyes, smell the scent of his shower soap. 'All done. Your jumper will likely need a wash too.'

'Stop fussing. It's only a little bit of sticky. Nothing soap and laundry powder won't fix.' It hurt to know that something so simple could turn him inside out. Had Diane been that bad?

He placed a hand on her arm. 'Fen, I have something I need to tell you that's been eating away at me for a long time. I'm just not sure the time is right with everything else going on, but maybe it is. Tomorrow everything could come crashing down around us and I'll never have the opportunity again to tell you how I felt.'

Her stomach hitched. 'At this point in our lives, there is no right time for anything. If you have something on your mind, we need to get it out in the open. No more closed doors, Kieran. No more secrets hiding in the shadows.'

His smile was grim. 'You had a door you couldn't open and I had one I couldn't close.' He let out a long breath and pinched the bridge of his nose as if to still a headache building behind his eyes. 'Once, when things were bad with Diane, I started an email to you. I never finished it or sent it. I left it open on the screen of my laptop when I went to see to Liam. He was a newborn back then. She came in while I was busy settling him and saw it.'

Fen chewed her lip hard. Diane's insane jealousy had often tainted her and Kieran's friendship, making him withdraw further and further as they'd got older. She could only imagine what Diane's reaction would have been if she was already so emotionally distraught. Sympathy for her nemesis pinched her heart. 'Poor Diane. She wouldn't have taken that well.'

'An understatement. Her nails left scratches on my back when she launched at me, her rage out of control. I barely managed to keep my grip on Liam as she wrenched at my arms and yelled obscenities at me. Diane was a woman possessed that day. She threatened me. Accused me of all kinds of things. Of having affairs, and not just with you. It took some convincing that I hadn't been seeing you behind her back. Nor did she believe that I had no intention of sending that email.'

Fen's throat closed over the ache of tears. 'Oh, Kieran.' So much hurt, so much pain, as if he hadn't suffered enough.

'She called me a liar, used every derogatory term in the dictionary, screamed and pounded at me, the walls, the windows, anything she could get her fists on, until the neighbours called the cops to report a domestic incident.' He ran a hand through his hair, his eyes dark with the memories.

'That's awful.'

'Yes, it was. I was blowing off steam in that email. It felt good to write it down even if I couldn't tell you about it for real. To get it out of my head. Out of my way so I could concentrate on raising my boy and finding a way to get my wife back.'

His pain and helplessness leeched through her. He

couldn't have known he wouldn't succeed. The same way Antoinette couldn't be saved from the life she'd chosen that caused her death. Because both Diane and Antoinette had been ill with a disease for which there was no cure, only medication.

'It's not your fault. Or hers. You tried to work with it, live around it, be the best husband and partner you could be to her.'

His eyes, when they met hers, were sad. 'All I succeeded in doing was to make her hate me even more. She told me that day she was going to drive off a cliff. I ignored it as an empty threat. She'd said those things before. Then she'd calm down, forget about it, and the roundabout of mood swings would start up again. I was caught up in a situation I couldn't walk away from. Not when she was so sick and Liam's life was in danger because of it. I did everything I could to protect everyone involved. I'd taken my vows. In sickness and in health.'

'Why didn't you say something to me? Send that email?' She'd been hurt by his silence, yet knowing Diane, she'd understood it at a level she couldn't explain.

'If I'd stayed in touch, who knows what Diane would have done. Nothing she did was rational, and it only got worse near the end. She wasn't aware of much outside of her own tormented world and the lies she made up in her mind.'

She reached for his face around Liam's sleeping warmth and stroked the roughness of his beard. 'You did everything you could, Kieran. Her death isn't your fault. I believe you *did* try, but some people you can fix, others are beyond repair.'

'Then why do I feel so guilty and angry about her dying?'

'Because you loved her enough to *want* to save her. She tried to take your son, which in the real world is all kinds of wrong, but in her damaged mind, it was the right thing to do. You have to forgive her for that or else you'll never forgive yourself.'

He covered her hand with his and pressed it to his cheek, rubbed his face against her palm. 'I've missed you, Fen. I wanted to send that email, to tell you I still cared.'

Warm tingles spread through her. 'I missed you too, so much, but you did the right thing not to send that email.' She drew his face to hers, pressed a kiss to his forehead, his cheeks, his lips, and eased back to watch his eyes close. When they reopened the sadness had been replaced with a green fire that reached in and tied her heart in knots. 'Why don't I put Liam to bed while you finish up here?'

Kieran lifted Liam's limp hands and wiped the remnants of honey and lint from them. 'Why don't we both go?' He stood and tossed the cloth into the sink.

Fen stood with the precious bundle in her arms and

followed him up the hallway to Liam's room, blood fizzing with expectation, her belly coiled with nerves. Maybe tonight that last barrier would fall and all that kept them apart could be laid to rest. God, she wanted that more than anything.

To finally find happiness with the one man who meant everything to her. Before the real world descended on them again tomorrow and reality brought with it the danger that still dogged their future. One unforgettable night to override all things forgettable to come in the morning.

Kieran pushed open the door, turned on the lizard lamp at the side of the bed and pushed back the covers decorated by woolly sheep. Fen untied Liam's dressing gown and gently slipped it down his arms before releasing it into Kieran's waiting hand. Her fingertips brushed his and heat swept through her. The atmosphere around them thickened, drew them into the warm magic cast by the soft lighting.

Fen placed Liam gently onto the soft mattress, hushing his murmurs of protest as she soothed his curls while Kieran removed his red dragon slippers. Then she pulled the covers up over him and tucked him in with a kiss goodnight. She straightened to find Kieran at her back, his warmth enveloping her, his hands cupping her shoulders to draw her against him.

She let him hold her as his arms came around her

and his lips found her temple in a soft, barely-there kiss. 'He looks so peaceful,' she whispered.

'It's that magic touch of yours,' he whispered back.

She turned in his arms and reached for his face, smoothing out the dark circles under his eyes with her thumb. 'Do you think it would work for you?'

'I'll be your guinea pig.'

'I don't know where we're going.' Uncertainty trickled through her. What if taking this next step ruined their friendship forever?

'I know where we've been.'

'Yes.' Apart. To hell and back with a return ticket. Multiple rides. Didn't they both deserve to get off that train for a stopover? She pressed into him.

'I know I never want to be without you again.' His words rode over her skin as he lifted her closer, his lips so close to hers she could almost taste the honey he'd licked from the spoon while cleaning up. 'Stay with me tonight?'

'Only tonight?'

'I want forever, but I don't know if we're ready for that yet.' He brushed her fringe back from her face. 'We'll need to talk about that sometime.'

'Tomorrow. Nothing we can say tonight will change anything that's happened. Tonight, I need you to hold me. I need to hold you. Because tomorrow we start another journey.'

She wrapped her arms around his neck and stood on

the toes of her boots to reach his lips. She drew them down to hers and kissed him with everything she had bottled up inside her. He took it, swallowed it and asked for more.

Then he swept her up in his arms and carried her away down the hall, pushing the door of his room closed with his foot.

Chapter Seventeen

Kieran woke to the sounds of rain on the old tin roof of the cottage. Something, somewhere had shifted and healed during the night, curled around the woman he considered his best friend, the heart and soul that had disappeared from his life and come back. A band aid on a wound he'd rather heal than let fester.

Fen murmured in her sleep and snuggled into him. He wrapped his arms around her. Lying there with silence around them and the rain making music in the background, he realised something else. No midnight crying from Liam. No four-year-old spread across his bed. No damp tears seeping through his T-shirt.

A moment of panic seized him. *Liam!* He eased away from Fen, stood and pulled on his track pants before making his way to his son's room. Liam lay fast asleep, his toy sheep hugged close, a thumb in his mouth and long lashes feathering cheeks pink with sleep.

Kieran leaned against the door frame with a sigh of relief. His boy's first full night of undisturbed sleep since forever. How cool was that? He pulled the door closed a little so the noise of the kettle and clutter of mugs wouldn't wake him. God knew they'd all needed a good night's sleep. And he'd had one. None of his own nightmares about Diane had surfaced. No sense of presence of her hovering in the room, waiting to raise bad memories. And the memory of her hadn't come between him and Fen last night as he'd half expected it to.

He filled the kettle with water, turned it on. The basket of cupcakes still lay covered on the table. He peeled back the red-and-white-checkered cloth to find a note pinned to it. *Good to see you've stopped pacing. Tell Fen not to rush home in the morning. Riggs has her chores covered.*

Kieran smiled, shook his head. Of course Liv would have picked up on his mood. He'd paced the rows between the vines yesterday unable to concentrate on the task at hand, worrying about how Fen was getting on in the city. The kettle whistled, and he moved to turn it off.

Fen appeared in the doorway, wrapped in his hoodie that reached mid-thigh. 'Everything okay?'

He abandoned the kettle and moved to her instead.

She looked warm and deliciously tousled. There was no stopping the rush of pleasure in knowing he'd been responsible for that look. That every dream he'd ever had about Fen had paled in comparison to making sweet love to the real being. He swept her up against him and tightened his hold on her. 'It is now. Sleep well?'

She grinned up at him. 'Like a baby.'

He nuzzled her neck, kissed a trail over her jaw, curled his tongue around the shell of her ear and smiled as she shivered against him. 'Me too.'

Her hands travelled all over him, touching every inch of skin she could find, fingers skimming over the material of parts she couldn't reach. He kissed her like a man taking his last drink. Savoured the taste of her freshly brushed tongue. 'Is that my toothpaste?'

She smiled against his lips. 'And your toothbrush. We've shared worse.' Then she kissed him until he forgot he owned a toothbrush. 'Let's go back to bed,' he suggested.

'Can't. I need to get back. We've got the book club coming for breakfast.'

'I'm not game enough to disobey Liv's orders. She said to tell you not to rush home this morning.' He let his hands run an exploration of their own, loving her curves against him. How they fit so perfectly with his. He wanted this morning to go on forever. 'She even gave you a note to excuse you.'

Fen laughed. 'She did not.'

'Did so too.'

'Mm.'

The hum against his neck almost sent him over the edge, made him want to forget all about murders, outlaw gangs and everything they still faced. To bury himself in her warmth like he had last night and only see a future together instead of a past that kept them apart. 'Say yes?'

'No.'

He pulled back and looked at her with a frown, ice creeping up through him, stealing his warmth. Had she changed her mind? 'No?'

'I hear Liam singing.'

On cue, the toilet flushed and he called out, 'Daddy, I peed!'

He groaned before calling out, 'Good work, mate!'

Fen slipped from his arms with a quick kiss on his mouth. 'Ask me again tonight.' She moved away out of his reach.

'Oh, I will.' He ruffled Liam's hair as the little boy shot into the room and scampered onto a chair next to Fen. 'Did you wash your hands?'

'Course I did,' Liam scoffed. 'I'm hungry.'

'You're always hungry, squirt.' A truth that had only become reality since they'd arrived in Wongan Creek. Nothing made him happier than to see his son's appetite returning. Kieran pulled a loaf of bread out of the bread bin. 'Vegemite toast?'

'Yeah. And a cupcake.'

Fen nudged Liam playfully. 'Do you think if I eat all my toast, I can have a cupcake too?'

'Only if you eat all your crusts. Daddy says so.'

She screwed up her nose. 'How about you eat my crusts and I have the icing on your cupcake?'

Liam eyed her for a moment. 'No way! That's not fair.'

Fen ruffled Liam's hair. 'I guess I'll just have to eat my own crusts then.'

'I have to eat mine because today is my first day at school with Benji and Casey, and crusts make you smarter. But you're already smart, Fen, so maybe you don't need to eat yours. I'm going on the big white bus so I'll be stronger if I eat my Vegemite toast.' He showed Fen his muscles.

Kieran turned away from the scene and looked out the kitchen window, blinking against the sting in his eyes. No-one, not Diane nor his mother-in-law, had ever had a conversation like this with Liam. Fen was great with Liam. She'd be the perfect mother.

Outside the window, the familiar sight of a marked car rolled down the drive, reminding him of the battle they still had ahead. He turned and walked away to place bread in the toaster, reached for the Vegemite, took the butter from the fridge, the movements automated, a habit formed from following the same routine every day. Reality had seeped in with the dawn. There'd be no sunshine through the clouds today.

The happiness he'd felt last night with her in his arms, would be destroyed by the forensics team packing up their crime scene, more questions from the visiting detectives, and the shadow of Beyond Hell's Reach standing in the wings between lies and murder. He'd do well not to forget the danger wasn't over yet.

'How about I get Liam dressed while you finish making his breakfast?' Fen's question filtered through his thoughts.

Another difference that shouldn't have his heart pounding with hope. Diane had never offered to see to Liam. She'd left it all to him. Kieran cast a quick look at her over his shoulder, his tone short. 'I think he'd like that, thank you.'

'You okay?' Concern furrowed her forehead.

'All good.'

She moved to his side, a hand on his arm. 'You sure?'

He nodded. 'Just thinking.' His gaze strayed back to the window where the dust cloud behind the police car grew and billowed as it drew closer.

Fen saw it too. She stiffened beside him, the smile slipping from her face. Another day, another challenge, another stone in the pond. They both knew it.

'I won't stop fighting until it's over, Kieran. Not now I know the truth. If you're concerned about safety, then you need to consider your choices. I won't stand in your way.'

No, she wouldn't. She would step aside the way she had for Diane and give him his freedom. He had no doubt she could fight this case on her own, find the answers she needed, but at what cost? 'We'll talk later.'

'Okay.' For a moment she let her head rest against his arm, squeezed his hand, and then teased and tickled his son out of the kitchen, into his room.

He listened to the murmur of their conversation as Fen guided Liam through the routine of getting dressed. He heard Liam laugh at something Fen said, the sound making his heart ache. How unfair that, on the brink of finding happiness, the damage of the past had to once again resurface. He hoped the detectives moved fast on the new evidence. That it would hold up in court in the face of an arrest and conviction. That no-one else got hurt while the wheels of justice turned in their excruciatingly slow way.

When Fen and Liam returned to the kitchen, he served toast and coffee in the mounting tension in the room, his thoughts turning to all the things that could happen in between investigation and arrest. He looked at Fen. She'd changed her clothes. Gone was his worn and faded hoodie, in its place her black jeans, dark jumper and the leather bands.

Liam tugged on Fen's sleeve.

'Fen, are you and Daddy going to fight?' His bottom lip protruded, his forehead creased in a worried frown.

Fen's gaze flew to meet Kieran's. 'No, sweetheart, of course not.'

'Are you angry with my daddy? You said you were going to fight. My mummy used to get very angry. With Daddy and me.'

'Oh, mate, no.' She frowned. 'Oh, I understand now. You heard me say I won't stop fighting. I'm not going to fight with your daddy. It's some other bad people I need to fight with. Your dad and I are friends. Good friends don't fight. They might squabble a little, but they always kiss and make up.' She ruffled Liam's hair.

He giggled and smoothed the curls flat with his palms. 'You're messing up my mane.'

'Eat your toast and drink your juice, mate. When you're done you can play in the playground a while.' The words came out gruffer than Kieran had intended.

'I don't want you to fight with Fen, Daddy. She'll go away. Like Mummy did. And then she won't come back.'

Kieran recognised the build-up to a tantrum. Liam's go-to place when he felt threatened. Damn it, it had been weeks since the last one. He'd thought they'd made such good progress. And now this.

Fen reached out to hug Liam. 'I'm not going anywhere, mate. We're not going to fight, but we do have a lot to talk about and it may be hard stuff to deal with. Now finish up so we can go outside and wait for the school bus.'

Her quick look at him had Kieran praying she was right. He didn't want to fight with her. He wanted to turn back the clock ten years and start over.

Liam waved at them from his booster seat in the school bus as Marge drove it away down the drive. They waved back. His first official day at school. Beside her Kieran stood, stoic and still. She nudged his rigid side.

'Is this what was worrying you in the kitchen earlier? He'll be fine. He has Casey and Benji to look out for him. Marge will be there with him all day and Janet has plenty planned to occupy his mind. And the cop station is right next door to the school. He'll be safe, Kieran.'

'But he's so little. What if something upsets him and he has a meltdown?'

She grinned up at him. 'No doubt Janet will call on Virginia to sort it out.'

'God, the poor kid.' He grimaced. 'I'd better get moving. I've got a ton of fertiliser to put on the ground where the new vines will go.'

Fen hugged his arm and stood on tiptoe to kiss his cheek. 'Go get smelly. I'll check on Liv and see if she needs my help before I head upstairs to clean out

Lucky's enclosure. I've got some fresh branches and rocks to re-decorate with.'

'Decorating for lounge-room lizards, hey?' He grinned before tugging her into him. 'Are you contemplating a new career?'

'He's a dragon,' she whispered against his lips. 'And he has more class than a lounge-room lizard.'

He kissed her hard then spanked her backside. 'Go. You're distracting me from the job. You'll get me fired. I hear the boss is a bit of a dragon.'

She pinched his arm. 'I'll tell Liv you said that.'

'I wasn't talking about Liv.'

She kissed the smug look from his face and left him standing as she turned in the direction of the cellar café. Inside, her mum moved things around on tables, wiping down surfaces. 'Hey, Mum.' She kissed Liv's cheek.

'Hello, sweetheart. Did Liam get off to school okay?'

'He was very excited. We had a few concerns getting him dressed this morning, but as soon as he saw Casey and Benji on the bus, he was keen to go.'

'He's making good progress. Things will settle down again soon, you'll see.'

'There's still a long way to go. Do you need me to do anything?'

'No, sweetheart. It's going to be a quiet day today, so I'm restocking the store and doing a bit of a clean out. I'll potter along here. We've only got a skeleton staff on today, and I've told them to come in a little later. We may get a bit of a rush around lunchtime if the weather warms up.'

'Okay then, I'll be upstairs with Lucky doing a bit of redecorating.'

'I'll bring you up a cuppa in about an hour.'

'Perfect.' With a wave, she jogged down the stairs and made her way to the house.

The house was silent as she entered it. She still couldn't get used to that. The lack of Muzz-noise. Taking the stairs two at a time, she made her way to the landing and pushed open the door to her room. She hadn't slept there since coming home from the city. Sleeping beside Kieran was so much more fun than sleeping with popstar posters on the wall, alone in a single bed.

Lucky wallowed on a branch in the corner of his enclosure, his beard flaring when he spotted her movement. She reached for the tub of crickets, picked one out and fed it to him then she reached inside and let him crawl onto her arm, up onto her shoulder.

'I've got some fresh stuff to put into your home, Lucky. And Liam will add some more when he comes home from school.'

She pulled out the old branches and dropped them into an empty cardboard box. Lucky nestled into her neck to hide under the warmth of her jumper as she lifted out the rocks. Picking up a plastic cup, she began to scoop the sand out of the bottom of the enclosure.

'Well, that makes my job so much easier.'

Fen whirled around, the scoop falling from her fingers as Lucky dug his claws into her collarbone. Fear pooled in her belly. Roach Sampson held Liv up against him, a knife glinting at her throat. 'Let her go. What do you want?'

'What I came for. What I've waited for since the day I killed that bitch, Antoinette. And now I'm going to kill this one too.' He nodded towards Liv. 'And then it's your turn. Don't make any stupid moves. There's no-one to protect you anymore.'

Fen dug her heels into the carpet, her chest tightening. Where was Kieran? 'You killed Luciano Romano.'

'Diablo was an idiot. He had no business protecting that piece of trash he stamped as his property. She didn't pay for her hits.'

'So you murdered her?'

'I *cut* her because she promised me a free fuck in lieu of payment and then wouldn't give me what she owed me. So now I'm going to take it from the little snitch she kept hidden.' The rank smell of stale sweat permeated the room, stealing the freshness from the air as he moved, dragging Liv with him. 'And then you're going to die along with your sweet mumma here. Dead girls don't tell tales, you see. A pity because you'd fetch a good price on the meat market.'

She wanted to slap the smug look from his face, but he held Liv a little too closely and she knew all too well the burn of a knife blade. She needed a distraction that would make him drop that knife. Then they'd stand half a chance. 'You've got balls breaking in here with the place crawling with cops.'

'Do you think cops will stop me? I've got friends on the inside. Pigs hungry for money and a piece of the action.'

'Let Liv go. I'll give you what you want.'

His hand came down hard on her wrist, grating the leather cuff against her scars. She cried out and Lucky skittered along the back of her neck.

'You don't have to give it, *sweetheart*. I'm a man who prefers to take what he wants.'

'Is that what you did to Antoinette?' Pain skittered up her arm as he twisted her wrist hard and she fell to her knees.

He removed his hand. 'Get up. No more questions. But you understand how I won't leave any witnesses?'

'It's too late. The cops already know. I remembered everything. How you cut Antoinette like a piece of meat. Because you wanted what Diablo had. Isn't that why you're president of the club now? Murdering innocent people, setting fire to property, stealing hard-earned incomes?' She pushed herself up off the floor, feeling Lucky settle on her shoulder under her jumper.

'Then a couple more bodies won't matter, will they now?' The knife glinted at Liv's neck.

Fen did a mental scan of the contents of her room. Unless Roach was afraid of crickets, she didn't have much in the way of a defence weapon. Her penknife had become police property thanks to the man who'd used it on Harry's dog. If the bite marks on Roach's arm were evidence, Robbie still had a strong pair of jaws. She could really use them now. 'You put a harmless pet in danger. Stabbed him with my knife.'

'Had a lot of fun with that. Useless mutt bit me. I wanted to leave you a message, *Fenella*. I'm going to cut you like I cut that dog. Like I cut the bitch that night. Cut, cut, cut. I bet you wish you had that knife right now.' He twisted the blade in his hand, grazing Liv's throat. 'I've got one right here you can use. It's sharp. And I'm going to sit back and watch you take it to your wrists. One. Last. Time.'

She stepped forward, catching Liv's glance. Her mum's eyes were wide with fear. Fen wouldn't let this bastard get the better of her and harm the people most precious to her. 'Why?'

'Why?' He laughed, the sound harsh. 'Because you're the last one standing. The last one between me and freedom. The last one who can identify Roach Sampson as a murderous bastard. Once you're gone, those files will disappear. The prostitute bitch's case will go cold again, back on the shelf where it belongs. The body in the bag will be a terrible case of the foster child so damaged by life, abused by the system, that she murdered the social worker responsible for it. Slashed her foster mother.' He pulled a lighter from his pocket and the flame flickered to life with a click. 'And then she burnt the place down before she turned that knife on herself.'

'No-one will believe it.'

'No-one will argue with the president of Beyond Hell's Reach because I'll own this town and the people in it. I've been looking for you for a long time, little girl. Your daddy's not here to save you anymore. The past has caught up with you.'

He shoved Liv away hard, sending her smashing into the desk and chair, scattering paperwork across the room. Fen moved fast, crashing into him with all the force she could muster, slapping the knife from his hand. It skittered out the door into the hallway.

Lucky leaped from her shoulder and found purchase on Roach's face, claws digging into his eyes. Roach screamed and tried to dislodge the dragon, but Lucky clung on as the man stumbled backwards and fell. Desperate for him not to get up again, Fen brought her Doc Martin down hard on his crotch and prayed the guttural cry would bring Kieran running.

Downstairs the front door slammed open. Feet

pounded through the house and up the stairs. Blindly, Fen delivered punches to keep the man down. Kidneys. Ribs. Solar plexus. Until she was lifted away.

'Woah. Easy, Tiger. It's okay.' Adrenaline kept her fighting blindly. Strong arms wrapped around her, Kieran's voice soothing in her ear. 'You can stop now, Fen. He's not getting back up. If he does, Riggs will taser his arse.'

'Liv?' Her voice came out strangled through the knot in her throat.

'I'm okay, sweetheart. A bit shaken and bruised, but okay.'

'Uh … Fen? Can you get Lucky off this bastard's face? I need something left of it to identify him with. Mostly, I don't want Lucky in the way if I have to fire the taser. I don't think he'll like the after-effects much.' Riggs' voice had her relaxing.

Kieran's arms loosened from around her and she stepped forward. Roach wouldn't be opening his eyes any time soon. He'd be lucky if he could see out of them again. She held out her hand to Lucky, her voice shaky. 'Come on, boy. Let go now.'

The dragon pulled in his beard and skittered up her arm. She stepped away, backed into the warmth of Kieran's solid strength.

Riggs shook his head as he rolled Roach over and slapped on the handcuffs. 'Bloody legend. The boys in the city will have a field day with this. Taken down by a bloody bearded dragon and a whippet of a girl. Only in the country. Gives a whole new meaning to the name Cranky Lizard, doesn't it?'

'Lucky's not a lizard, he's a dragon.' Shivers raked Fen's spine as the heat of the adrenaline wore off.

'He's a bloody legend, that's what he is.' He hauled Roach up. 'Stand, you bastard. I'm getting too old for these shenanigans. One wrong move and you'll feel the force fifty thousand volts can deliver.'

Fen felt the press of Kieran's lips to her head. 'You okay?'

She nodded.

'Good. Grab the first aid kit and see to your mum while I help Riggs get this bastard down to the car. And, Fen? Could you please put Lucky back in his enclosure? I'm not holding you again until he's safely out of the way. I like my face the way it is.'

Chapter Eighteen

Fen stood on the café verandah with Liam and Kieran. A long afternoon of questioning and statements had preceded a restless night, but today Roach Sampson was well on his way back to jail in Perth and the search for Luke had been escalated.

She'd persuaded Liv to have a lie in this morning, her body sore and bruised from the battering she'd taken. Riggs would be by later to check on them all. Fen smiled. She hadn't missed Riggs' concern for her mum that went beyond the call of duty or that he'd come back to the vineyard after leaving Roach in the care of the detectives to spend the night in Liv's guest room again.

A kind of surreal, unsettled peace hovered over the winery estate in the foggy morning aftermath of the events of the day before. A night in Kieran's arms, held tightly and curled into the protection of his warmth, had done little to still the reality that it wasn't over yet. Not until a conviction and sentence could be passed. For both men and the members of the club who'd assisted them. Only then would she relax completely.

At least Liam had been at school and out of danger yesterday. He'd grown so much since he'd arrived and didn't need any setbacks to stop him healing completely. Fen squashed down the niggly feeling that twisted her belly and focused on business as usual at The Cranky Lizard.

'Are you sure you'll be okay with Liam for a while?' Kieran kissed her hard and stepped back. 'As soon as the machinery is loaded and out of the way, I'll be back for him.'

'Liam will be fine. He can help me set up tables on the verandah for this morning's CWA book club.'

'He'd like that.'

'He's a champ. If he sticks around after he's eighteen, we'll have him running the show at the bar. The ladies love him.'

Kieran smiled that smile that sent a warm glow through her. 'I'd like to be here to see that.'

Fen reached out and squeezed his hand, comfortable in knowing the bond between them was healing and growing deeper again. 'You're welcome to stick around. Go now. Liam and I have work to do.'

She waved him away. Beside her, Liam looked up at his dad with a grin on his face. The little guy had wormed his way firmly into her heart. Just like his father had. She could finally look towards a future and the possibilities her growing relationship with Kieran presented. Perhaps she could be a wife to Kieran and a mum to Liam one day. Not a replacement mum, but a new mum, like Liv had been to her.

'Yes, go, Daddy. We're very busy now.' Liam tugged on the leg of Kieran's jeans.

Kieran laughed. 'Okay, okay. See you in a short while, mate. You be good for Fen, okay?'

Liam rolled his eyes. 'Course I will.'

'Right. See you soon.'

He ruffled his son's curls and gave Fen's hand a squeeze. A part of her wanted to hold on tight and keep him there, an inexplicable sense of *déjà vu* twisting through her. But that would be silly when most of the bad stuff lay behind them and Marge's busload was due to arrive in half an hour. She let him go.

'Come on, Liam.' She held out her hand. Tiny warm fingers wrapped around hers. 'Would you like to lay out the plates this time?'

'Can I?' His excitement quickly turned to a pout. 'What if I break them? Will you be mad?'

'Not if it's an accident. But you won't break any, will you? Because we'll be doing it together.'

The smile she'd grown to love reappeared as he tugged on her hand. 'Come on, Fen, we'd better hurry.'

They worked steadily together, the tables soon set in

cheerful summery shades to detract from the grey of the skies.

'We need more plates.' Liam placed the last blue plate onto the yellow-and-white-checked cloth. 'We haven't got enough.' He pointed to the three empty spaces between the silverware.

'Oh gosh, you're right.' Fen checked her watch. She'd have to duck into the storeroom to get some more. That would mean having to wash the dust off them first. Beside her Liam yawned his boredom. Surprised he'd lasted this long with the task, she decided to cut him a break. 'Why don't you go and see what Lucky is up to while I go and get those extra plates?'

Lucky was enjoying some outside time in his kid-safe enclosure near the play equipment. Liam would be okay in the playground with plenty to distract him. Besides, it wouldn't take long to quickly grab the plates from the storeroom and she could see him in the playground through the windows of the café.

'K.' Liam scampered across the verandah to the play area.

Fen unhitched the safety gate and he slipped through the gap. She hitched it closed again, waiting for the click to make sure the gate had hinged closed. 'Wait here for me, okay?'

'K, Fen.' He disappeared up the tube to the slide and she could hear the rattle of the plastic tumblers on the noughts and crosses board as he stopped to play with them, happily chatting away to Lucky.

She hesitated a moment longer. Perhaps she should just take him with her. No, he'd be fine there. Pushing down the growing sense of unease, she crossed into the café kitchen, ducked into the storeroom and hauled out the box of extra plates. After the events of the last few months, paranoia was clearly getting the better of her. She could still see the fear in Liv's eyes and the blade at her throat when she closed her eyes.

Fen sorted through the plates, setting aside the ones that were chipped or scratched. She made a note to shop around for new crockery, perhaps consider having The Cranky Lizard logo put on them. Plates sorted, she made her way back into the kitchen and washed them off under the lukewarm water and reached for the cloth to dry them.

Beyond the window, between the bare vines, Kieran and the hands loaded the diggers onto trucks. She couldn't wait to see new leaves budding in each of the rows come spring, even though winter brought its own beauty to the valley.

Fen dropped the cloth onto the bench, made her way back onto the verandah and finished the table settings. Now to get Liam and find him a place between the ladies where he'd be safe while she prepped the morning tea.

Wiping her hands on her apron, she made her way to

the playground. Her heart lodged in her throat at the sight of the open gate. Damn it, she'd latched it, hadn't she?

'Liam?' Deathly silence met her call. The unease in her stomach churned. 'Come on, mate. The ladies are on their way. No time to play hide and seek now.'

Nothing. She looked up the tube to the slide. Empty. The open gate. *Please, no. Please don't let Liam have found a way to open the gate.* She ran the length of the play area, looking over the fences to make sure he hadn't climbed them and fallen over. Nothing. The unease turned to panic that gripped her chest in a vice as she turned to find Lucky's enclosure empty, the door ajar. She looked over the top of the structure. Beyond the fencing lay the pond. On the surface, Liam's red puffer jacket billowed above the water.

'Oh, Jesus, no! Liam!'

Fen climbed the fence and vaulted over, the shock of her boots hitting the hard ground reverberating up her spine. She ignored the jolt and ran down the slope to the pond. The ice-cold water robbed her of her breath as she waded in knee-deep, grabbed hold of the jacket and hauled the boy into her arms. The ache of dread and holding back tears closed her throat. She couldn't bear to look at his face. Not yet.

'Kieran!' She screamed so loudly it echoed down the valley, only to be drowned out by the truck's engine as it kicked into gear. Laying Liam's limp body down onto the grass, she had no choice but to look at him. His lips were blue, his skin holding a grey hue. No, this couldn't be happening. She loved him too much to lose him. She checked his pulse, her fingers icy cold. Or perhaps it was Liam's skin that was cold, she didn't know.

'Help!' she called out again, but the noise from the vineyard combined with the bus coming up the drive carried her voice away again.

Desperate, she began resuscitation, counting the compressions between breaths. It felt like ages as the hollow inside her grew, but eventually Liam coughed and threw up pond water. Heavy footfalls reached her ears, but she concentrated on Liam, placing him on his side, soothing the curls on his head until his stomach was empty. Then she swept him into her arms, held him to her chest, buried her head in his curls and cried as she rocked him back and forth.

His silence terrified her, his skin clammy. She wished she'd worn a jacket, something to cover him, to warm his little body.

'Kieran!' she called, but her voice came out on a sob, cold stealing over them as the wind turned the water soaked into her damp jeans to ice.

'You take something from me, I take something from you. That's fair, isn't it, Fenella?'

The voice, no longer gentle as it had once been, chilled the blood in her veins. 'Luke.'

'I hate it when people don't listen. So you have to pay.'

She held Liam closer, willing her body to warm him. 'And you think hurting an innocent child and murdering social workers is the way to make me pay? You're the criminal here, Luke.'

'It wasn't my fault.' Luke shrugged. 'He fell in the pond. Happened while he was chasing that nasty little pet of yours.'

'He's afraid of water. He wouldn't be near the pond if you hadn't lured him here.'

His laugh was harsh, ugly. 'You think you have all the answers, don't you? It would be so easy to pin this one on you. A mentally unbalanced woman who self-harms, driven over the edge to murder her boyfriend's brat. What would your new man think then, *Fenella*? Or do you prefer Rosa?'

'It's over, Luke. The police are closing in on you. Right now, there are security cameras everywhere taping this with a live feed to Riggs' office.' She crossed her fingers that Riggs had set it up to be so and tried to keep calm. 'The footage will show the truth of what happened here. No-one will believe I did this. Please, I need to call an ambulance for him.'

His grip on her arm would bruise later. 'Get up! Do you think I care if the brat dies? I'm going to finish what Roach started, because I don't like loose ends either.'

He hauled her to her feet with Liam in her arms. She

lost her balance and fell against him, their combined weight unexpected on the slope of the lawn, making him stagger back, his nails grazing her arm as he lost his foothold on the dewy grass.

'Bitch!'

He went down hard. Fen turned to run. Footsteps echoed on the verandah boards as the ladies piled outside ready for their morning tea. If she'd dropped the café blinds to block out the wind like she'd intended to do, the ladies wouldn't have seen them a few metres away below their line of vision. Liam's fists curled into her shirt. He whimpered. She held him tighter, ran harder. *Please God, let him be okay.*

'Help me!'

In her peripheral vision, Luke clambered to his feet, running after her, gaining ground as she struggled under Liam's dead weight, losing it again as the smooth leather soles of his boots slipped under him.

'Yoo-hoo!' Virginia Turner stepped up to the railing. 'Oh dear. Call the police, Marge. That rascal, Luke, is back.' She turned and headed for the stairs, her cane firmly in hand.

In her arms, Liam's little body went limp. Fen couldn't find her voice. Guilt washed over her, flooded her lungs, filled her soul. She'd left him alone. She hadn't been able to take care of Kieran's little boy. Just like Diane. He'd hate her, never forgive her, for not protecting his son. She cursed herself for encouraging him to become so attached to Lucky that he'd be lured into danger.

'Stop right there, you animal.' Virginia stepped in front of her and Liam, a plump barrier between them and Luke. 'And don't even think I'm going to be the pushover Martha Wallace was. I'm not afraid to use this cane on your arse.'

Too many witnesses and nowhere to run, Luke slid to a halt. Virginia slammed her cane into his chest, winding him and sending him flat on his rump.

'Stay down. Someone get me a pack of cable ties. We don't want the bastard turning on us.' Virginia planted her cane firmly in the centre of Luke's stomach, her quiet, authoritative commands able to be heard as the truck's engine faded away down the driveway.

'Top drawer in the kitchen, next to the knives.' Warm hands touched hers. A jacket covered Liam's body, another dropped around her shoulders. Liv's arm came around her. 'Are you okay, love?'

Fen nodded. Her throat ached. 'Liam …'

'Let me see him.'

Liv checked the little boy over. 'He's okay. He's breathing, but a little cold. Let's get those wet clothes off, so we can put a dry blanket around him.' She turned to the group. 'Someone go and get Kieran. Marge, bring blankets. Bella, put the kettle on to boil and make some sweet tea for Fen. Has someone called an ambulance?'

A whiff of floral perfume drifted over her as the

woman she recognised as Travis Bailey's mum knelt beside her and squeezed her hand. 'I'll go find Kieran. It'll all be fine, sweetheart.'

'No, it won't. He'll be so worried. Liam didn't deserve this.' Fen shook her head, tears burning her eyes, falling over her cheeks.

'What happened, love?' Liv's calm voice soothed her along with the gentle touch smoothing her hair.

'He fell in the pond ... I took my eyes off him for a minute ... I thought he'd be safe in the play area ... Lucky got out. And then Luke was there. Where's Lucky?' Fen's grip tightened around Liam as he coughed and shivered.

'Lucky's right here, Fenella.' Liv placed him on her shoulder.

She felt the tickle of Lucky's claws against her neck. The dragon burrowed into her damp jumper. 'Kieran?' Her teeth chattered from the cold.

'He's on his way. Barbara's gone to get him.' Liv smoothed Fen's hair back from her face. She dabbed at a speck of something on Fen's cheek, the softness of the cotton handkerchief soothing against her ice-cold skin.

'Daddy!' Liam's voice was a soft cry into the fabric of her shirt.

'He's coming, baby,' she promised.

Oh, dear God, what had she done? For the second time in his life, Kieran would have to face the fact that his son had nearly drowned. She lifted her head to see

Kieran's long legs eating up the distance between the vines and the pond, at a full pace run.

As he reached them, she looked up at him, her heart pounding with fear, misery eating into her bones. Shock had etched a shade of pale into his tanned features, emptied his eyes of the affection she'd seen there earlier today. He leaned down and took his son from her. She let the boy go, felt her soul go with him. It didn't matter that Kieran would never forgive her. She'd never forgive herself.

'What happened, Fen?' Terror added an edge to his tone. Damn it, how had Liam ended up in the pond? He hugged his little boy closer, the cold, clammy feel to his skin bringing back memories of another time he'd rather forget.

Liv laid a hand on his sleeve. 'Go easy, Kieran. They've both had a very big shock.'

Marge approached with two folded crocheted blankets over her arm. 'Doc Benson is on his way over to check Liam. He'll get here before the ambulance does. The sarge is on his way too.' She handed a blanket to Liv and threw the other over Liam where he cuddled against Kieran's chest. 'Let's get them inside where it's warm. There's a lovely fire going in there. Virginia will take care of the deadbeat.'

He tightened his arms around his son until a wriggle from Liam told him he held on a little too tightly. But the vision of Fen cradling him in her arms, holding him, crying … God, the outcome could have been so much worse. He couldn't dwell on that, not again. 'What happened, mate?'

'Lucky ran away, Daddy. I had to catch him.' He coughed, a hacking sound that echoed from his little lungs. 'And then there was a bad man there.'

Virginia prodded the man lying prone on the ground. 'The one we're about to tie up. Have you got those cable ties, Marge?'

Fen clutched the edges of the jacket around her shoulders together, her hands shaking, blue with cold. 'I don't know if he fell in or if Luke pushed him. I'm so sorry.' She forced the words out from between chattering teeth. 'I only left him in the playground for a few minutes …'

A part of him wanted to go to her, drag her into his arms and tell her it was okay, it wasn't her fault. The other wanted to shout and scream his frustration and disappointment. Not at Fen, but at himself for leaving Liam. For thinking it would be okay. For believing the danger had passed. But now his son's recovery could be set back months, years, because he hadn't been there to watch over him. Again.

Doc Benson breezed in and dropped his bag on an empty table. He opened it, pulled out a stethoscope and placed it around his neck. 'Lucky I was just across the creek. The Bailey baby made an early appearance. Barbara, you're wanted over there. Sorry, there was no time to call and warn you. The little bugger was determined to arrive in a hurry. Poor Travis is still in shock.'

Barbara's hands flew to her face. 'Oh! Oh wow. It's a boy?'

Doc nodded. 'Congratulations. Ed's coming over to pick you up.'

How could they be talking about this now? Anger, irrational and unwarranted, surged inside him. His son had almost drowned. He looked over at Fen. She stared at the mug in her hands, her fringe hiding her face, her knuckles white from the way she gripped the cup, and retreated so far into herself, he'd be lucky to reach her again. Doc Benson claimed his attention.

'Now,' said Doc. 'Let's have a look at this young man. Took a dip in the fish pond, I hear? I bet that water tasted a bit yucky.'

Liam nodded against Kieran's chest. 'Pooey.'

'Well, that's what fish do in water.' Doc Benson warmed up his stethoscope between his hands. 'Now, let me have a listen to your chest in case you swallowed a fish and it's swimming around in there.'

Kieran held Liam while the doc examined him, took his temperature and prodded around as doctors do. He watched Marge wrap Fen in a hug which she received reluctantly. Her face was paler than usual. Ghost-white under the black of her fringe. Her eyes seemed empty, soulless as she cast a quick look his way before staring off into the distance again.

It wasn't her fault. He wanted her to know that. Not like Diane. But the short burst of sirens announced the arrival of the ambulance and Riggs, raking up old memories of hospitals and morgues, funerals and goodbyes. It would have to wait. He had to put Liam first.

Doc ruffled Liam's curls. 'Let's take a ride in the ambulance, hey? That'll be cool, right?' He looked up at Kieran. 'Just to be sure there's no water left on the lungs, I'd like to get an X-ray and a few tests done. There's always a threat of secondary drowning in these instances and I don't want to take any chances. But I reckon this little guy is built tough, so he'll be right. Won't you, mate?'

The same scenes played over in his head that had played twelve months ago. Tests, X-rays, machines pumping away, his little boy fighting for his life following a lung infection. More than anything, he wanted to throw his bags into his rental car, strap his son into the booster seat, and drive. Away from the memories. To somewhere where there were no ponds or bodies of water in any shape of form, no danger stalking them. He wanted the impossible to keep his son safe.

He allowed the paramedics to tend to Liam,

followed them to the ambulance, held his hand as the doors closed on Fen. She sat huddled in a blanket, held tightly by Liv. She'd be okay until he came back. He let the steady sound of the machine monitoring his son's heartbeat soothe his nerves as they bumped over the gravel road onto the main highway into town and pushed down on the rise of *déjà vu*.

At Wongan Creek's small hospital, he settled himself in for the wait while Doc Benson and the nursing staff checked and rechecked Liam's vitals. As dusk crept in outside the windows, Kieran watched his son sleep, so small and fragile against the crisp white sheets, the occasional cough making him restless.

He'd tried to call Fen, but she wasn't picking up her phone. Liv was unreachable too. Virginia had reassured him everything was okay, that Riggs had arrived to arrest Luke who was now in custody, awaiting charges to be laid. It gave him little comfort and didn't stop him from needing to hear Fen's voice.

'How's he doing?' Doc's voice reached past his thoughts.

'Restless, but no vomiting or any trouble breathing.'

'That's good news. He'll be okay. The X-rays have come up clear. I'd like to keep him overnight though to make sure, given his history.'

Kieran nodded. 'Sure, Doc.'

'Get some rest, son. He's going to need you for a while to get over this scare. Kids are resilient though.

Take the bed next to his. We'll kick you out if we need it.'

'Will do.' He stayed in the chair as Doc Benson patted his shoulder and disappeared out the door.

His mind played the scene over and over in his head. Fen holding Liam close, stroking his curls, rocking him back and forth, tears on her cheeks. Then when she'd seen him, looked at him, he'd seen guilt and fear in her eyes. He didn't want her to feel that way. He had no doubt that Fen loved his son. More than Diane had, because she hadn't loved Liam at all.

Chapter Nineteen

F en sat on the rock overlooking the creek, the sky dull, the clouds heavy with unshed rain. Under the leather, her scars burned hotter than the ache in her heart. Would Kieran come back to The Cranky Lizard or would he head straight back to Sydney? If only she'd kept a closer eye on Liam. The only upside to the whole mess was that Luke had been flushed out.

Liam would be okay. Doc Benson had confirmed it when she rang the hospital. But she hadn't been ready to hear Kieran's voice yet, despite the missed calls on her phone. God, if she hadn't been able to revive Liam, if Luke had succeeded …

No, she wouldn't think of that. Across the paddock, Harry's sheep grazed, content under the laden sky. Harry would be home, warm and dry, inside with Travis and

Heather, Robbie and Casey, admiring Heather's new baby. Next door, Harley and Tameka would be planning the opening of their new brewery in the spring. They'd all been through so much already.

Life had changed but would go on regardless, and she'd be in it alone. The word shouldn't hurt so much. It shouldn't reach in and grasp her soul in its dirty fist. No more laughter with Liam. No more Kieran to wake up to. Ever again. This time the lizard's tail wouldn't grow back.

The first drops of rain fell, ice-cold chips that bit into her skin. She turned up her wrists, feeling the splash of raindrops against her skin, allowing the cool to ease the burning itch.

'It's wet out here. You'll catch a cold.'

Her fingers curled into her palms at the sound of Kieran's voice from behind her, her heart beating out an erratic rhythm. 'You came back. Where's Liam?'

'Did you think I wouldn't?' Kieran eased down beside her on the rock, his thigh hot against hers. 'He's waiting up at the house with Liv.'

'How's he doing?' She clasped her hands between her knees.

'Good. He'll be fine.'

'How can you be so certain?'

He nudged her shoulder with his. 'Because Doc Benson said so. And the first thing he asked about when we pulled into the drive was if he could go and check on

Lucky.' Kieran reached an arm around her back and pulled her closer. 'Why are you out here in the rain?'

She relaxed into his warmth, her mind full of questions, but it didn't matter why he'd come back. Only that he had. 'Thinking.'

He'd never forgive her for putting Liam's life in danger. Damn it, she'd never forgive herself. When she'd hauled him out of the water, unconscious and not breathing … the thought clenched around her heart and brought a sting to her eyes. Jesus, if he hadn't recovered … she couldn't have lived with that.

'Sometimes thoughts are our worst enemy.' His arm tightened around her.

She shook her head. 'Not this time. I'm having the pond filled in.'

'You don't need to do that. The blame here is entirely on that bastard, Luke. It's not your fault Liam slipped away. He was lured away, and he did what any normal boy would do. He went after what he cared for most. What he was afraid to lose. We can't wrap him in cotton wool, Fen. He has to be a boy if he's going to grow up out here in the country.'

'If it happened once, it can happen again. What if, next time, we're not so lucky?' She couldn't bear to think of it.

'There are other ways to make it safe. A grid across the top, a fence around it. We can fix it, Fen.'

She lifted her head from his shoulder to look at him,

soaking up everything Kieran, from the neatly trimmed beard along his jawline, up across the strong cheekbones and into those green eyes that saw everything. 'We?'

He reached for her hands, still clasped tightly between her knees, and separated them. She welcomed the warmth of his skin, shivered as his fingers wrapped around hers.

'We'd like to stay if you'd like to keep us. Liam wants to adopt Lucky as an honorary brother.'

Doubt shoved its way through the glimmer of hope that grew inside her. 'Don't make grown-up decisions based on a four-year-old's needs, Kieran.' She tried to tug her hand from his, but he tugged back.

'I'm not. I'm making this decision based on a long-ago fifteen-year-old boy's infatuation with a troubled, kindred spirit who made his life somewhat bearable until she owned his path to happiness. But I was too blind to see it, Fen. I was blinded by Diane, her beauty and charisma. I loved her without a doubt, but not the way I love you.'

He released her hand and slipped off the rock to stand in front of her, the stone formation level with his waist, perfectly positioned for him to stand between her knees. He placed his hands on her thighs. Heat crawled up to warm places that shouldn't be feeling it. Not yet. Because wanting him and loving him wasn't enough. She had no desire to be his second choice again.

'Please don't say anything you're not one hundred

per cent sure of, Kieran. I don't want empty words because you're confused about where you stand or because you're influenced by Liam's feelings. He'll grow up and forget me.'

His hands slid around behind her, splayed across the denim that hugged her hips and drew her closer until they touched. Heat chased away coherent thought and she stiffened her knees against his sides to stop her legs curling around him and drawing him closer. Need, hot and dizzying, spread through her as she placed her hands on the thickly corded muscles on his forearms.

'What I feel for you has nothing to do with how Liam feels. I've denied myself this for too long. I thought if I let myself love you, I might destroy you like I did Diane.' He held up his fingers to her lips as she opened them to protest. 'It took me a long time to understand that Diane was already sick, long before the Vincents took me in.'

'I'm so sorry, Kieran. Things could have been so different for the two of you.'

'No. We were never right for each other. I know that now. All those years ago, when you kissed me goodbye in the storeroom, I regretted letting you go. I owed it to Diane and her parents to see it through. But that day when I left you behind … it smothered something inside me, Fen.'

'I hated Diane for taking you away, then I hated myself for thinking I had any right to keep you.'

'I wish we could go back and change things.' He buried his face in her neck and she slipped her arms and legs around him.

The need to hold him, feel him close, overrode whatever lay ahead. 'But we can't. We can only fix the future. I'm so sorry I let Liam out of my sight. I was so scared when I saw him lying in that water.' She shuddered again at the memory.

Kieran lifted his head and took her chin in his hand, forcing her gaze to his. 'You saved him. You didn't hesitate to jump in and do what you had to do. He's alive because of you.'

'But the long-term effects, the mental harm from almost drowning again ...'

'The difference is you held him. You dragged him out of that water, held him and gave him life, then you held him some more. You didn't back away. He didn't have that when he went into the river. In his own mind, he knows you loved him enough to do that. No-one has ever loved him like that, except for me. He loves you, Fen.'

'I love him too, but I'm still not sure I'm mother material. What if there's too much of my own mother in me?'

'There's a lot of Liv and Muzz in you too. Never forget that. Parenting doesn't come with a user manual, but together we'd be stronger, better. And knowing how much you love him is all Liam needs to grow. Knowing how much you love my son makes me love you even more.'

'What are you asking, Kieran?'

'I'm asking if you'll let me stay, if you'll be a mum to my son. If you'll be my wife, my life-partner, so I can spend the rest of our lives showing you how much I love you. I don't want to drive out of town into an empty void when everything I love is right here, when my heart and everything in it is in Wongan Creek.' His hands cupped her face and drew her closer.

'How can you be so sure?' Her resistance faded with his lips just inches from hers.

'Because without you, I'm running on empty. Please say yes, Fen.' The words drifted across her mouth before his lips settled on hers and everything he'd said was echoed in his kiss—love, longing, forgiveness, acceptance and a taste of forever.

Behind them, Liam's whoop echoed down the valley, cockatoos took flight as he raced towards them, oblivious of the soft rain falling around him. Kieran lifted her off the rock, his arms tight around her even as he broke the kiss. She slipped her legs from his waist until her boots touched the ground. Little arms wrapped around their legs as Liam pushed his face between them. One arm still holding Fen, Kieran swept the little boy up with the other. Liam's arms reached out for her and the last particle of ice around her heart melted as she stepped back to take his weight.

Liam crushed her neck in a hug. 'I wanna stay with you and Lucky. Can I? Can I?'

'I think we can work something out.' Her heart pounded against her ribs and doubt edged around her mind, but damn it, she couldn't picture a future without them. They'd survived so much, together and apart, surely they could work through this.

Kieran's arm slipped around her waist and they turned towards the homestead. On the verandah, Liv stood with Riggs by her side, grinning widely, one hand on her heart, the other held tightly in the sarge's, her fingers curled around his.

Liam wriggled in Fen's arms and she let him slip down and run to Liv. 'My daddy's going to ask Fen to be my mummy.' His stage whisper drifted down towards them.

Kieran's hand slipped around Fen's as Liv raised an eyebrow and said, 'Well, he'd better get to it then while we put on the kettle for a cuppa to celebrate. Are you coming with us, Liam? I'm sure I've got some lizard cookies in a jar in the kitchen.'

'K. Can we get Lucky down too? He won't want to miss the party. Is that okay, Fen?'

'Of course it is. Be gentle with him, okay? Let Liv help you get him out.'

Liam ran into the house ahead of Liv, leaving Riggs in charge of putting the kettle on. With a grin, the sarge followed them inside.

Kieran turned Fen in his arms and held her close. 'So, is that a "yes"?'

Fen smiled up at him. 'Was there a question?'

He grinned back. 'Fenella Rose-Waterman, will you marry me, with a ready-made son to raise, and can we please have more babies together?'

She pushed on his shoulders with feigned resistance. 'Steady on. Can we enjoy the one we have for a little longer?'

He nuzzled her nose with his before capturing her lips and a mind-drugging, body-arching kiss that promised lazy hours of loving later. 'Say it and stop torturing me.'

She cupped his face with her hands and closed her eyes, drew in the scent and feel of him, of what she had to look forward to waking up to for the rest of her life. 'I love you, Kieran Murphy. Will you be my forever tail that doesn't break off? Will you be there for me when I fall or fail? Will you let me love your son as if he were my own, because I already do.' She opened her eyes to see the glimmer in his. 'And will you please stay right here in my heart, and never leave?'

'I think we can agree on that.'

'Thank you.' She reached up and kissed him, a featherlight touch because she wanted to hear those magic words again and not distract him from them.

'Is *that* a "yes"?'

'Ask me again.'

'Will you marry me and make me the happiest man this side of Wongan Creek?'

'Yes.'

THE END

Whispers, Secrets and Shadows (Wongan Creek Series) can be purchased from your favourite bookseller. If they don't have it, ask them or your local library to order it in for you.

Dear Reader

This book has been written and edited using Australian / UK English grammar and punctuation conventions because the story is set in Australia. For more information on the differences between UK and US language and punctuation, please consider reading this article: https://tinyurl.com/56tkbh6a

If you enjoyed this book, please consider leaving a review on BookBub, Goodreads or the platform you purchased it from. If you would prefer to email me, please visit the contact page on my website at https://juanitakees.com/contact/. I do love to hear from readers and welcome your feedback.

Kind regards

Juanita Kees

Other Books by Juanita Kees

Wongan Creek Series

Whispers

Secrets

Shadows

Unfinished Business

Exposed

Tagged

Silenced

Bindarra Creek

Home to Bindarra Creek

Promise Me Forever

The Calhouns of Montana

Montana Baby

Montana Daughter

Montana Son

Contemporary Romance

Finish Line

Paranormal Fantasy

The Gods of Oakleigh